WATCHED OVER
BY ANGELS

Ancient tales of the Thanet Kingdoms

John H Stedman

ISBN-13: 978-1540705747

ISBN-10: 1540705749

Cover design © J H Stedman

Design & formatting by Socciones Editoria Digitale
www.kindle-publishing-service.co.uk

Dedicated to my Mother
Hazel Joan Violet Stedman

Contents

How do you really know what's true?

Google 'Thanet' and you will find information on the area and its main towns: Margate – the traditional seaside resort for generations of London and Kentish families, now with a re-born Dreamland amusement park; Ramsgate with its picaresque harbour and cargo ferry to continental Europe and then Broadstairs with its sheltered sandy bay and cliff top houses made famous by the novelist Charles Dickens.

Search a little further and you will discover that it was on the shores of the Isle of Thanet that Christianity first arrived in the British Isles when St. Augustine landed in 587 AD. Those interested in geography might like to note that the island is situated at longitude 1.25, latitude 51.37 – on the eastern tip of Kent in south east England and that Thanet now hosts Kent's own international Art Gallery.

In fact Thanet is no longer a real island. Long ago the Wantsum channel that separated the island from the mainland silted up and now only a narrow dyke remains of the waterway that in Roman times was nearly two miles across. Today the road passes over the land seamlessly and only a sign 'River Wantsum' informs visitors they are entering a special place.

For what the internet fails to reveal, as it focuses on the geography above ground, is *why* this is a very special place. The real wonder and magic of Thanet in fact lies underground where its 'true' history is recorded, back through every world of the three Kingdoms till the beginning of time. Hidden below, deep in a mysterious world of caves, the entrance to the secret Kingdoms of Thanet has been discovered by a girl. Her name is Simone.

Where it all began

It was after 6:30pm on Friday 30th July 2004. Most of the day-trippers had left the golden sands of Botany Bay and were either streaming back to Margate train station or were already in the long queues of traffic leaving the island, heading back towards the Medway towns and London. It was the end of a normal summer's day in Cliftonville.

The evening sun glowed on the chalk cliffs as the wind moved round to the North West. The tide was almost in now as Simone walked alone around the headland and paddled through the waves into the sheltered bay. 'The cove,' as the children called it, was a favourite roosting site for wading birds and gulls. When the tide came in it was cut off from approach from either side. She liked this cove and always thought of it as her secret hiding place and the hours spent here each summer with her close friends, scouring the tide-line for washed up treasure, held some of her happiest memories. The raucous cries of the herring gulls filled the air and echoed around the cliff face - the familiar and comforting sounds of so many summers…

Simone sat down on the still warm sand, leant back against the cliff and breathed in the cooling air from the sea. With eyes closed her thoughts turned to the previous week. She had never been to a funeral before. It had all seemed so unreal. She had watched and listened, shared in her parent's sadness, tried her best to comfort her Nan but at nearly fifteen years old she could not think of the best thing to say, except 'I'm so sorry.' She had naturally just cuddled her Nan and held her hand throughout the whole service.

This was Simone's first experience of loss. She had watched her Dad, always a figure of strength to her, standing by his Father's graveside, tears rolling down his face. Her Mum had bravely fought back her tears to chant a beautiful prayer. That melody had given Simone strength to support her Nan who stood weakly, gazing down – lost. She had watched her Dad bend down to pluck a rose from a wreath, kiss its petals and drop it onto the coffin. She had liked this gesture and bent down to pick flowers for her Nan and Auntie for them to drop into the open grave as their last goodbyes. Then she too kissed a rose and let it fall. Other mourners approached and taking a handful of stony soil dropped it into the grave. The loud hollow sound of stones striking the wooden coffin came as a shock and she had instinctively flinched with fright. Her Nan had been equally surprised and shocked at this awful sound and had squeezed Simone's hand as if to reassure them both.

Now, a week later she was alone, trying to make sense of so many things. Trying to understand the new emotions she was experiencing; trying to accept that her sheltered, innocent childhood had gone, and she could never get it back. Neither could she slow down the physical and emotional changes she was experiencing. Growing up filled her with a wild mix of happiness and sadness. Happiness for the thought of her future as a woman and the freedom that would bring. Sadness for the cost of that new life – leaving the security of her childhood behind. Change, it seemed to her, came at an alarming rate. Growing up seemed relentless and very confusing.

Before she opened her eyes, Simone tasted the salt on her lips and tried to empty her mind, listening to the sounds of the sea, the gentle waves and echoing bird calls. When she opened her eyes she saw in front of her a young gull searching through the flotsam which had been driven in by the tide. His mottled brown and grey feathers were ruffled by the wind as he balanced awkwardly, mostly hopping on his left leg, while his right dragged behind him. She watched as he suddenly stopped, grabbed a clump of weeds in his beak and took off over the sea. Lifted by the wind he turned back again towards the beach and glided down to drop the tangle of weeds in the sand next to her hand. The bird circled around twice as if watching her then flew up and disappeared over the cliff.

'Was this some sort of sign?

He'd dropped the tangled weeds right by my hand. That wasn't an accident!

Then he circled above me. He was watching to see if I would pick It up.'

Simone realised she was speaking out loud and looked around to see if anyone could have heard. *No, she was alone.*

Picking up the small bundle she began to unpick the tangle. Slowly and delicately she pulled it apart, discarding the weeds until only a colourless band remained.

It felt warm on her damp hand and as she picked it up it shone and sparkled – her touching it had brought it to life! She slipped the band over her hand and marvelled as the bracelet flashed rainbow colours with each turn of her wrist.

Spellbound, all she could think of were the long summer holidays when her friends Joined her to search the tide line; fantasizing about finding treasure that had drifted from a foreign land or exotic jewellery washed overboard from a sinking pirate ship.

Unbelievable!! Now she had really found it but there was no one to tell!

Talking to an Angel

"Don't be sad. Your Grandad passed through. He is in the next world now."

Simone jumped up and spun round. The cove was empty, yet she had heard a voice. A gentle female voice and somehow, though naturally she would have expected to be frightened by such a strange event, she wasn't. She felt perfectly relaxed and calmly asked,

"Who's there? Where are you?"

"Look closer" came the same voice "come closer." And Simone stepped right up to the cliff face. "Now open your heart. Touch your bracelet and close your eyes........and see me"

With closed eyes and open heart, Simone watched as a young woman walked towards her, smiling. "Who are you"? Simone heard herself asking. "Where have you come from?"

"My name is Tala, and I come from the realm of the Angels, Simone."

"You know my name? How?"

Tala smiled at Simone's directness. "The realm of the Angels is where everything is recorded: in fact everything that has ever happened in Thanet throughout all the Kingdoms since the beginning of time."

"Why do you need to do that?" asked Simone.

"The Guardian explains that we record so that people may one day discover this wisdom and learn from their mistakes. It has always been so. And when people from your world die, their souls pass through our Angel realm and leave behind the record of their lives. Then they pass on to the spiritual worlds."

"What, like heaven you mean?"

"That's what people call it but it's not really a place," explained Tala. "It's worlds within worlds that souls journey through for eternity. Every soul begins this journey after their Earth death but at different levels, depending on how well they have lived."

"Have you ever been to Heaven?" asked Simone.

"No, Angels were created to live between your physical world here and the spiritual worlds where your Grandad is now. We have our own existence and we cannot enter your world or the spiritual worlds. We must always stay in between. Always in between."

"But if Angels live between two worlds, how come I can see you?"

"Especially with your eyes shut," said Tala who began gently laughing.

Simone opened her eyes and it was no different. There was Tala standing before her.

"Come Simone, come into our realm and I will explains. Take my hand and hold on to your bracelet with the other." Simone held Tala's hand and immediately felt as if she was being transported through a barrier; slowly pulled through a series of invisible veils. Each veil she passed though slowly warmed her skin like the delicate caress of a summer breeze then a final veil of delicate vibrations…as she passed through the cliff face into a faintly lit cavern. As she let go of Tala's hand she felt a tingling sensation running up her arm. She knew what it was but struggled to believe how it could be possible. *Kindness* – it was kindness she could feel. Kindness from the Angel's hand.

"I sense you are worried about time, Simone. Please don't worry. The moment you crossed to this realm, time stopped in your world. No matter how long you stay with us on your return your Earth time will begin again at that same moment. No one from your world will ever know you have crossed over." "But why me?" asked Simone.

"There are two parts to that answer. The 'how' I can explain, the 'why' requires the wisdom of the Guardian. One thing I can tell you, Simone, never before has anyone found a way to bridge two worlds. You alone have crossed from your world into the realm of the Angels. It is so wonderful to see an ancient legend come true. It is recorded that the Dawn witches collected moon dust and flew back to earth sprinkling it over the sea when making their wishes and asking for blessings."

"You mean like children throwing coins in a fountain and making a wish?"

"Exactly" replied Tala. "And it was believed that as their moon dust touched the surface it formed into a bracelet and sank to the bottom of the sea. And the legend said there it would remain until found by a pure hearted maiden who would be given the key to their kingdom. The middle kingdom, known as the Kingdom of the Witches."

"You mean fairy tales can come true?" Asked Simone.

"This is no fairy story, you have proven the truth of this ancient tale. You have become the story, Simone.

I was watching you, feeling your sadness and I saw the injured gull choose you to receive the gift of moon dust. There can be no doubt that you were the maiden he was guided to. The moon dust bracelet is your key to cross over to our realm and your invitation to enter the Kingdom of the Witches."

As Simone studied her glowing bracelet she became aware of silent movement all around her as other Angels joined them and soon she was encircled by beautiful smiles.

Simone continued, "I feel so different. It's weird – like all my sadness and confusion have been rinsed off and I feel older somehow." Looking into Tala's smiling face she asked, "How old are you, Tala?"

Tala began to laugh and then Simone heard other Angels laughing gently. "That is such a sweet question to us. You see, I am the same age as when I was created. We do not measure time in years like you, but in kingdoms, and kingdoms stretch back to the beginning of time. So I am both as young and as old as the kingdoms, as all Angels are. And each angel has a special role to play in our realm. For instance the Guiding angel maps our caverns here below your Island. The Recording angel ensures all events are stored here in our crystals and nothing is ever missed or lost and many others have varying responsibilities – all to serve the Guardian and preserve our Angel realm."

Tala continued. The first Kingdom recorded is known as the **Kingdom of the Ancients.** Worlds of magic, star flying and the mysteries of ancient Kings and the struggles of warrior tribes are woven throughout the universes in this Kingdom."

The second Kingdom recorded is called the **Kingdom of the Witches**". Tala's expression grew suddenly serious as she continued. "It began with the dark and terrible 'War of the Witches' and finally ended in the peaceful 'Dawn Witch' era."

"You mean the Dawn witches were the ones who flew to the moon and collected stardust to drop over the sea?" asked Simone.

"Indeed they were and they also established what you might call reserves on the island to protected rare creatures and studied and practised healthy eating, forbidding all animal products. All this, thousands and thousands of your years ago."

"The third Kingdom we call the **Divided Kingdom**. That began as a time of great confusion, disunity and strife and sadly still continues so today. Yet it was also once an age of miniature worlds, teeming with wondrous creatures; many of which survived until humans first set foot on the Isle. Then some fled to the sea while most creatures hid deep underground."

"You said that the Divided Kingdom continues today with disunity and strife – does that mean in the Kingdom world and in our human world too? Tala."

"Yes in both, sadly. Until people realize that there is but one Human race and the earth is but one Country, the beginning of the **Kingdom of Unity** will be delayed."

"Each Kingdom" continued Tala, "flows into the next, just as the streams fill the rivers and the rivers run to the sea. Our duty as Angels is to watch over this knowledge and faithfully record every action, every thought and every dream. We only record, nothing more."

"The Kingdoms you describe sound wonderful," said Simone excitedly. "But are these creatures still here? Can I find them?"

"Yes, a few are still here, but well hidden. You may find them eventually with patience and faith and some may even find you - as a reward for some future kindness you show to another creature."

"How would that be possible?" asked Simone.

"The Guardian has taught us that there is an unchangeable Law of every universe: that an act of kindness by one creature for another, creates its own reward."

"But what happens if someone is unkind or cruel, Tala?"

"Such deeds are destructive in every world and they carry their own punishment."

"Sorry, I don't understand what you mean."

"Well," continued Tala. "The person who does wrong things to others will come to feel the pain he or she has caused and also come to know of the reward they have lost by not doing the right thing. This is Justice in every universe."

"You mean every bad deed is always punished?"

"Of course", answered Tala. "Not always at the time, maybe much later in their lives and in ways they would never suspect, but no one can escape from the universal law."

Simone looked down, deep in thought. These were complex ideas to consider but she instinctively accepted them. They seemed fair to her young mind and they felt right in her heart.

Suddenly the silence was broken. "Behold – the Guardian" echoed the announcement from within the cave and the Angels stood up in unison. The circle parted and the Guardian entered slowly. He raised his left hand and brushed the hood of his cloak back to reveal locks of silver white hair. The lights brightened and Simone could see that the midnight blue of the Guardian's velvet cloak was edged with silver. In his right hand he carried a long crystal staff which he tapped on the floor. "The Council of Angels is now met," he announced. "Be seated Angels."

The Guardian turned to Simone, who had remained standing, and walked towards her. He was taller than she had first thought and as she looked up into his smiling face she was transfixed by his eyes. They were of the palest blue and radiated pure kindness. Simone returned his smile and then bowed her head, sensing she was in the presence of someone magical.

"We are the Council of Angels and we welcome you" the Guardian began in a gentle voice. "To serve the Kingdoms we shine light on good deeds and we illumine kindness. We record all this so that creatures can eventually come to learn what is good and true. So they may be able to 'follow the light' as the Ancients first taught. Until this moment," he continued, "Angels have always existed separately between your human world and the Kingdoms on the other side. Always in between. Nor since the beginning has any creature entered our world. You stand before us now the first creature to have ever crossed over." "But why me?" asked Simone nervously.

The Guardian slowly moved his head from side to side and said, "I heard Tala explain to you 'how' you were chosen, 'why' you were chosen?" he paused and a smile crept across his lips, "Why, you? I truly cannot say. I think in your human world you might call it a miracle." The Guardian raised his arms wide and turning to greet all the Angels arrayed around him, loudly proclaimed "We call it a wondrous miracle!!"

On hearing these words the happiness on the faces of the Angels lit up the cave like daylight and Simone gasped as she glimpsed the hundreds of Angel smiles, rank upon rank, disappearing into the far distance in every direction. And she saw how their smiles lent a glow to their skin colours that ranged from pale olive, through burnished copper to deepest ebony and hair, now highlighted in the unseen breeze, from lightest gold to red and chestnut to raven black...... All breathtakingly beautiful.

The light dimmed as the Guardian continued. "I hear the voices of the Ancients summoning you, from the Kingdoms. This is beyond my understanding, yet I must obey. My duty is to prepare you to enter the Kingdoms below." Stepping back into the circle the Guardian tapped his rod three times and gave the order "Record her Kingdom name and prepare a key for her to pass through all veils. "Turning to Simone he asked "How do you wish to be called?"

"My name is Simone but my family and friends call me Sis."

"It shall be so," announced the Guardian. "Record her name in Crystal. Henceforth throughout all the Thanet Kingdoms she shall be known as 'Sis'."

"Come now Sis, we must prepare you for the key ceremony and to witness your 'Promise of the Heart' pledge that the Guardian has written just for you. And," Tala went on "I have been told by the Watching Angel that a Crystal is to be drawn from the sun's rays to record your initiation and promise. Imagine, made of pure sunlight it will be kept only for you to store all your memories from every world – for ever."

So many questions rushed around Sis's mind. The whole wonderful experience was so totally overwhelming that she had no choice but to let go and be swept along in the joy and total magic of the moment.

The promise of the heart

Dressed in an Angel's gown of shimmering flax blue Sis returned and stepped back into the circle where the Guardian waited expectantly. He asked her "Do you come to this Council with a free and willing heart?"

"Yes, I do" replied Sis.

"Do you understand that this key to the Kingdoms is granted to you alone and must remain secret, never to be spoken of in your human world?"

"Yes, I do," she replied solemnly.

The Guardian turned toward the Attendant Angel and commanded her, "Bring forth the truth stone and reveal her sunlight crystal."

The flat stone was laid on the floor and stepping onto it Sis accepted the long glass Crystal from the Guardian's outstretched hand.

"Will you put your whole trust in the wisdom of the Guardian and his Angels?" "I promise," answered Sis.

"Then now before this assembly of Angels, hold the sunlight crystal against your heart and repeat after me: 'I make this promise of the heart, to be true to all worlds.'"

"I make this promise of the heart, to be true to all worlds," Sis repeated slowly.

"To believe and trust – where all is possible, all is secure," continued the Guardian.

Sis repeated his words.

"And lastly" added the Guardian. **"Do you promise never to look unkindly upon another being but only to see their goodness that you might help them become yet better?"** "Yes, I do," answered Sis.

The Guardian took the sunlight crystal that now sparkled with Sis's promises and called out, "Keeper of the Thanet records, take this crystal and plunge it deep into the waters of knowledge. Now Sis, choose your sister Angel who will be your guide and companion."

Without hesitation Sis answered "I choose Tala."

"Step forward Tala" said the Guardian. "You will be Sis's guide to all the hidden veils. You will be closer to her heart than her own dreams. He took Tala's hands in his and looking into her sapphire eyes said, "We entrust this special girl to your safe keeping.

Now take her to the dream chamber."

Tala took her hand and led her into the cavern and down a few stairs to a small room. Inside was a long bed over which were spread silken sheets and dazzling pale blue pillows. The room was lit by soft lights that seemed to be oddly moving to and fro like the ebb and flow of the tide, somewhere above them.

Tala whispered, "Lay your head down Sis and sleep the sleep of Angels." Barely had she closed her eyes than she fell into a trancelike slumber as Tala covered her with a delicate brown robe.

In Sis's dreams she travelled through the Kingdoms, flew on a tour of wonders and was given a glimpse of endless worlds. She saw a kaleidoscope of places, creatures and colours and wondrous plants and flowers. She flew over strange seas and mountains, coloured deserts and ranges of stars and clouds and tangled cloud forests...

All things and places so real she could not only see them, but feel them and touch them too.

"Wake now and behold the lightest dream robe in all the worlds" called Tala.

Sis sat up and looking down saw that the robe was gently swaying. It has no weight but all warmth. It was made from wafer thin brown wings: all packed tightly together, all delicately moving. Then it happened. One by one the butterflies opened their wings and a magnificent pattern of yellow, blues, tangerine, and pink unfolded. The robe was made of living butterflies that now edged apart, wings flapping in an explosion of brilliant colour.

"Unbelievable. Oh! I have never seen anything so beautiful," said Sis breathlessly.

"This" said Tala, "is a tiny glimpse of the wonders of creation that are yours to discover."

Tala bent down and taking a miniature brush collected the coloured dust that had fallen on the floor from the wings of the waking butterflies. Very slowly she swept it onto a thin sheet of paper. "Give me your hand Sis," and Tala painted three strips of colour onto the back of Sis's left hand. Three stripes: pink, blue and yellow. Then she gently blew on Sis's hand and in each of the stripes a filigree outline of a butterfly appeared. Again she blew and the outlines took in the colour and she was left with a perfect pattern of three butterflies. "There, Sis, you have a key for each kingdom, Come now we must return to the Council."

"Show forth the keys," requested the Guardian. Simone held out her hand and the butterflies glowed with an iridescent sheen. "It is done," announced the Guardian proudly. "The wish of the Dawn Witch Queen has been fulfilled. Now to return here from your human world, just place your finger on the Kingdom symbol you wish to enter, whisper 'Tala' three times and you will find her here, always waiting for you. She will guide you to the Kingdom veil and will wait there for your return. Angels are forbidden to enter any Kingdom. When you enter Sis, you enter alone. Now you are one with us. We will never leave you by yourself. We will ever watch over you."

"May I ask a question, Sir" asked Sis.

"Certainly, but please call me Guardian. This is my title for I have no name."

"When I enter the Kingdoms, will I be safe, will I be able to speak to the people I meet?"

"Yes" replied the Guardian. "You will be safe, Tala will be watching over you and following your every thought and action from behind the veil. Once you enter into a Kingdom you become a natural inhabitant of the time and place, so you will not look or sound strange or be any different from them. Whatever language is spoken you will speak and understand as they do. Only memories will return with you and these Tala will collect in your sunlight crystal."

Now it is time to return to your home, back to your human family. Go now, trust us, your Angel family. We will always watch over you."

The power of trust

Simone could not remember wading back around the chalk headland and trudging across the sand to the concrete walkway cut into the cliffs. It was her habit to sit on the cliff tops and shake the sand out of her plastic beach shoes. From here she could look out to sea and count the various cargo ships that were anchored off Margate sands. This evening however, once she had crossed the car park into the street, she just ran straight home without stopping.

The following evening she enjoyed a relaxed dinner with her parents and brother, and after helping to clear the table suggested to her Dad that maybe her brother could have first choice to choose the TV programme tonight as she was tired and wanted to have an early night.

"Thanks Sis" her brother replied.

"That's kind, darling, I know it was your turn. I will be up in a moment" said her mother.

"A little later she came upstairs and leant down to kiss her daughter goodnight. " Night, Night". She smiled to herself, remembering back to her own childhood. Like Simone's now, her world then had been full of wild imaginings and pretending – and pretending always felt more real than the 'grown up world around'. And she felt grateful as a mother to see her daughter free and healthy to enjoy this special 'growing up time.'

As a wife and mother now it seemed her own world was just work and responsibility – *so very different*. But being a 'mum' was her greatest reward and she loved every minute of it! She waited a few minutes stroking her daughter's hair and then quietly left the room, closing the door behind her.

Simone listened for the sound of her mother's footsteps on the stairs and then she heard her talking to her father in the kitchen. She waited to make sure she was completely alone before stretching over for the small pencil torch in her bed-side drawer then, pulling the sheets over her head, she switched it on. The butterflies glowed in the dark as Simone moved her finger over each of them, unsure which to choose.

I wish I could see Tala again, just to talk, I really miss her. "Tala, Tala, Tala," she called and closed her eyes tightly, as a young child when making a wish on a rainbow.

"Where shall we go Sis?" asked Tala, as she threw her arms around her new friend.

"I am so happy to see you Tala. It's only been a few days but I missed you. I missed you all" she said to the angels who now crowded around her.

"We missed you too but don't forget although we see and record everything, we cannot enter your world. It is for you to cross the veil into our Angel realm. You alone have the key to unlock all veils."

Sis looked around and asked "where are we?"

"You have come through to the angel chambers, 'deep caverns' we call them, that stretch under the Isle and out to sea to the north, east and south," said the Guiding angel. "Would you like to see them Sis?"

"Make sure you hold on to her hand tightly" said Tala. Then turning to the Guiding angel said, "Here, use this silk rope to bind your wrists together."

Like children everywhere, Sis had day-dreamed, imagining how it would feel to fly. Now her day dream became real and she took off, bound to the fastest angel of the realm. Like a film played at treble speed, they flew without slowing for corners then dived down vertically into massive caves, then up again to caverns pierced with needles of sunlight.

This was like a continuous ride on a whirlwind. She had absolutely no control, yet bound to the Guiding angel she felt no fear, just amazement, as miles upon miles of narrow tunnels, caves and caverns, flashed by. Their take off was so fast that Sis automatically held her breath and did not realise what she had done until the Guiding angel shouted "Sis, you can breathe out." Then they stopped on a ledge at the bottom of a wall.

"Look here, it's the map room" said the Guiding angel. "There, that is the 'Kingdom of the Ancients'. She turned and continued. "Over there 'The Kingdom of the Witches' and behind you' The Divided Kingdom.'"

They walked hand in hand around the massive room. The maps were suspended on each wall, hanging like giant banners. At the base of each was a wheel. "Go on turn it Sis". Sis grasped the wheel and it turned easily in her hands. On each movement the map changed as she moved forwards and backwards. "It's like a living map."

"Exactly" said the Guiding angel. "Every detail is perfect. That is why it is so important to record everything. With your key you can choose to enter any Kingdom at any marked moment. Next time you come I will show you some wonderful records, but now we must get back."

They returned at a slower pace, allowing Sis to really see this underground world. "Don't you ever get lost down here?" She asked.

"Never", replied the Guiding Angel. "To guide and create maps is my service to the Guardian and I have wandered these caves beneath the Isle since they were created and have mapped and measured every hair's breadth."

On their return they were met by Tala who smiled broadly and asked "Well Sis?"

"I can't tell you – it was amazing! And the living maps…Wow!" She had so much to tell Tala and became so exited her words could not catch up with her thoughts and she started mumbling and everyone laughed.

"Next time I will take you to our libraries" promised the Guiding angel.

"I didn't see any books" said Sis.

"Of course not, everything is saved in crystals. If everything that we wanted to record was to be printed in books - can you imagine - there would be enough volumes to fill all the Thanet caverns millions of times over. Even that might not be enough. No," explained the Guiding Angel, "the Guardian allows us to make crystal copies of our own interests. These form our libraries, our stores of wonders and favourites. 'Our special things', we call them."

"What's your special thing Tala?" asked Sis.

"My love is for the natural world. Each cloud formation since the beginning of time has been both unique and ever changing - as are the seasons. And then the endless warm colours of sunset and the pure silver shades of dawn that shed their splendour across land and oceans alike."

"You make everything sound so beautiful, Tala."

"Oh, but it is, Sis. Creation is perfect."

"Mine for birds" said the Guiding angel. With my crystal, alone in the dream chamber, I can follow the Albatross circling around the southern oceans. Dive with the Peregrine Falcon, the fastest bird in the human world and best of all, hover with Hummingbirds. They are the jewels of the air, so beautiful! The peoples of South America have many different Spanish names for hummingbirds. The sweetest of all is '*Besaflor*' - it means flower *kisser.*"

"My love is for trees", added the Recording angel. "They are as living storehouses and absorb all life, sounds and memories around them. Through my crystal I listen to the trees in the dream chamber and they give up their secrets to me. Nothing in all your human worlds can compare with the sheer loveliness of the Sakura – the Japanese Flowering Cherry. Imagine Sis, whole hillsides awash with pure white blossom and when the winds come - an endless blizzard of fragile tree snow." The Angels all sighed, imagining such a pure white windblown landscape.

Sis went quiet too, then broke the reverie by asking: "So, if you cannot judge and if, as the Guardian said, you cannot interfere,

how it is possible to have favourites?"

Tala smiled, "No doubt you will be studying philosophy at University when you are older. That's a good question." Come, sit here, I want to introduce you to someone who can answer you."

The 'someone' appeared from behind and sat next to her. "Hello Sis," he said and laid his arm around her shoulder.

"I'm so happy to see you, Guardian. I just flew with the Guiding angel. It was out of this world."

"Indeed it was. *Indeed it was.* You asked an intelligent question Sis. Angels as well as the Guardian must view all creation fairly, otherwise how could they record accurately? Yet each is also an individual and like you, has a unique character and special qualities. So it is only natural that we are drawn more towards particular things or Kingdoms. Yes, we are allowed to have favourites, it would hardly do if we all liked the same things. That really would be boring, wouldn't it?"

"What's your favourite thing, Guardian?"

"Butterflies of course," he answered, glancing down at her hand. "I thought you might have guessed that."

Sis liked this explanation. It made her feel closer to the Angels, knowing they too could have favourite things.

"There is a difference though," added Tala "we must value and treasure everything and then we are allowed to love some things even more."

"That means that you cannot dislike anything?"

"Correct", said the Guardian, "in fact, the language that the Angels were speaking before you came, you could call it *Angelesque,* has no word for 'dislike'. We can only say it in English as we are speaking now. We appreciate everything and like some things even more. Simple isn't it?" asked the Guardian. Sis remained silent. "What's wrong?" He asked.

"It's too hard. I could never be as good as an angel. There are some things I really hate." As Sis uttered this word a flash of lightning shot around the cavern roof and Sis sat up shocked. "What was that? You can't have lightning underground, can you?"

"Everything is possible" said the Guardian. "Remember your promise of the heart. Believe and trust, where all is possible all is secure?"

"It was that word you uttered," Tala explained. "The 'H' word has no meaning here. It contains nothing good, nothing positive, and nothing to help creatures to become better. As soon as you said it, it was rejected by this realm, cast out on the lightning you saw.

"Come Sis" the Governor said kindly. "You cannot expect to learn everything at once. Remember I told you, 'trust, trust', that is the greatest knowledge we can ever bequeath to you."

"But isn't it just as important to tell the truth? It would be a lie for me to say I liked bees and wasps, they really frighten me. I say I *H* them or *I can't stand them*".

"There is another way" suggested the Governor. "Let me ask you. Do you believe that anything in creation is completely bad, I mean *really* bad in itself?"

"I suppose not", returned Sis, screwing her face up in deep concentration.

"Therefore, if you were to recognise something good or beautiful in the thing you disliked so much, would it not soften your feelings?"

"Well it might", admitted Sis.

"Then close your eyes and stretch out your right hand" said the Guardian. Sis did as he asked. "Without opening your eyes tell me, do you trust my word?"

"Of course" replied Sis.

"Then hold this trust in your heart and open your eyes, now!" Sis obeyed. What her eyes fell on was a nightmare, an unspeakable nightmare. Sheer terror gripped her. She was unable to move, unable to scream. Her whole hand was covered in bees. A black and yellow, buzzing, crawling, furry mass that began to move up over her wrist. Her natural reaction would have been to shake her hand, scream and run. That is if her heart hadn't already stopped! She felt the Guardian's hands reassuringly closing around her left hand. He spoke quietly, "Trust. Trust me and you can overcome all fears. Breathe deeply and believe in my words with all your heart. Believe in your chosen Angel, Tala. Look now into her eyes. Take our strength, be one with us and banish your fears. Did I not promise you we would never leave you alone?"

Somehow Sis looked back to the heaving horror covering her hand. Focussing on one bee she slowly moved her hand towards her face and studied the intricate coloured patterns adorning the insect.

"Look closer Sis" the Guardian encouraged her, and Sis held her hand right under her chin and saw the real beauty of the transparent, whirling wings as she sensed the lightest movement of air. '*Like a microscopic fan*', she thought.

"They are amazing" Sis exclaimed.

"Yes" said the Guardian, "all creation has beauty. We just have to learn how to see it. You can let them go now". Sis lifted her arm out again as one by one the bees flew off. As the last one left, she was filled with a wonderful sense of fulfilment.

"That is the power of trust, Sis. No power in the universe is stronger. Trust rests on love, and love is the force that binds together all existence."

Sis closed her eyes again, trying to recapture this wonderful sensation that had miraculously banished her terror. The Guardian, still holding her hand, spoke softly. "Return to sleep my dear one. Return to sleep…"

Simone turned over in her bed and noticed a torch light under the sheets. Without thinking, her eyes closing again, she felt for the pencil shaped torch and switched it off. If it is possible to sleep with a smile, then Simone did, all night…. And she awoke with a smile on her face, rushed her breakfast and went straight on the phone to arrange with her friends the day's activities. Activities, once her friends had arrived, which invariably involved a constant streaming in and out of the house, going down the road to the beach, coming home again to shower, leaving sand in the bath and piling dripping swim suits in a heap in the wash basin.

Then there were the discarded wet towels as the noisy group of girls prepared to return to the beach, this time for a picnic. Later she would either be asking if her friends could stay for a sleep-over or begging her parents to be allowed to sleep alone in a tent in the back garden. *Yes, it was definitely school holiday time!*

'Holiday time' was also when Simone had promised to clear out her bedroom. It still hadn't happened yet. Starting a few times with the best intentions, Simone's activity had always ground to a halt as soon as she began tidying up and going through her photograph collection. That invariably took the rest of the day and all that happened was the photographs were put back in boxes - but in a different order.

Unlike her older brother who was always throwing things away, some of which his mother would rescue from the bin and save for him to use or wear later, Simone had to keep every scrap of paper, every feather or memento of visits anywhere. She insisted she *needed* each piece of work kept from infant and junior school and as she knew where everything was in her room she wasn't really convinced of the need to 'clear her things up.'

Her 'things' defined her childhood, held her memories and she needed to keep them all. Even more so now as she seemed to be accelerating through her teenage years. She also instinctively knew whenever her mother had tried to tidy her room herself while Simone was out. She would rush to the dustbins to retrieve whatever had been hidden in the rubbish. In time she developed a sixth sense. This led her to also check inside all the black sacks her mother filled and hid in the garage to be taken to the Charity shop.

Simone had to wait a few days until her friends had returned to their homes and her bedroom (still covered in sleeping bags and littered with crisps, sweets and chocolate wrappers from the previous nights' sleep-overs) was quiet. So many times when she and her friends had been talking, whispering and laughing together into the early hours of the morning, Simone had almost let slip her secret. It was so difficult. She was bursting with excitement but unable to share any of it. Now, she was alone again. The rest of the family were already asleep as she drew her curtains to darken the room and lay back on her bed. The night was unusually humid and the air still. Even with her window wide open the curtains hung without movement. Slowly, Simone's eyes became accustomed to the dark. She held her hand up, placed her little finger on the pink butterfly and whispered three times, "Tala".

The Kingdom of the Ancients

"We're so pleased to see you, Sis" said Tala. "Come to the map room and we can plan your journey into the Kingdom of the Ancients. Here, take my hand." They flew together, this time at a more relaxed pace and Sis was bemused to see her white nightdress turning to a subtle shade of pink. By the time they landed on the platform entrance, her nightdress was the deepest pink.

"You are ready already" joked Tala, "let's study the map".

Tala slowly turned the wheel to the left as Sis looked on fascinated. Gradually the map became clouded and dark until only a soft blackness with occasional points of lights remained. "Here is the beginning of the records. We have nothing before this – no crystal, no pebble memories. The river of knowledge starts somewhere here", explained Tala as she pointed to the edge of the map. "The only way to travel upstream into the Age of the Ancients is to go into the river and find a question mark floating down and swing it round. Only questions can return to the source - the spring of all Knowing." "That sounds a bit scary," said Sis.

"Or very exciting" answered Tala. "Entering the other Kingdoms is much simpler than this, don't worry, I will watch over you and you only have to whisper my name once to return to me. Then you will hold the sunlight crystal and all your memories will be safe."

"But what if I get stuck somewhere or something frightening happens and I can't get out?"

"Why, Sis – you already know the answer yourself. Think!" Sis's face relaxed into a grin. "Trust, trust", she said.

"Yes, yes", laughed Tala, "and remember what the Guardian said, 'the more you trust, the more you will understand'. In time you will trust so perfectly, it will change into pure faith - what angels call 'Iman'. You belong now in all Kingdoms and you have nothing to fear. Come."

Tala took her by the hand and flew from the map room down and down through darkening tunnels till they alighted on a stony river bank. The sound was almost deafening. A cacophony of music, song, speech and all the familiar sounds of nature mixed with other sounds so strange Sis had no idea what they were. All came from within the river and as the waters cascaded over mountainous boulders, the sounds increased, then softened and quietened as the waters slowed and eddied in pools.

"I must leave you here Sis. The veil falls before the river bank.

Go now."

Silver Aynjels of the glass road

Sis walked gingerly forward and felt a weird vibration from her head to her toes. She was through the veil. She instinctively looked back for Tala but the veil reflected only her own image back. *What's happening to me?* Her hair turned to metallic fronds streaming away from her head. Her eyes were growing and turning deep blue. Her skin hardened into a dull grey colour. Her arms and legs grew longer and she felt a new strength flowing through her body. Her fingers lengthened and her nails became golden. She touched her nails and they felt hard and glistened. They were pure gold. She glanced down, her toenails were gold too and her night dress had changed and tightened into a metallic suit, smooth and golden - so slippery her hands could not rest on it.

Power surged through her. Remaining still felt unnatural to her now. Every fibre of her being screamed to move, to race, to fly – to be gone!

She peered into the river searching for a question mark. Carefully, she stepped into the shallows but her feet remained dry. What swept against her were waves of sound and she waded deeper enjoying the music of the Ancients – for now she knew what it was. A beautiful concert of stars reverberating around the universe, echoing endlessly and reflecting off star clouds with wondrous notes and phrases.

Without thinking, Sis dived forward into the river of sounds and swam and twisted and sped. The music flowed through her and around her. She was part of this symphony and it ran rhythmically through her veins. What joy she experienced. She was so enchanted she little noticed the sounds were sweeping her downstream. She stopped and searched again across the surface. Then she saw it, a bright orange question mark drifting towards her. She stretched out and her strong hands held it. She turned it around and hung on as it raced upstream.

Now the music sounded in reverse. The ribbon of sound grew narrower and suddenly she was speeding uphill faster and faster till she saw distant lights sparkling ahead. The lights grew brighter as she slowed and the question mark came to a stop. She stepped out onto a large smooth boulder and leaning forward, peered into a small cave from which sprang all sounds. Sis had found the spring of all Knowing!

Around the cave entrance sat a group of children. Sis watched as they waited for any sounds to splash off a rock then their nimble fingers would pick up the droplets of sound and gently place them back into the stream. So engrossed were they, that they did not notice Sis's approach. Suddenly, as one, they stood up and bowed to her. Then the tallest lifted his head and said, "We catchers serve you truly, Oh Aynjel. Look please, our hands are empty of all sounds. Nothing will ever pass our catching. No droplet of knowledge will ever be lost. This is our pledge." Sis was surprised to hear herself replying, "I bring you greetings from the Lord of all the Ancients. He is well pleased with your devotion, Oh Catchers and sends you each a heavenly smile. Yours is a sacred duty and your actions are sung of in all catcher realms across the universe."

"We are honoured indeed, Oh Aynjel. Take with you our love for the Lord of all the Ancients, that it may light your path between all star alleys."

Sis smiled and the catchers, one by one, caught her smile and tossed it into the air. The smiles exploded into countless tiny star sparks that shot across the velvet sky, each one brighter than the last, until Sis had to shade her eyes with her hand against the stunning brilliance.

As the star bursts grew dim, the alleys the catchers had spoken of appeared in the skies above her. Clear pathways edged with golden light. Instinctively, she raised her hands together, fingers pointing upwards like a diver preparing on the high board. She sprang up, diving upwards. Her speed was incredible. Stars flashed by her and clouds of giant sky moths scattered in all directions as she passed. Every now and then she was joined by consort Aynjels of various shining colours who followed her, twirling around her playfully. It reminded Sis of the films she had seen of dolphins swimming alongside and in front of sailing ships. Approaching the alleys the consort Aynjels waved to Sis and veered off, spinning into the mist.

As she neared the alleys, her fingernails glowed as molten gold and her suit shimmered and rippled. Like a magnet, the alley drew

Sis in deeper and the star clouds seemed to wrap around her, slowing her descent till she landed on a smooth glass road. It was illumined from underneath by blue glowing branches. She stared in sheer wonderment upon a glass road supported in space by blue trees!

Just then, three young Aynjels approached her, skip-floating more than walking. They were dressed in silver and all had blue hair. They stopped and smiled at Sis. "Are you coming to the festival and the tree planting songs?" asked the eldest. "You are dressed so beautifully for star-flying. Where have you come from?"

"I've come from behind the spring of all Knowing," said Sis. All three stared in disbelief, looked at each other quizzically, paused and then laughed together.

"That's a sweet joke but we know from your gold nails that you are a Queen Aynjel from the Jewel planet of Soltan. We have never travelled that far but we have heard songs about the catcher Aynjels there."

"Can you tell us a story? Please, please," entreated the youngest Aynjel.

The eldest explained "In our sector, it is so very rare to receive visitors. We only meet other creatures at tree planting times. Please, tell us a story."

"Alright," said Sis, "but first you must teach me a tree planting song, just one, so I can sing with you at the festival then I will tell you an ancient tale. Is that fair?

"Let's sit down and you sing each line so I can copy you." The Aynjels all sat at the side of the glowing glass road looking at Sis expectantly. As they fidgeted and settled down, other silver Aynjels dropped in through the clouds until a whole group encircled Sis.

Suddenly there was an explosive 'crack' and a flaming spear crashed through the glass next to them, tearing a jagged hole in the road and setting fire to the branches beneath. The silver Aynjels jumped up and the youngest started to scream with fright. 'Crash.' Another spear hit the road, this time leaving a gaping hole and igniting fires in a row of trees. The road shook and swayed like a suspension bridge in an earthquake and all the Aynjels stumbled around desperately trying to cling to one another.

"What's happening?" shouted Sis in alarm.

"It's the Vaspers. Look there! It's a fire chariot and it's full of spear-throwers. They have come to destroy the road," said the nearest Aynjel.

"They hate our community" continued the boy next to her, "They've come to steal our roses. Help us, please help us," he sobbed.

"We're alone. All the elders are away. We only have this road to connect to the known horizon. Don't let them destroy it – please Queen Aynjel," begged another Aynjel who clung tightly to Sis's arm. "Protect us!"

A strange anger welled up in Sis. She leaped into the air, aiming for the Vaspers' chariot. Spears rained down on her, glancing harmlessly off her smooth golden suit and spinning off in all directions. The Vaspers roared, "Stop that Aynjel." But it was too late. Sis was already under their chariot and using all the new Aynjel strength that was surging into her, she pushed and the chariot started to edge backwards. The Vaspers howled and cursed at her and threw everything overboard to dislodge her but to no avail. They picked up speed, helplessly reversing away from the damaged road.

Sis let go and the chariot sailed off into the blackness. When it was out of sight she flew back down to the silver Aynjels who were still shaking and huddling together, nervously peering into the gaping holes in the road. Where the blue trees had burned, pieces of the road splintered off and dropped into the black void. It was a terrifying sight for the gentle silver Aynjels.

From behind the group, an old lady walked forward and offered Sis a blue rose. "It is pure aquamarine. We grow them in secret at the side of the road planted in meteorite dust", she explained. "It's the greatest treasure we have and it is for you, Aynjel Queen. We owe you our lives. Those Vaspers deserve their fate. They have a terrible suffering to come," she added with great bitterness in her voice.

"Who are they?" asked Sis.

"Vaspers. They're the last of the warrior hoards. The others, the Valrons and Vermins, made peace with the Council of the Galaxies. Only the Vaspers refuse and still raid the star clouds and destroy our glass roads."

"Is there no one to protect you?" asked Sis.

"The Elders try to fight but mostly we hide below in the trees."

"But why did you say they deserve their fate? What's going to happen to them? "I'll answer that," came a voice from behind. As she turned, Sis was faced by the same old lady who was now smiling. She turned round, confused for a moment and then as the two stood together, a few Aynjels began to giggle at Sis's astonishment.

"Yes, identical twins. I am called Wenz and my sister, Henz."

Sis studied their faces intensely. She tried to look at every tiny detail, but even up close she could detect no difference in their physical appearance at all. Every tiny crease on their skin, deeply ingrained with fine blue powder, was an exact reflection of the other, like a mirror image.

"You really are absolutely identical,"

"Yes" said Wenz. "We are known as cluster twins, the first to be born in this river galaxy."

"And that's what saved our lives," added Henz. "We were captured as children in a raid on our settlement. Our family were glass builders helping to construct the new road. Everyone was killed except us. The Vaspers had never seen twins before so they kept us as pets for their children."

"Pet slaves, more like!" Wenz spat out the words. "They fed us only enough to keep us alive to work, and the work never stopped."

"How did you get away?" asked Sis.

"A Zarion merchant who traded with the Vaspers took pity on us and smuggled us out. These Silver Aynjels welcomed us into their community and we have been here ever since, learning to grow aquamarine roses that they trade for glass."

"We can never regain our childhood," said Henz. "The Vaspers stole that from us." She looked into Wenz's tearful eyes. "But we

31

can make a difference to the lives of these young Aynjels." She rested her hands affectionately on the shoulders of the nearest youth and looking up into Sis's eyes, said "because of these silver Aynjels our lives have purpose again."

A small boy with head bowed, shyly walked up to Sis and asked, "Have the Vaspers really gone for ever, Aynjel Queen?" Sis looked over to Wenz expectantly.

"Have they really gone for good, Wenz?"

"Yes. They can't come back", answered Wenz. "You see, when, as young fighters, they are first given their flame-spears, they swear an oath 'never to retreat'. Their chariots are built to only drive forward. Now they travel helplessly backwards to their star camp to face shame and utter humiliation. I've seen it happen once before," she said shaking her head sadly. "All the Vasper tribes will come out to witness their retreat. One by one every member of the tribe will ceremoniously turn their back on them. They will then be branded on both arms with the point of a flame-spear and each bound with chains to a piece of dead star rock. Then they will be thrown into the void of nothingness, to die slowly. They will never be spoken of again. It will be as if they had never existed. They are the cruellest creatures, even to their own."

Sis felt uneasy. No, it was more than that, she felt guilty. *Yes, she had saved the young Aynjels, but at the cost of condemning at least twenty Vaspers to a horrible death.* She searched inside her heart for an answer. *How?* She thought, *could it be right to hurt people, however bad they were, in order to save others?* Something was wrong.

She closed her eyes seeking inspiration. None came. Only the words of the Guardian, 'Trust, and trust' came to her mind. She had this growing feeling that to leave the Vaspers to a horrible death was wrong – *but what was right? Hadn't they killed countless numbers of peaceful Aynjels?* Nothing was clear in Sis's mind. The wonders of the river of sound, traversing the ancient Kingdoms, the beautiful giant sky moths floating so gracefully through the star mists and the incredible glass roads held up by blue-light trees. It was all so fabulous, way beyond anything her imagination could ever have conjured. Yet even this wonderful dream world was riven by hatred and cruelty.

A nagging impulse stirred in her and her arms lifted almost involuntarily as she pointed in the direction of the receding chariot. The Aynjels looked on shocked as Sis powered into the blackness up and up until her brilliance disappeared. A hushed silence fell upon the group. Sadness and disappointment hung like a cloud around the Silver Aynjels. None spoke. No one moved.

Sis could hear the wailing and moaning of the Vaspers long before their chariot came into view. Flying over them, she saw that they were hurling their spears overboard, jettisoning their swords and daggers. Their brilliant armour once worn so proudly was being ripped from their tunics and flung over the side. All the vestiges of their merciless warmongering were being torn away and discarded into the winds and swirling dust. The final symbol, the streaming blood-red banner was torn to pieces by the warriors' strong hands in their last act of aggression. With nothing left of their former glory, their pride shattered, they lay down defeated to await the inevitable.

Again, Sis's feelings were tangled and confused. The terrible killing warriors were once easy to fear. Now their plight was not frightening, but pitiful. Slowly she was beginning to understand the Guardian's wisdom when he said 'never judge' and why the Guardian and Angels only ever recorded and could never interfere. Interference could be helpful at one time and yet wrong at another. Nothing was certain, nothing absolute.

What was it the Guardian had told her? Sis asked herself. Then it came to her and she repeated out loud. "Trust - no power in the universe is stronger. Trust rests on love and love is the force that binds together all existence."

Without a second thought Sis flew to the rear of the chariot and with both arms outstretched, pushed against it. The massive craft came to a halt and the Vaspers stood up peering nervously in all directions as Sis sprang up and stood on the front facing them. In their physical size they dwarfed the delicate frame of Sis. In strength of mind, Sis as the Queen Aynjel, towered above them all and they read it in her eyes. The warriors' stares fixed on Sis. She glared back at each of them searching for some understanding, trying to read their expressions, till at last the silence was broken.

"I greet you Aynjel. As King of the northern Vasper tribe I accept defeat and place my men at your command. Here is my oath stone". The King pulled from his neck a large diamond medallion. Sis accepted it from his outstretched hand and nearly toppled forward with the weight, even holding it with both hands. "It is a sun diamond, only one other has ever been found in all the universes. It is beyond price. What now is our fate, O Queen Aynjel? We have no home, we are outcasts for ever."

"On behalf of the Silver Aynjels, I accept your surrender. Now, you must make amends. "Return to the glass road," she ordered. The chariot moved forward, edging downwards towards the silver Aynjels who now lined the road on both sides. Looking down, the warriors could see right through the gaping holes in the road to the emptiness beneath and smell the smouldering tree branches, some still glowing red in the darkness. It was a desolate sight.

The chariot drew up alongside the road and Wenz and Henz pushed through the crowd to confront the King. Wenz roughly pulled her sleeve up and pushed her scarred arm into the King's face. "Look! Look at your greatness. Such bravery", she taunted, "branding a young girl's arm with a red hot spear. What kind of creature are you?"

"You don't deserve to live in the same universe as these kind Aynjels" screamed Henz. "We don't want you here – go! Go. Die slowly beyond the triple moons." As they finished their invective, the twins struck out at the King, beating his chest and arms with their flailing fists, spitting and kicking him.

The King stood unmoved, accepting the abuse, trying to ignore the raging hatred of the old women. In past battles, he had been merciless to his foes, his inbred instinct always 'to kill or be killed'. For the first time he was truly powerless to act and did nothing till, exhausted by their efforts, the twins fell to their knees, crying and sobbing. With one hand, the King helped them to their feet, looked into their watery eyes and said, "From this event forward till my end, I promise no warrior of my clan will ever harm you again. On the sun diamond I swear it, we will protect you with our very lives."

The King knelt in submission to the twins. Behind him the nineteen warriors exchanged embarrassed and confused glances before awkwardly kneeling down behind their King.

Sis laid the colossal sun diamond on the road and walking up next to Wenz and Henz said, "Yours is the choice. The King has given his word. Can you trust him? Can they stay here and protect you or do you seek their destruction? For all you have suffered, it falls to you alone to decide. What will it be?" All the Aynjels held their breath. The tension in the air froze all feelings.

Henz and Wenz looked at each other. There was no need for words, their thoughts and feelings were as one. "Suffering must have an end. The Vaspers shall live," they called out together.

"They will stay here to help us rebuild our lives", announced Henz.

The King rose and speaking in a solemn tone said, "From our warrior hearts we thank you. We will repay your trust".

"Traitor! You're not worthy to be King," screamed a red haired warrior, who jumped up holding a glass phial above his head. The Aynjels near him rushed away and he stood, eyes blood-red, shaking and shouted, "A warrior would rather die than live as a slave. You've no pride. I'll poison you all and you accursed King - you first!"

He rushed at the King and grabbed him round the shoulders, grappling him to the ground. They struggled as the King held his attacker's wrist to stop him pouring the liquid. For one moment, the phial was poised above the King's face. They rolled over battling desperately for the phial. The King twisted the warrior's arm with such force that his elbow shattered with a sickening crack and the phial flew into the air. As the warrior screamed in agony Sis instinctively dived forward to catch the glass phial just before it hit the road. The King scrambled to his feet and was again bowled over by his crippled assailant. They fought for their lives with terrible screams and moans. A knife flashed downwards and the blade cut a deep gash in the King's shoulder. Another flash and it came down again. This time both of the King's hands held the warrior's wrist and twisted the blade away from his own throat, back and upwards towards the chest of the crazed warrior. With all his strength the

35

King pushed up and the dagger sank full length into the warrior's heart. His life ebbing away, he collapsed onto the King's battered body, pinning him to the floor. The other warriors rushed over to help their King.

"Don't touch him! Move away," shouted the King as he struggled from beneath the lifeless body and staggered to his feet. Blood poured down his arm. He stood unsteadily, and then rolled the body with his feet toward the yawning hole in the glass. With a final kick, the warrior's body fell over the edge and sank out of sight. "There will be no burial ceremony for him. He has shamed us all."

Sis stood trembling with the phial clasped in her cold hands. She was used to watching action films about war and fighting, but to see someone being *really* killed was very frightening. She couldn't stop herself shaking and her body felt ice cold. She felt sick with fear and turned away from the crowd trying to keep her composure.

"Queen Aynjel," called the King, "do you have the glass phial? Please, bring it to me." Sis turned and walked unsteadily towards the King who was being supported on both sides by his faithful warriors. Carefully the King took the phial from Sis and examined it. "You don't know what you've done. Every creature in this realm now owes their life to you. If that phial had broken, it would have been the end of all settlements, in all sector horizons, for all time."

"What on earth is it?" Asked Sis.

"Dream poison," answered the King. "It's the ultimate weapon, kept hidden on my war chariot. It's been kept there for many sun cycles and I forgot about it when we rid ourselves of all weapons."
"You also forgot the dagger that nearly killed you," added Sis.

"I gave orders for all weapons to be destroyed. I expect to be obeyed. The warrior who shamed us was adopted by our tribe when he was young. He was a fearless fighter but jealous of those in authority above him. He could never accept defeat. Now he has paid with his life and will not be mentioned in the 'scrolls of death', the ultimate humiliation for any warrior - because he dies without honour."

"Why is the dream poison so deadly? Sis asked.

"One drop slowly diluted in water and sprayed in the clouds or in the wind mists and everyone who breathes will be affected. First it makes everyone happy and they behave childishly, like the drunken Leeboks who drink solar wine. Then it affects their minds and they become hateful and distrustful and begin to believe everyone is plotting against them. Even families turn on each other. Ultimately the whole society turns against itself until all are destroyed. It's like destruction from within, a kind of slow, communal suicide. And the poison – it stays in the air and water for generations."

"That's so wicked", gasped Sis. "How could anyone dream up such a thing?"

"Well, is it any less wicked to kill with a spear or knife than to kill with poison? Our civilisation was built on war, on killing before we were killed. Dream poison was created for the dreaded day, when our civilisation was surrounded and threatened with total annihilation. Then it was to be used to destroy everything. If we were to die, we wanted all of our enemies to die with us and no future generations to be born – ever!!"

Sis eyed the harmless looking glass phial in the King's massive hand and asked "How can such a terrible weapon ever be destroyed?"

"The only way would be to seal it in molten glass and hurl it into the roaring Ribbun Abyss. It is said that the Abyss leads to the edge of the Black Universe where no life forms can exist. It could do no harm there. But it is a long and dangerous journey and none of the Vaspers are capable of star flying." The King raised his eyebrows, waiting for Sis's response. Neither spoke.

For the first time in the Kingdom of the Ancients, Sis's confidence failed her. She knew from the King's expression that he wanted her to carry out the mission. Equally she knew none of the silver Aynjels could match her for speed or endurance. She was the logical choice but the very thought of such responsibility weighed her down. She was empty of all enthusiasm or energy. *Maybe the dream had stopped?* She looked over the King's shoulder into the blackness and heard again, faintly but clearly, the words 'trust, trust'. The deeper into the void she stared for an answer, the stronger the answer came.

"I will go. Have the phial sealed" said Sis confidently.

"Excellent", said the King. "Thank you. I will have my navigator draw up star maps for you. You will have to traverse the star deserts of Han, then over the twin crystal seas to the very edge of the Abyss. You could face many dangers, you must be prepared for anything."

Journey to the Ribbun Abyss

The sun diamond was placed for safe keeping in the house of the elders, guarded by two Vaspers at all times. The King and the other warriors assisted in the glass streaming workshops, their great physical strength proving a real asset in the road repair. They were each able to carry glass slabs that would ordinarily require six Silver Aynjels and a slab sledge. They could also bear the weight, one on each arm, of two planting Aynjels suspended on thick ropes hanging over the side of the road. In this way the planting Aynjels could make quick work of grafting new branches onto the blue trees.

The phial sealed, it was placed in a strong carrier strapped to Sis's back. The King adjusted the bag and checked the fastenings. For the last time, Sis studied the maps and memorised her route.

"Go with our blessings. We shall keep the crystal fires burning to guide you back to us," promised the King.

The twins stretched up to kiss Sis on either cheek. "Fly! Become the stellar wind." Called Wenz.

"Rid us of this danger" shouted her Sister. "Hurl it into the Ribbun Abyss!"

Everyone stood still, their eyes following the golden light that showered off Sis as she leapt into the black sky and in an instant was gone. She flew at lightning speed, the pure thrill of flight rushed through her like an electric charge. Such freedom, such power - this was pure joy. "Wonderful" she shouted, but the sound disappeared into the blackness before she could even hear her own voice. The space below her lightened and she could make out a gleaming desert, stretching away in all directions. She passed through several solar systems, new suns appeared, each with planets and moons, and then another system and a new sun, and yet another. All the while she continued to cross the star desert of Han; a featureless, flat landscape that went on and on.

She had no way of knowing how long she had been travelling. There had been sunrises, many beautiful sunsets. Then as she watched twin suns rising together she caught a glimpse, far in the distance, of sparkling water. The twin crystal seas at last!

The star desert ended abruptly. There was no wide shoreline, just sand then suddenly sea. Sis turned downwards to rest on the warm sand and hung her feet in the cooling crystal water. From her side pocket she pulled out a thin flask and sipped the liquid the Aynjels had prepared for her. It was an energy drink that tasted both bitter and sweet simultaneously. It also gave her an immediate burst of energy and rather than resting she took off again flying low over the first crystal sea.

The sea below her was stunningly beautiful and as Sis floated above it the melody line from her favourite choral piece, Barber's *Agnus Dei* came to her mind and she began to sing to herself. It seemed the perfect setting for the music. The combined beauty filled her heart and she could not help herself crying with happiness. Her tears flowed and streamed behind her like dewdrops trapped in trailing cobwebs. Then she heard it. From beneath the sea came the other voices singing all the accompanying parts of this masterpiece. Twice the music rose with a crescendo. The third time it was resolved in a glorious burst of harmony. Held in an inspired state, Sis turned round and flew back to the beginning of the sea. Over and over again she returned to sing with the sea, circling through the music till she almost lost consciousness and started to fall from the glowing sky. She came to her senses just in time to prevent herself crashing into the sea. With a jolt she steeled herself, stretched her arms and flew off. The sounds died away as she sped on.

Beneath her the crystal sea streaked by and gradually the water colours deepened until finally ending against a black rock face. Up she flew and over the cliffs and before her spread the second sea. This was different. The water rolled and splashed revealing huge creatures cruising on the surface. Sometimes there would be an explosive sound and giant plumes of water shot up as the creatures fought. She winced as a big fish leapt up into the air to escape gaping mouths that shot up out of the depths beneath it. She saw whole flocks of orange birds plucked from the surface by long yellow snakes and dragged under. The waters boiled and swirled, every now and then a billowing red cloud would spread as another creature was slaughtered. *How could these seas be twins? The first radiated life and music. The second absorbed and took life into itself like a liquid tomb. It was horrible and she began to worry how long it would take her to cross.*

The question haunted her as she flew onwards sensing her energy and her strength were fading. She stretched upwards trying to gain height and see beyond the obvious horizon. There was something large, too big to be any sea creature, in the farthest distance and she willed herself to fly towards it. What came into view set her heart racing. It was an Island jutting out of the wild sea. Waves crashed against its rock-strewn beach and ran on to the cliffs. Spray shot into the air leaving a hanging cloud suspended over the cliff face. Sis felt the moisture clinging to her suit as she flew through the mist and up on to the highest point on the island. It was dark now and only the swinging moons, Sis counted three, gave any light. She was totally exhausted. Even so she was careful to lay down on her side cradling the dangerous cargo in her arms before her eyes closed and she floated into a dreamless oblivion.

The dual suns were high in the sky by the time Sis stirred, their rays beat down on her from a hazy sky as she sat up to look around. She was on top of a plateau heavy with vegetation, all laden with dark green moss. It grew on the rocks, over every branch. Even the stalks of the giant grasses which ranged down to the shore were covered with a fine green mesh.

Sis got to her feet and tightened the strapping around her waist and reassuringly felt for the glass bottle on her back. She was just about to walk down the moss hill when all around her groups of small beings sprang out of the grasses encircling her. They eyed her curiously and pointed at her, mumbling.

"We haven't seen you here before" said the bearded man nearest to Sis. He came up to her waist in height and was dressed in a long moss coat. His pointed and very small shoes were made from tree bark and his hair and beard were dark and curly which contrasted with his pale skin and orange eyes. He was so pale, he looked as if he had never been out in sunlight. "We are the Collectors for the caves of Kelvin. These are the Monitors of the wells" he said, pointing to the group next to him. They were considerably taller and very thin and carried rolls of ropes around their slender waists. "Have you come to our Isle to give or to take?"

"To give or to take what?" asked Sis.

"You could take from us our ideas and hopes. Or you could litter our Isle with rubbish and use it like a stellar dumping ground as the Waldrons do. They even send over loaded water sleds to fill our wells with their rubbish and left-over rotting food. All they care about is keeping their 'Waldron Rise' clean and pristine, while our pure wells stagnate."

"I come neither to take nor give" said Sis. "I took rest here after trying to star fly across the sea of death. I am travelling to the Ribbon Abyss on a mission to save the silver Aynjels and their way of life."

"Then we bid you welcome. I am Tullis, chief cave Monitor and our caves are your home." He lifted his arms out in a kind of welcoming gesture and asked Sis, "How are you called. Have you been named?"

"Yes, my kingdom name is Sis."

"And our wells your fountains" added his deputy. "Forgive our rudeness." My name is Sebix and I'm Tullis's sister. Come, you must eat with us".

Sis looked down at the empty flask on her hip and gratefully accepted their invitation. "Thank you", she said.

It was a short walk through the undergrowth to the beginning of the cave system. An easy stroll through the long grass and tangled roots for Sis's long legs, but an arduous hike for the small Collectors who every now and again had to use their long knives to clear a pathway.

From the nervous faces of the children and women who peered out from the caves, Sis could tell that they were wary of strangers. Once they were all inside the candle lit cavern and the leading Collector told the community how they had found Sis asleep and that she was a star traveller, the atmosphere changed. The young children crowded around her, feeling her shimmering golden suit. A confident older girl even ran her hands across Sis's metallic hair in amazement. "How can metal be so soft?" she asked.

"That is a wonders of the Aynjel realm," replied Sis. "Haven't you seen Aynjels before then?"

"No" the adults replied in unison. "No such mythical beings have ever visited here – not in our lifetime anyway."

"Ours is a world of cleaning and protecting the wells and trying to prevent the Waldron's rubbish sleds from landing here." Said another.

"Even our children have a part to play. With their sharp eyes they are our look - outs, our danger- spotters", a young mother added.

"What dangers are there here?" asked Sis.

"Where shall I start? They are above us, below us, and on every side."

The leading Collector continued to explain. "We are unable to make boats big or strong enough to sail across the sea. We have nothing that will protect us from the surface killers; the yellow jumping sea snakes or the terrible dragon fish that breed in the Trench of Trevor. They patrol the inland waters surrounding our Isle, swimming in hunting packs. They have even been known to swim up to the beach to grab their prey."

"But surely you're safe here on your Island?" asked Sis.

"Not when the perma clouds thin at night and the Waldron's' Scorpion - bat can get through. It happens rarely, but when it does, agh! It's too frightening to describe in front of children." "I've not heard of perma clouds" said Sis.

"They're like fixed covers of cloud that hang over our Isle and protect us from aerial danger. Nothing normally gets through, but the Waldrons are always watching for a chance. They sit up on high towers watching, waiting for the opportunity to open the cage and to call down the Scorpion-bat that lives above the cloud. Normally it feeds on small creatures like wind riders or cloud bouncers who live in the perma clouds. But it likes nothing more than the chance to hurt us and the well Monitors. No Scorpion-bat could survive long in our humid atmosphere but its attack is so swift that even the shortest time span is fatal." He put his small hand to his face to hide his lip movements from the children and said in a hushed voice "the Scorpion - bat is no bigger than a blackbird but the sting in its monster tail is deadly, its claws are like razors and its needle teeth, poisonous. It can sting, rip flesh and bite with frightening rapidity causing untold carnage before it returns to its lair in the clouds."

"We have nowhere to hide from it", Sebix continued. "It sees in the dark, can fly through all tunnels and caves, climbs down wells and can sense any warm-blooded creature hiding in even the deepest vegetation. Now," she said, "if any of our look-outs see the perma clouds thinning we stay in this cave and light fires at every entrance to ward off the bat and wait for the safety of daylight. If only we had done that at the time of the last attack."

"What? You mean you were attacked. What happened? "Asked Sis.

Tullis beckoned to her to move away from the surrounding group and sit next to him, out of hearing range of the children.

"No alarm was raised in the early evening and everyone had settled down to sleep. We had been working all day clearing the caves and were so tired we didn't even have a story-ring. That's a fireside meeting when we all swap stories that our parents told us – the children usually love story rings. Yet that evening everyone was asleep before the second sun set. In the night the Scorpion bat came down and stung everyone in the first two caves, then flew through to attack the well-Monitors who were huddled together next to the rain well. By the dawn of the first sun, so many lay dead, their bodies stiffened by the poison and their bellies moving and swollen as the bat-grubs grew quickly inside them."

Sebix, wiping her streaming eyes explained. "That was a terrible day. Not only had we all lost loved ones, young and old, but we were unable to bury them fittingly for fear the grubs would hatch and destroy us all."

With her voice shaking, Sis asked "What did you do?"

"What could we do" said Tullis. We had no choice. Some bodies were dropped down the whispering pit and consumed in the eternal fires that burn under the Isle. Others had to be taken to the shore, wrapped in bark coffins and pushed out to sea towards the Trench of Trevor. That is the deepest part of the sea and lies close to our shoreline. We returned up here to watch them. Once they floated near the trench, the water came alive with rows of dragon fish, their massive teeth-filled mouths taking bodies whole. In a 'times flash' they were gone."

"We call that 'the Day of Misery' when all hearts were broken. There were very few of us who had not lost a son, daughter, father or mother. And everyone- Collector and Monitor alike, lost many friends."

"I am so very sorry" Sis said in a hushed voice. "I can't imagine anything more awful."

"And it didn't end there" added Sebix. "The Waldrons came and threatened that if we didn't leave, the next time they would let out both Scorpion- bats and none of us would survive. That's how we learned that they kept two Scorpion bats and also that the Waldrons were uncomfortable breathing in our humid air so they couldn't bear to stay here long. They said they watched every movement we made from their sky towers. They didn't want our island to live on but needed it to use as a rubbish tip!"

Tullis continued. "None of us know where their island is. They sent their rubbish sleds over in the night so we have no idea from which direction they came. But we know it must be a very high island to reach up into the sky and be close to the perma clouds. How else could they control the Scorpion bats?"

"Of course," agreed Sebix. "But even more - who else might they be in league with is the question? The memories of our Ancestors protect us from such horrors as Witch-Savages."

She put her fingers to her eyes as she made the ancient wish plea and everyone repeated,

"Protect us, Oh Ancestors."

Sis picked disinterestedly at the food on the table before her. The meal had been most welcome. Welcome that was before she had listened to the tragic story. Now a nagging doubt began to creep into her consciousness. *'If this Island was so high, why hadn't she seen it as she flew in? It was dark, but surely she should have noticed it. Were her powers failing?* Not wishing to appear ungrateful she sipped the moss tea from the stone cup, but could not eat anymore. She looked around at the Collectors faces. Their sad orange eyes were damp with tears. No one was eating, just slowly drinking tea and staring at the table. Without warning Sis raised her hands, clenched them in a fist and shouting "No!!" crashed them down onto the table. "No!!" and she buried her face in her bruised hands and sobbed uncontrollably. "They must pay. They must be punished," Sis yelled loudly and her voice rang around the cave labyrinth. She stood up violently and the bench tipped over on to the floor as she strode out of the cave entrance. She screamed at the top of her voice into the pitch black sky - "Waldrons! You will pay for this." The sound of her voice slowly sank into the moss and the surrounding blackness.

Her body shaking, Sis turned back to the Collectors who had followed her outside and were now staring at her, shocked and confused. They had no idea what to think or what to say. Sis tried to compose herself. She lifted her head and said "I am very grateful to you all, I did not intend any discourtesy. I'm sorry. Oh! If only I knew where the Waldrons were" she continued in a threatening tone, "I swear I would! ... She stopped herself midsentence as she desperately tried to think and reason beyond her blinding anger. At first nothing seemed to appease her crazed thoughts of revenge. Her hands were clenched into vice-like fists, arms shaking, she turned around to stare into the inky blackness of the night. Wishing, hoping, and pleading for guidance to help her. Nothing came.

Then she felt a small hand pulling at her wrist and as she looked down she saw a young boy's tear stained face who nervously whispered "We trust you Aynjel."

The sound of that word "trust" from the lips of an innocent child melted her anger as she bent down to pick him up. Holding him close in her arms she knew, this was her answer.

She felt suddenly strengthened and said, "This young boy, this precious child, has reminded me. We must never lose trust. I give you my word, I will find the Waldron's Island and rid you of the Scorpion- bats for ever."

The first sun was slowly burning off the sea mist as Sis set off on her mission. Looking down below her she could see the Monitors and Collectors waving as she began to methodically fly around the isle in ever increasing circles but no new island appeared. *'How could an Island hide?'* She smiled to herself for thinking of such a silly idea and flew down to the beach to try and think clearly.

She sat on a damp rock and tried to focus her thinking... *We know the Island exists, the Waldrons came from there. So why can't we see them?* Trying to concentrate she stared at the surface of the sea and became almost mesmerized by the dancing lights of the sun's reflection on the waves; like a ripple of stars. "Trust, trust" she repeated over and over again to herself. Then she stopped. A growing sensation, like a physical magnet was drawing her off the island to fly low across the sea, almost touching the waves till she saw in front of her the surface flatten and the sea become a mirror. As she drew closer and looked into the mirror the Waldron's isle towered above her, and its reflection sank into the sea. All around the Isle hung a thick sea fog that totally cloaked it from view from any direction above the sea. Only inside the cloak of fog could the Isle be seen and she flew upwards and round and round the island. On descending down to the sea she could see in the mirror the moss Isle not far away, again reflected above and below the sea. Holding all these images in her mind, dipping below the fog shield she flew back. Back to the waiting Monitors and Collectors.

"Bring me the largest sheets you have and quills with ink," she asked excitedly.

"I have found the island where the Waldrons live." Sis sat at the big table to draw. All the Monitors and Collectors crowded around Sis watching expectantly as she made her initial sketches. The children jostled and shoved one another and crawled along the floor between adults' legs – all vying to be the first to see the map.

When finally she completed her map. She rolled it up and told the crowd around her – "first I must show the leaders waiting in the joining hall, then we can begin to plan our attack on the Waldrons." On hearing this the children as one jumped up screaming with excitement.

"We're going to attack the Waldrons, we're going to attack the Waldrons!" This childish exuberance sent a chill down Sis's spine. Suddenly she remembered the deadly phial strapped to her back and her unaccomplished mission. *And she, a Queen Angel was stirring*

47

up creatures to wage war on others. Hadn't she herself been caught up in the hysteria of last night and sworn to kill the Waldrons? How she yearned for the Guardian's wisdom now.

The obsession of the Waldrons

Approaching the thickening perma clouds, her flight slowed. Then she slowed even more as she drifted over Waldron Rise. She could clearly see the two enormous towers reaching up from the hard stony surface. It was a strange Isle, much taller than wide, like a pillar rising from the sea, with steep fog-clad sides. She could see a road cut into the rock side winding round and down to the jetty, against which were moored flat, dirty barges.

The Waldrons she saw were tall and thin like the well Monitors, only they all wore brilliantly whitened clothes and had no hair. It was difficult at first to separate men from women, they all dressed identically and used the same brushes, only the more feminine shape and gait gave some of them away. She noticed they were all constantly brushing themselves and each other and bending to pick up small items from the polished stone paths. Every few paces were big, white waste bins, around which were constant activities. Every other Waldron seemed to have a broom and to be continuously sweeping, not just the floor but also the tower sides, as high as they could reach. As she flew lower she noticed that at every level of the huge living towers, Waldrons were hanging by rope cradles sweeping with hand brushes.

Sis hovered behind a thin cloud and watched. She had come here vengeful. When she had left the meeting her mind was clear, her mission, simple. Now she held back, pondering the strange things she was witnessing. Nothing seemed clear anymore. Eventually, almost against her own understanding she began to feel sorry for them. *They did nothing but sweep and clean endlessly, and it was an obsession that could never be satisfied. What kind of life was this? Imprisoned by the need to clean constantly, they could never reach the end, never be satisfied with what they had done. They were real slaves with no hope of freedom'.*

This wasn't what she'd expected. The Waldrons far from looking dangerous appeared weak and pathetic. She didn't know how to react. In all the time she observed them not once did any smile or speak or even acknowledge another.

Sis was really bewildered. With their limited outlook, the Waldrons would not be capable of considering the needs of others, but were driven only by the need to find more space to dump their rubbish. They probably did not even see anything wrong with their actions. *Yes* thought Sis, *the Deputy was right all along. The scorpion bats are the real enemy.*

She floated slowly upwards to the beginning of the perma clouds. It was like a secret world in the sky. She watched with amusement the hedgehog shaped cloud bouncers playing and wondered how they could ever see through the long, thick hair that permanently hid their faces. She was amazed to see bright red surface skaters hanging upside down on the cloud's surface that reminded her of the pond skaters she had watched as a child. Among the clumps of cloud fern hopped, what looked to Sis, like very long haired rabbits. They had floppy ears and a flattened tail that dragged behind them as they dived in and out of their burrows in the cloud wall. There were insects too. Shiny yellow cloud dragon flies that landed on Sis's arm and small puff moths, perfectly camouflaged with their speckled grey wings.

Sis looked down to the top of the two Waldron towers. There was a thick twined rope leading from each up into the perma clouds. She dived upwards and came out above the cloud, right into the double mid-day sunlight. She closed her eyes against the fierce light, and then slowly opened them to see at the end of each rope a small cage. Moving closer she discovered that the metal mesh cages were covered in finely woven silk in double fold. Inside were small shapes moving and she heard a strange buzzing sound. She had found them!

Moving closer she flew nervously around the cages trying to steal a glimpse of the Bats inside. Grabbing the silk cover she only moved it a little before a weird cackling, spitting sound erupted from within and a horrible stench of stale sick oozed into the air. Sis pulled back in disgust…and for a moment hovered between the cages to calm her senses. From inside the cages came the sound of wings flapping, not like how the feathers of a large bird sound, but a dry, rattling noise, like stretched skin grating over bone. There could be no doubt- these were the Bat horrors. No doubt in her mind either, that from the sounds and smell, Sis dreaded having to look at them.

She thought about grabbing the cages, but they were too far apart to be clasped together at the same time and still she was shaking, unable to move. Then she saw in her mind's eye, the image of the bees that had covered her hand and arm and she found herself repeating the Guardian's words, "trust, trust" that had helped to banish her terror.

Her mind was racing now. She was thinking clearly again and flew around inspecting the cage coverings. *There must be an opening or trap door for the bats to get in and out – yes –there!* Underneath the cages a rope went through a ring and was tied to a trap door. A simple tug on the rope or better, slicing through the rope, and the bottom would drop out and the bats would be free. At the thought of that fear again welled up inside her. And again she repeated, 'Trust, Trust' till her hands stopped shaking and she tentatively began to pull the heavy cloth aside.

And there it was! Hanging upside down – the Scorpion bat. Its thick body was covered with bony, blood coloured armour. Its jagged wings hung open like a dead creature baked black by a desert sun. In each of its front claws it held a dead cloud-bouncer. One it pierced with its monstrous stinger curled back over its head, the other it gnawed at with its poison fang-like teeth, its mouth dripping – *that was the smell!*

It was as if the bat was practising, jabbing and piercing the dead animal, over and over again. It stabbed so rapidly it reminded Sis of a Woodpecker hammering wood for grubs. Only the bat did not pause as the woodpecker does. It jabbed its sting through the grey skin of the lifeless body and just didn't stop. Now she understood clearly how so many Monitors and Collectors had been killed on that single night. She dropped the cover back with a sigh of relief, turned and flew down to the meeting hall.

The assembled Collectors and Monitors were drinking moss tea and laughing together. In the corner, copies of bark maps were being given out to a queue of creatures as they lined up patiently to collect their copy.

"I have seen the Scorpion bat and it is everything you said it was," announced Sis in a serious voice. Hearing this, all talking stopped, and everyone became serious again, even the children stopped playing and looked up at Sis.

"You really saw the scorpion bat - really?" Asked a young monitor girl, who clearly did not want to hear the answer?

"Yes I did, and close up. It would be hard to imagine a more dangerous creature. We must be very careful to catch them safely and make sure we see them going into the Abyss." "And did you see the Waldrons? Asked Tullis.

"Yes, all of them, but without the bats they are no threat to you, I can assure you of that. Now tell me, what is the strongest and lightest material you have on this Isle?" Her mind was racing now, trying to visualise how a trap could be made to catch and safely carry the Scorpion bats. All the Collectors looked puzzled. The Monitors who were more studious by nature were deep in thought. Then a voice called from the back.

"It must be the web of the lizard crag spider. We make ropes from it and they can even take my weight when I am drawing". The crowd parted and Dant, the cave artist, came forward leading a woman by the hand. Kassy blushed shyly at all the attention and the appreciative comments from the crowd. My wife Kassy is the expert. She teaches spinning and weaving."

"Kassy, can it be woven into very fine meshed net about as wide and long as me?" Asked Sis.

"Yes it could, I'd need to get my old loom out, haven't used it since the children were born.

"I will need two" explained Sis "and both must have a hollow edge. We'll need to pass a rope through so they can be tied and sealed as a bag."

"What, you mean like our climbing pouches?" Asked Dant, as he pulled from his waistband a deep pouch with a string-tie.

"Exactly," said Sis, "only they must be strong and the string- ties tight enough to hold an angry Scorpion bat."

"I will go and get the children so they can start immediately. They will be happy to be involved in something as important as this."

"Wait" called Sis. "Can you make the weave of double thickness, Kassy? I've seen what the sting can do" "Yes, but it will take a little longer".

"I leave tomorrow at first sunrise. I want to catch the bats at dawn. They are bound to be most sluggish then after their night's feasting."

Before retiring, Sis drank honey in her moss tea and enjoyed a barbequed meat dish. She dared not ask what meat it was. She just concentrated on fuelling her body and even had two plates of moss pudding. *Tomorrow would bring a double challenge: to catch the bats and find the Abyss.* She filled her side flask with honey and moss dew, checked over the navigator's maps, and tested the sharpness of the small blade which she hid in her flying boot. The two net traps were tied to the phial straps and wrapped around her waist. She was ready for the morning.

Even though she was tired and the moss bedding very cosy and warm, sleep did not come easily that night. Sis was impatient for the morning light. As she lay in the dark she thought about the mirror on the sea. A mirror that reflected a world above and a world below. She repeated in her mind '*there was another world, identical to this beneath the mirror*'. She said it so naturally, so matter of fact. Now in the depth of night, sleepless on a strange Island, the reality behind that simple statement came as a lightning bolt to her senses...

"Was it possible that everything in this Kingdom of the Ancients was replicated in the mirror world beneath: every being, every realm and every world? At this very moment was there a mirror Sis? An Aynjel Queen on a quest to save the silver Aynjel's way of life? And was she watched over by a mirror Angel? Could Tala and the Guardian exist at the same time in two identical worlds...?

A young man, the son of the deputy Monitor, shook Sis's arm gently. "It's nearly sunrise, Miss Aynjel."

"Thank you. What time did you wake up" asked Sis.

"I never slept. I guarded you all your sleep long" he said, blushing slightly. "You are our only hope to rid us of the bats so I was your guard in the darkness. Here, I brought this warm tea for you." Sis felt flattered.

"Thank you" she repeated and leant over to kiss him delicately on the cheek. She had meant it as a sisterly 'peck.' It seemed a natural thing to do, as he was a similar age to her brother, but it felt very different. She looked up at his proud face. *He was really handsome.* He held her hand and called on all his ancestors to protect her. "And may they see you return to us" he asked of the sky.

"I don't even know your name" exclaimed Sis.

"It's Than" he said. "It's a very old Monitor word for moss."

"So Thanet is a place where moss dwells?"

"Yes" he said, "if you translate it from the ancient dialect. How did you know that?"

"I study language too," she said with a cheeky smile.

"Bye Than," and she lifted off into the dawn. Than watched her and waited to see if she would look back. She did, and they both smiled.

Sis would only have one chance. She had to capture the Scorpion bats one after the other then both had to be dropped into the Abyss for the realms to be freed from their evil. There was no room for error, no possibility of a second chance. If one got out – everything would be lost.

Sis rested on the cloud at its thickest point. It was like sitting on a bouncy cushion she thought. Around her cloud bouncers played, oblivious of the terror lurking in the cages floating above them. Sis untied the nets and wrapped one around each arm. The blade she held in her teeth. She closed her eyes and asked for help from the Guardian and Angels. In her mind she saw her loving guardian Angel, Tala, patiently waiting behind the veil. She sensed all their love was with her. *Her duty was to 'trust, trust' and 'believe, where everything is possible – everything secure'.*

Silently she drifted below the first cage and with a practised flick, threw out the nets under the base and immediately flew up pulling the net around and up to cover the cage completely. Then a simple slicing through the rope and the trap door dropped and the bat fluttered screeching into the spider web sack. Immediately she pulled the top of the sack down, off the cage and tied a double knot, tightly and then a final knot, just to be sure. She tied the draw string to her belt then moved over to the second cage. With the practice of capturing the first bat, Sis soon had the second safely tied up. But the noise and the smell as the bats thrashed about in the net sacks was sickening. Sis held them at arm's length as best she could. "One more thing" she gasped and pulled from her hip pocket another string-tied bag full of a strong-smelling dried leaf. Carefully she guided each of the spider web sacks into the leaf bag and tightened the string. She listened, the buzzing died down and then there was silence. The deputy had secretly had a third bag woven and had filled it with dried poison - fern. In the bag were enough leaves to kill a tribe of Collectors or Monitors, but no one knew if it would work on Scorpion bats. *At least it's quietened them down*, Sis thought.

She tied the ropes to her belt and double-checked the knots. She left enough strings to allow the bag to float harmlessly behind her. Her final check on the phial pack satisfactory, Sis burst into the brightening sky.

Far below her the first Waldron cleaners of dawn soon discovered the cut rope ends coiled untidily across the tower roofs. They were petrified, unable to imagine how this could have happened - they ran around in total panic. Some were even thinking, although not admitting out aloud, that maybe the scorpion bats had bitten through the ropes and escaped. Pandemonium reigned across Waldron Heights. Everyone was trying to hide. For the first time in living memory cleaning was abandoned - for the whole day!

Bargaining with a Galaxy Turtle

The navigator maps had indicated two signs for the approach to the Abyss. One, the Fish Shaped Galaxy with green stars that Sis had just passed, was easy to recognise. The second, the Black Star in the Derwent Galaxy was not. Her route was to take her under the Black Star, through a light tunnel, past Net Point and out onto the Plain of Ribbun that ended at the Ribbun Abyss.

Sis drew up and rested on a large rock. It was smooth and warm and had a square-cut pattern. With the silent bag hanging down below her feet she took a drink of honey and rested. As she sat she began to sense that the rock was moving and she looked down. Giant leathery flippers waved below her and a head appeared, lifting up in front of her. "It can't be. Not this big!" gasped Sis. But it really was - a giant galaxy turtle! Instinctively Sis wanted to try to cuddle the great big thing, but that would be like trying to hug a house. She slid down its shell and flew right in front of it. It's big, dark eyes did not blink as it trundled across the galaxy. It took no notice of Sis who was now dashing around it excitedly.

"You are gi-normous" said Sis. "I wonder how old you are." Still the Turtle seemed oblivious of her. "Can you tell me, please, where is the Black Star? I'm lost and I really need your help."

The turtle slowed to a halt and said slowly "you ask more questions than a brood of Hag Welders... and that's saying something!"

"Please, I am alone and lost. Can you help me?"

The turtle let out a deep sigh. "We are all ultimately alone. I am always alone. I haven't talked for over 400 triple moon rises. I like alone. Alone is good." His flipper gently moved forward.

Sis persisted. "Do you know where the Black Star is?"

"And if I know, what do you have to trade with me, eh? My knowing must be worth something?"

"Well what do you want?" asked Sis curiously.

"I'm hungry" growled the Turtle. "Fat lot of good you are, have you got any wave weeds on you?" he mocked.

"You can see I haven't. I don't even know where they grow"

"Of course you don't. Well, for your information, they grow on the shores of Lake Nega, on the Black Star's moon. That doesn't help you much does it?"

"You are very grumpy" said Sis. "How long will it take you to swim the galaxy to the shores of Lake Nega?" "About ten moon rings".

"How long's that?" asked Sis.

"A very long, long time and I am so tired and so hungry, I'm going to sleep. Just go away and leave me alone."

"Don't, please. How can I find the Black Star?"

"You can't by yourself. It's through the meteorite marshes of Goddon and then you must approach very slowly. There's no light around the Black Star."

"Actually I don't want to go to the Black Star itself, I need to go under it to find the light tunnel," explained Sis.

Hearing this Turtle perked up. "I've been there. Lovely lights and pools full of black lilies, delicious."

Sis was beginning to lose her patience. "Why don't we help each other? I will push you and you steer us." Without waiting for a reply Sis flew behind the giant's shell and pushed. Nothing happened.

"You have to help me get started. Get your flippers moving, come on!"

The Turtle lazily moved his flippers and was surprised to be suddenly moving so quickly.

"Faster" he called out and Sis pushed with all her strength. Now they picked up speed to such an extent that the Turtle could not move his flippers fast enough. So he drew them in, occasionally lifting the front right or left to steer.

In the thin air between the galaxies, it was easy for Sis to maintain speed once she had the momentum, and it required little effort now for Sis to drive the great turtle forward.

"Slow down" shouted the turtle as he held both left flippers out to steer down to the right. A brilliantly lit tunnel approached and they sailed in, slowing until the turtle dropped his flippers on the ground and sighed. Sis slipped to the floor and looked around - a *tunnel in space. How was that possible and where did the lights come from?*

For such a large creature the turtle moved quickly and with a splash wallowed in the first pool, tearing out black lilies by the roots. In no time the pool was empty and he moved on to the next. Sis, carefully checking her spider web bag and her phial straps, *they were all sound,* rested against the wall and sleep overtook her. When she awoke the turtle was a speck in the distance. She flew towards him over a row of empty pools. The turtle was rolling in the very last pool, the fifty-third! He had devoured all the lilies from one whole side of the tunnel. As Sis stood above him he moaned "I've eaten too much, my stomach hurts. I'll stop now and save the pools on the other side for when I come back."

Sis gasped. "How is it possible to eat so much? Can you move?"

"No" replied the Turtle, "can't move at all. See there," he lifted his head to motion to the end of the tunnel. "There's Net Point to the left, and beyond that, behind the high hill - the plain of Ribbun. I will wait for you here and guide you back."

He dropped his head and began to snore almost immediately.

With a short run Sis launched out of the tunnel. As she rounded Net Point she heard terrible screams and howls. Dropping down behind a pile of rocks she peered over. A deep valley stretched to the left and on the hill crest on both sides stood groups of creatures. A net was stretched across the valley, trapping birds and animals as they moved through. The netting was sticky and once touched held the unfortunate victim in an unbreakable hold. From above, howling creatures hurled rocks on them, then flew down to drag the bodies up the hill to eat. They screamed as they ripped the bodies apart and ate them, fighting viciously among themselves and sometimes biting and tearing at each other.

Sis looked on in horror and as a small sun rose she saw that the creatures were Witch-Savages, the wild creatures that the Monitors had dreaded. And they had every reason. These creatures were truly terrifying. They stood upright but used all four clawed limbs to tear flesh. As the sun rose even higher, Sis could see that their faces were blood-soaked and there was blood and entrails glistening in tangled rivulets down their filthy clothes. They had stopped eating but continued to hurl down rocks onto their trapped victims. Now they were killing for the sake of it. Eventually they tired of even this and slunk away into their lairs between the rocks.

Sis took the chance to move. Keeping close to the ground she flew with all haste and made it to the plain of Ribbun. Now she accelerated, flashing across the plain, until she felt herself being buffeted by sudden wind gusts – bursts of hot then cold air. She could feel a force that was dragging her forward. As she fought to slow down she could see clearly to the end of the plain and the sharp stone edge of the yawning Abyss.

She landed heavily and clung to a rock to watch everything flying up and being sucked into the Abyss. Nothing escaped: sand, rocks, dust - everything was pulled in. The ground beneath her trembled and more of the plain broke off and crashed into the Abyss. It was growing, getting wider. *How could she get near enough to throw in the phial with the deadly dream poison without being drawn in herself?* The Abyss was unstoppable. Devouring everything in its path as, like a living thing it, moved closer.

Sis had believed all the danger had passed. She had come so far and had never imagined that getting the bats into the Abyss was going to be the most dangerous part of all. *The ultimate test* she told herself. *I must trust. I must believe.* It crossed her mind to just hurl the bag and phial at the Abyss. *"But what if the vial leaked or the bats escaped? It did not bear thinking about.* So she watched and waited, every now and then crawling backwards from the inferno. *Had she really come so far only to fail at the last moment?*

"I thought you said you were coming back" moaned a voice behind her. She had never been so happy to hear any voice. She turned and the massive galaxy turtle's bulk blocked out the sun. His eyes looked kindly at her as he asked "What kept you?" "That" said Sis, pointing to the roaring Abyss.

The turtle just stared. "That I don't like, let's go back."

"I can't until I see these two evils thrown into its heart and it's impossible to get close enough to do it without being sucked in myself."

"Huh" puffed the Turtle. "You may be, but not me! I've eaten so many lilies, roots and all. I must be heavier than the seventh green moon in the Fish Galaxy. If I was to stand facing away from that 'earth eating thing' and you held onto my tail, do you think you could do it then?"

"Yes, I believe I could."

"Come on then, I'm already feeling tired again." Sis loosened the phial fasteners and wrapped them around her wrist. In the same hand she clung to the draw string of the spider web bag. Her other hand clutched the strong tail of the turtle who, having balanced his flippers evenly, carefully started to back up towards the Abyss.

The heat and sound and smell were awful. Worst of all was the frightening vibration in the air above and through the earth below as more and more of the land was devoured. The Abyss crept closer, the heat was becoming unbearable and softening Sis's flying suit. Even her hair started to glow. She could wait no longer. Twisting round, she threw first the bag and watched as the Scorpion bats were vaporized in the raging flames. Then, swinging the phial by its strapping, stared as it sailed out into the flames. There was a massive mauve flash as the poison was devoured by the boiling rocks. It was done!

With her free hand she banged on the Turtle's shell and he gratefully moved forward with quicker and quicker movements until they were airborne. Now out of danger, Sis started to fly and once again pushed the turtle through the air. The lazy creature who couldn't ever be bothered to fly fast himself, once again relaxed and enjoyed the luxury of Aynjel speed, all the way back to the tunnel of lights and his next meal.

They sat together in the tunnel of lights. They were a strange pair; a gold-clad Aynjel and a giant galaxy turtle. After ten pools of lilies the turtle lay down to snooze. Sis leant against his massive shell and felt the rhythm of his snoring though her body. She too slept heavily, relieved and grateful she had fulfilled her mission.

She was woken by being pushed to the floor as the turtle turned to begin breakfast in pool eleven, then twelve, then thirteen. Sis drank the last of her honey elixir and thought over everything that had happened. *As much as she had been able she had trusted and believed. She had tried her best to be true to her 'promise of the heart'.* Then the words of the Guardian came back to her, 'beware lest you judge anyone…judgement belongs to another realm… beyond even the Guardians' understanding.'

She had made judgements. In this she had totally failed and, even worse, who had she helped to become better? But it was no good feeling sorry for herself and dwelling on her failures, she must put all her energy into trusting and believing – and to keep trying not to make judgements. "And to try and make people become better" she announced out loud.

"What was that?" asked the turtle, with his mouth still full.

"I was just thinking out loud" Sis called back. The turtle blinked and trundled on to lily pond number twenty. Sis caught up with him as he was transferring pools yet again.

"Don't you ever stop eating?" Sis asked abruptly.

"Don't you ever stop talking?" replied the turtle. This time his mouth was empty and he allowed a little smile to crease the corner of his mouth.

"Wow, that's a first – you really smiled!" laughed Sis.

"I can smile when I have time between meals and that's not often" replied the turtle who let out a short gurgling sound as he spoke. Sis guessed that was the nearest he ever got to a laugh. She felt honoured!

"I have to go back, my friends are waiting for me" said Sis.

"Tell me the way, please."

"No" answered the Turtle. "I can't."

"Why can't you?" Sis pleaded, genuinely disappointed.

"Because I'm going with you, I have got to see the twin crystal seas you told me about and moss covered Isles. Delicious!" "Do you mean it?" asked Sis.

"I've proved it. I'm leaving more than thirty lily pools uneaten.

61

Don't see how I can be more serious than that. Do you? Come on." As they entered the meteorite marshes of Goddon they came upon dust clouds that stung Sis's face like a sandstorm. It turned thicker into a kind of grit-fog. The particles began matting her hair and getting under her hands causing her to slide around.

"Slow down!" She shouted to the turtle banging on his shell. As he slowed she lost her grip and slid off. She stood on the turtle's front flipper and called to him. "It wasn't like this on the way to the tunnel. The dust is all over me, we can't fly like this. It's awful. Can't we go another way?"

"There isn't one, said the Turtle. This marsh stretches for seven light cycles, no one knows how long it is, but it's the most intelligent marsh in the whole galaxy. It's a reverse marsh. It doesn't stop anything passing through one way but makes it impossible for anything travelling the other way. Sometimes it reverses itself – then it gets really confusing and catches you out. Some say it's operated by Marsh-witches to catch their prey. It's so easy to get lost. And then there are the meteors which shoot across the marsh- white hot chunks of rock come at you from all directions. Really not very nice," he added with mock seriousness.

"Please stop teasing me, it's not fair," she said to the Turtle. He glanced down and realised that she was not pretending.

"It can be dangerous, but I will get you through, trust me." The sound of this word comforted her. "I have to pull my head and flippers in to protect myself and drift through the marsh. You strap yourself on to my front flipper and hide behind and "don't stick your head out."

"Don't worry, I won't" answered Sis, as she crept behind one of his front flippers and tied herself tightly to its leathery skin. Then the turtle pulled in his flippers, tucked in his head and began to glide.

At first they made good, if uncomfortable progress. Sis could see little around her, but was comforted by the turtle's heartbeat. It was so regular and strong. She could hear the sound of rocks crashing into the shell above her and occasionally the whole shell would roll to the side with the force of the impact. The marsh was getting thicker and their movement slowed to walking speed. Above her, Sis heard scratching sounds and shrill shrieks and calls.

Through the small gap in front of her she could make out shapes scrambling down ropes and hitting the shell with sharpened pieces of rock. The shrieks grew louder, the banging more insistent. She could feel the turtle's heart racing faster and heard his short, sharp grunts as his huge body was covered with ropes being pulled from all sides.

"Marsh-witches, a hunting party" shouted the turtle. Sis could barely hear his words above the crashing sounds of the rocks pummelling against the turtle's shell. She could not move. Pinned between the turtle's shell and flipper, Sis felt protected but angry at her uselessness. *What could she do?* There seemed to be hundreds of Marsh witches, and now they were not moving at all. Then suddenly the shrieks, the hammering of the rocks - everything stopped. The taut ropes fell slack. Even the turtle's racing heart beat now slowed. There was an eerie silence.

Slowly, very slowly, the turtle extended his neck to look around. There were catching- ropes hanging everywhere. They streamed off his back and from every large meteorite around them and the Marsh-witches had vanished. Then the marsh reversed and the skies were clear in front of them. The turtle wasted no time and with powerful strokes flew through the sky. Sis held on for her life. Below her she saw the reason why the Marsh-witches had fled. On the meteorite clumps and rocks a battle raged. A formation of Witch-Savages had stretched their killing nets between several large clumps and was chasing the larger Marsh witches into the nets.

It was no contest. Repeatedly the Marsh-witches reversed the marsh. However the Savages had killing parties on both sides so there was no escape. Whichever way they ran they were confronted by the Witch-Savages who attacked them furiously with a rock barrage and soon the nets were full of lifeless Marsh witches. A few were eaten there and then, the rest were wrapped together in the nets and dragged away. When they were finally clear of the effect of the marshes of Goddon, Sis took over, pushing the exhausted turtle through the pure, fine air, as they passed the Fish-Shaped Galaxy and were bathed in green star light.

The rest of the journey was uneventful except for the turtle pointing out to her the electric jelly fish feeding in the clouds of

Cecilia. Their bodies were an opaque blue and their endlessly long tentacles colourless but deadly. Sis watched as whole shoals flew by, encircling small bat moons and filling the sky above the moon with a mesh of poisoning stings. They blocked out all the suns causing the maggot-bats to emerge from caverns deep in the craters and fly upwards in the false twilight and straight into the ribbon of stings. They flapped down to the surface, paralysed, whereupon the jellyfish domes would float across and suck up the bats. Once a moon had been cleared they shot off, dragging their lace-like tentacles behind them, searching for the next maggot-bat colony.

Sis flew in front of the turtle and pointed. "There, that's Waldron Rise and just behind it lies the Island of moss."

"I'm so hungry, I could eat the whole Island," muttered the turtle, "and that sea looks so refreshing, think I'll take a swim." "Not in that sea you won't," said Sis sternly.

The Turtle looked at her in surprise. "I'm a Turtle and I swim. You watch, I swim even better than I fly and faster!"

"It's not what you think" replied Sis. "It's a very dangerous sea full of creatures that will kill you - even big old you. Promise me you will not go near the sea?"

"Alright, not for the moment" he said to please Sis but inwardly couldn't imagine that the sea held any danger to him, a giant galaxy turtle. However as they landed on the plateau he forgot about swimming altogether and plodded off tasting anything and everything green.

Than was at the head of the group running up the hill to meet Sis. They threw their arms around each other in happiness and relief. The children arrived next jumping up and skipping in excited circles around her. Then the adults, all the Collectors and the Monitors moved up the hill to greet her. The air was full of laughter and questions. As Sis began to tell them the story of her travels, the same question repeatedly rang out from the crowd: "The Scorpion bats, the Scorpion bats. Have they really gone forever?"

Sis climbed up a rock around which the whole group gathered and announced in her loudest voice, "I promise you I threw the bats deep into the heart of the Abyss. With my own eyes I witnessed them destroyed in a flash. You are free from their evil forever." Everyone cheered and jumped for joy.

"That mountain's moving" screamed a young child, and the adults turned round to look.

"Don't be frightened" shouted Sis, "he is our friend, a true and trusted friend."

"He's a giant and he's come to eat us all up" shouted a boy and all the children ran away as fast as they could.

The Turtle stopped eating and turning round looked sleepily at the crowd, blinked his eyes and said "What's all the noise, can't I eat in peace?"

The Collectors stared in awe at the size of the grazed path behind the turtle. "He's eating our Isle" said a shocked Collector. "Imagine how much dust and rubbish he's stirring up that will float down into our caves!"

"He's so big he might split the ground and fall into our caves," said another Collector.

The turtle turned back ignoring all the muddled comments and started eating again. This time he tasted whole birch saplings – chewing first the roots, then the trunk and branches and finally, and slowly, the succulent leaves. "Oh, very nice" he said, and proceeded up the slope, devouring every living thing before him. Sis had to think quickly. There was a real danger that the turtle would in fact strip the Isle of all green and destroy the historic homes of the Collectors and Monitors. Sis flew over to him and looking up into his contented eyes asked, "Please stop eating for a moment and come and meet my friends."

"Don't seem very friendly to me" he grumbled.

"It's because they're frightened of you. You're the biggest creature they've ever seen and on top of that you're eating up their Island. Come and meet them, please".

The turtle turned begrudgingly and moved down to the crowd. Seeing Sis walking with the giant reassured them. When he stopped and Sis climbed up his splayed flippers and flew up onto his giant shell, they visibly relaxed and sat down to listen to Sis. Their initial fears evaporated as they listened to the stories of their journey and the turtle's vital part in the destruction of the Scorpion bats.

Sis concluded "It would not have been possible without you. We owe you everything". She lay her head on his shell and spread her arms out. Seeing this, the children reappeared and rushed up to the turtle, scrambling over his flippers and gazing at his huge beaked mouth. The turtle had never had so much attention in his long life. His mouth opened in an embarrassed grin.

"What's your name?" called up a small girl sat perched on his left flipper.

"Dunno", replied the turtle very lazily.

What kind of creature are you and where do you come from?" questioned a confident boy who had clambered onto his right flipper.

"Well" said the turtle proudly, warming to their interest in him. "I am a giant galaxy turtle. I think, but I am not sure, that I hatched in the sparkling clouds of Soltan, I remember it as a warm and comfortable place. I've never had a name - don't need it. I hardly ever meet another turtle or anyone else for that matter. Anyway, where do you get a name from?"

"Your parents name you" replied the little girl. He looked down at her and lifted his left flipper up and down bouncing her. She screamed with delight and all the other children jumped up to climb on. The turtle smiled. It was so easy to make the children happy just by swinging his flippers. The parents looked on with pleasure as the children played. All fear gone, the adults approached the turtle's giant form and stroked his shell and felt his leathery skin. He was no stranger now.

"You must have a name" called out the girl.

"What's your name?" asked the turtle. "I'm called Levron."

"That's pretty, reminds me of the Levron trees that grow upside down on the discs of Ratter. They're difficult to eat because you have to fly upside down to get at them, but they really are tasty."

"Don't you ever think of anything other than food?" asked Sis.

The turtle thought and thought and thought again. Everyone waited until, shaking his head, the turtle replied, "No, can't say I do." Everyone laughed. Not just at the answer but at the honesty of the lazy giant.

"Than, have you seen anything of the Waldrons?" Sis asked her friend.

"No Aynjel, we haven't. It's just as if they are not there."

"I will fly over and have a look. Do you want to come with me turtle?" she asked.

"Leave me alone I want to sleep" he mumbled and he lay his head down and closed his eyes as the children played around him.

Sis looked down as a young boy tugged on her golden suit "Please Aynjel, give him a name."

Turning to Than she asked "what's the Ancients' words for 'Gentle giant'?"

"Suppose it would be 'Zar Kala'."

"That's good." Sis looked at the little boy's expectant face. "His name is Zar Kala". The boy ran off to tell his friends and the name was quickly whispered across the crowds. Then one enterprising boy stood on his friend's shoulders and with a piece of chalk wrote the turtle's new name on his shell. "If you want to make him happy" Sis suggested to the children "go and gather all the moss you can for a surprise dinner for him when he wakes up."

"Can I come with you to see the Waldrons?" asked Than bravely.

"I don't think your mother would be very happy with the idea" said Sis. "I'm sure she would think it was too dangerous".

"Yes" said a voice from behind. "But I trust you to look after my son. Go. Be careful."

"Thank you mother" said Than and turning to Sis whispered "Let's go, before she changes her mind."

Sis took his hand. "Just don't let go" she warned and they flew straight upwards and then out across the sea.

Than was dumbfounded. Every feeling, every sight overwhelmed him. He had never been off his Isle before and now he was in the sky flying with an Aynjel!

They approached above the fog and glided into land in front of the living towers. Feet firmly on the ground again, Than could feel his legs shaking and still his heart was pounding. Nothing stirred around them, the roads and paths were swept clean. Everywhere was immaculate, not a blade of grass out of place on the smooth lawns. The polished wooden towers gleamed, but there was no movement, no sounds, just an empty silence.

"I don't like this" said Than, and he stepped in front of Sis protectively. "It could be a trap." They scanned the area, still no sign of life and no sound.

"Let's look inside" suggested Sis. Given the choice Than would not have entered, but he followed and overtook Sis to go in first. The creaking of the old wooden door opening echoed emptily around the ground floor. On every level they found the same gleaming polished floors, tables and chairs. On the stairway, at the entrance to the top floor was a polished metal box. Smoke rose from inside it as Sis bent down and picked out a half burnt piece of parchment.

'You're the language expert Than, what does it say?"

He took the parchment from her hand and walked to the window to read it in the sun's lights. "Sis, see if there are any more pieces left over from the fire."

Sis fanned the smoke away and peered into the embers, picking out the largest smouldering fragments she could reach. Then rubbing the burning edges off against the hot metal box, took them over to Than. He looked at them before laying out all the fragments on the floor.

"What does it say Than? Why have they burned all these parchments?"

"I don't believe it," he shouted. "They've gone – the Waldrons have left".

"How do you know? You're not making sense. The whole place is so tidy and polished. You don't clean everywhere before deserting your home."

"Oh yes you do, if you're a true Waldron. Look" and he handed a fragment to Sis.

"Look, under this picture the writing says 'clean up before you go, sweep up and save your dreams.' And this, 'fear cannot find its way on a clean path.'"

"What's this one?" asked Sis, turning a fragment over to reveal a sketch map. It showed Waldron rise and a group of sleds roped together, heading eastwards.

Suddenly she said "Wait here Than" and dived out of the window upwards to the perma clouds. She pushed herself right through and saw the cloud bouncers and breeze hoppers still playing innocently. She dropped back into the sky and flew along the stony shore far below, there were no sleds. She scanned the sea all around to the horizon and saw nothing then returned to Than who was still reading.

"This one describes how the Waldrons lost their faith in their cloud protectors. This one quotes the witch's omen story that predicts that Waldron Rise will fall and crumble into the sea." He paused and looking up to Sis asked "Have they really gone?"

"Yes, there is absolutely no sign of them. They've definitely gone."

"Let's go back quickly. My people will be so happy. I can't wait to tell them."

He grabbed Sis' hand and started running towards the window. "Let's fly home".

It was a double celebration across the Isle. Than was asked to repeat his story over and over again. His mother felt proud as she followed him around. Both Collectors and Monitors looked up to him for the first time and the word 'hero' was on everyone's lips.

He was offered so much moss tea it would have filled a small lake. No one slept – even after both sunrises the celebrations continued on.

Sis had found the turtle eating his way out of a massive moss tent the children had built around him, and sipping moss wine from a row of the largest cooking pans that the children could find.

"Do you like your new name?" Sis asked and the children called out "Zar Kala, can we play?"

"I need some time to get used to having a name. It feels quite good. I just have to remember it now. Do I keep it for good, this name I mean?"

"Yes" answered Sis, Your name is Zar Kala. It's all yours and soon the whole world will know it."

Sis did not remember falling asleep and had no idea how long she has slept but she felt wide awake now as the smell of breakfast cooking drifted across the plateau. She was ravenous! Splashing water on her face she called out "Zar Kala, I'm going to the first cave for breakfast." There was no reply. Looking up she peered outside and saw the large flattened area where the turtle had been romping. It was empty except for a few half- chewed clumps of moss and a row of dry cooking pots. Sis turned to go, assuming her friend had wandered off somewhere. *Shouldn't worry,* she told herself *the children will never leave him alone.*

Later, as she came out of the cave Sis was met by a group of excited children calling out "Where's Zar Kala. Where's he gone Aynjel?"

"I thought he was with you", she answered.

"No, we haven't seen him since the third moons' rise."

Sis stood silently. She was beginning to feel worried and then it clicked in her mind, *I reckon he's gone for a swim.* Looking down at the children's faces she said, "Don't worry, I think he's hiding, I'll find him for you" and she flew up into the morning air and glided across the channel between the Islands.

Ahead of her on the beach of Waldron Rise she could make out a large, dark shape. Drawing closer she saw it was Zar Karla's massive form being washed in and out on the tide line. She froze with fear. All kinds of horrible thoughts raced through her mind: *had he been killed by the dragon fish, or had the yellow jumping sea*

70

snakes squeezed under his shell and stung him or perhaps some other hideous sea creature poisoned him? With tears streaming down her face she landed on the turtle's shell with a 'bump' and slid down to where his head should be. It wasn't, neither were his flippers showing. She feared the worst and screamed "Oh no, not my friend" and dropped her head into her hands, sobbing.

"What's my name? I've forgotten it," the turtle said as he stretched his head and flippers out.

"Oh! You're alive. I really thought the dragon fish had got you" and she leant over to stroke his leathery face. "I am so glad to see you, my own Zar Kala."

"Yes that's it! Thank you. I was trying to tell a group of marine turtles I met in the sea – totally forgot, it's difficult, this name thing."

"Did you swim or fly over?" asked Sis.

"I swam of course. That's probably why I feel so tired, plus I did eat seven dragon fish, phew! Do they fill you up?"

"What?" shouted Sis? I thought they would kill you."

"It would take more than those bullies. Once they know you are not frightened of them they swim away. The marine turtles call them 'bluffer fish'; everything they do is an act, always trying to look frightening with all those teeth! Call their bluff and they run straight down to the Trench of Trevor. This part of the sea is safe now. Tell your friends to come across."

"But what about the poisonous snakes, the yellow jumping ones?

"Ehhh… Zar Karla let out a little burp. Sorry," he said shyly. "It's the snakes- really hard to digest."

"You mean you've eaten them too" asked Sis in real astonishment.

"Yes! I am afraid I really over did it today – ate them all. I'm so full I have to sleep now", and he relaxed in the gently rocking waves. A delighted and very relieved Aynjel, Sis sped back to the plateau to spread the good news.

It took a few days for the rafts to be constructed. Everyone helped. The adults cut down trees, the children collected driftwood and vines. The Monitors scoured all the wells for discarded climbing ropes, even Collectors gave up wood hidden deep in the Kelvin caves. For the first time since anyone could remember, the whole Isle was united and happy. All kind of songs rang out around the Isle and the beach swarmed with activity as the three large rafts were completed and loaded up. Suddenly a large wave broke across them and washed the rafts up the rocky foreshore.

"I thought you were coming over" boomed the Turtle as he lifted his head out of the water.

"Zar Kala" screamed the children, and they plunged into the water to climb onto to his flippers.

Zar Kala dropped his head and admitted, "I missed everyone. Alone isn't so good now, I don't like it anymore. By the way", he added teasingly, "I found four Dragon fish on my way over."

"And you ate them all I suppose?"

"Of course not, I gave two to the marine turtles and then," he chuckled, "ate the other two myself. My turtle friends have offered to help, I'll call them." He took a deep breath and lowering his mouth under the water blew as hard as he could. The water bubbled and foamed as one by one the marine turtles climbed onto the shore and lined up in ranks facing the sea. "They might be a quarter of my size but they are very strong and fast swimmers" "They are most welcome," said Sis.

Everyone seemed happy to allow Than, their new hero, to organise the rafts and ropes. Zar Kala would pull one and then six marine turtles would pull each of the other two rafts. The remaining turtles would patrol in front and behind, protecting the flotilla. Than gave the order, shouting loudly "To Waldron Rise" and they slipped into the water, into the unknown.

Sis landed on the beach ahead of the rafts. The fog above clung to the steep hillside blocking out both the suns and all sound. Only the gentle lapping of the sea against the shore and the jingling of fine gravel under the receding waves could be heard. Sis sat down to wait and suddenly felt a strong desire to return to the silver Aynjels. *Was the glass road finished? She could not even remember how long she had been away. They didn't know yet that the dream poison had been destroyed. A new feeling began to press on her, that she was needed back. She had to return.*

Thanet. An island is born

With the arrival of the rafts Waldron Rise came alive. The children ran around the shore looking for caves and secret entrances. The marine turtles brought Zar Kala samples of the local seaweed to taste but it wasn't long before the aroma of the sweet vegetation growing up Waldron Rise became too much for Zar Kala to resist. With the marine turtles following him the base of the rise soon became a chomping mass of shells.

Sis found Than on the top floor of the tower with his mother and older relatives surveying their surroundings. Above the fog to the west they could see back to their Isle of moss and beyond to the cliffs of separation. To the east the sea stretched endlessly till it melted into the mist on the horizon. Peering into the distance for one moment Than thought he could see a coastline but it disappeared in the mist before anyone else could see it. To the north the light dimmed and the sea appeared bleak whilst to the south the sea appeared brighter and greener in colour. Sis watched them from the doorway then slipped out unnoticed and flew up to the roof. Seeing the enthusiasm and new happiness of the Collectors had only confirmed her desire to return to the glass road.

Alone again, she stared out to sea then looked down at the children far below who seemed like ants scurrying across the beach.

Getting ever closer, Zar Kala and his new found army of friends ate their way up the slopes towards her. As the green of the foliage disappeared, chalk rocks were revealed, dotted with countless small cave entrances like a white honey comb. She watched for a while and noticed that as the turtles moved higher so the fog lifted. Just then she heard footsteps behind her. "Than, you look so sad, isn't this a happy day?

"Yes, of course it is", he answered.

"Then, why the sad face?"

"I know you will leave soon and I will miss you and worse still, I don't know if I'll ever see you again". Than spoke quickly to hide his embarrassment, he was struggling to believe he had actually found the nerve to express his feelings so openly.

Sis's silence confirmed his fears. They looked at each other, their hearts fluttering, and then both looked away at some imaginary spot on the horizon.

Their dream state was suddenly shattered by a strong vibration that shook the floor and rattled all the windows below. Sis rushed to the side and peering over saw Zar Karla hovering half way up, ripping mature trees out by their roots and the disturbed top soil cascading down to the beach. His friends, the marine turtles, continued up at a slower pace, their black shells now covered in grey chalk dust. Drawing back Sis sensed danger. She peered over the edge again. The fog that clung to the moist vegetation was almost gone. In fact only the top quarter of the height remained green. And still they came. It really looked like an army marching, or rather eating, its way into battle.

Sis leaned out even more and counted. Led by Zar Kala at their point, the marine turtles now numbered over two hundred. *Where had they all come from?* Then the second vibration came and it was stronger and the whole tower began to sway back and forth.

"Than", she ordered, "get everyone out of this tower and down to the beach. I will look after the second tower. Please go quickly and tell everyone to walk carefully, we don't want to start a panic." Sis watched with admiration as Than guided everyone to safety, carefully checking each floor before descending to the next. Fortunately there were only a few Monitors in the second tower and that was soon cleared. On the beach Sis waited for the last Collector to come down the path then shouted "Move away. Get back onto the rafts."

No one needed asking twice. They clambered on and pushed off into the shallows to wait and watch. Behind them Sis sprang up and hovered next to Zar Kala. No one could hear what she told the gentle giant but it was effective as he immediately flew down to spread the' order to retreat'. With surprising agility the marine turtles turned and clambered down to the beach and then crawled to the water's edge. Everyone waited, nervously looking up at the towers which were clearly visible now the fog had gone completely. A deep and powerful rumble shook the heights and large pieces of chalk broke away and hurtled down. The towers trembled and swayed before collapsing with a terrifying sound. A huge grey dust cloud erupted and once again the top of the heights was hidden from view.

As the first sun sank in the western sky, its golden rays painted the chalk face and cave entrances. Only Sis seemed to notice the streams of sunlight coming out the other side! Waldron heights really were hollow. The thin walls of this huge chalk stack had been held together by the intertwined root systems of all the vegetation which had grown and meshed together. Now the fragile edifice trembled and lumps of chalk were dislodged to smash into pieces on the beach below. *Sis felt that she had to do something, but what?* She closed her eyes, took deep breaths and tried to concentrate. *Trust, trust,* she murmured repeatedly, but no inspiration came to her.

"Good job we got off there in time. The whole things going to come down soon", said Zar Kala as he lumbered up alongside.

"That's it", exclaimed Sis. Which way will it fall? That's what we need to find out"

"Oh, the marine turtles will tell you. They're used to islands collapsing, happens under the sea too and they told me they even get underwater earthquakes – now there's a thing."

His last words rang emptily through the air as Sis was already on the shore line enlisting the help of the marine turtles.

"How" she asked "can we calculate which way the rise will fall? We must get everyone over to the opposite side."

"Well, you have to read the ripples" said the first turtle. Then he let out a whistling sound and the others began lining up behind him. Eventually a line was formed that went from the foot of the heights right down to the sea bed. Then the first turtle hit the base of the stack with his flipper five times. The vibration passed through every turtle then under the sea to the last turtle resting on the sea bed and it was he who felt and interpreted the ripples in the sand beneath his two back flippers. There was no mistaking the readings and he turned and swam back to the beach.

"What's the answer?" asked Zar Kala.

"It will fall towards the sun sets" was the reply from the panting turtle.

"That's west to our homes and exactly over the rafts" Than exclaimed and rushed off to tell Sis. Immediately Sis ordered Than to check the beach for any children left playing. She took off calling for Zar Kala to follow her. The marine turtles were already there at the drifting rafts, they grabbed the ropes between them and pulled. Sis and Zar Kala flew along the beach. The turtles swam alongside dragging and pushing the rafts around to the eastern shoreline.

"Are you sure of this?" Sis asked the turtle next to her.

"Never been wrong yet", he replied, then added "What are you going to do about the tidal wave. It's alright for us, we just stay underwater, but you up here, don't fancy your chances!"

Sis's reply was lost in the rumbling roar of the heights collapsing into the sea in a perfect west facing line, just as the turtles had predicted. The ground shook, dust and spray enveloped them and everyone standing was thrown violently to the ground. The second crashing sound was even more frightening as a wall of water swept them up, flinging the heavy rafts into the air; the passengers tumbling into the sea. Sis was pulled under by the crushing power of the back currents and was spun around in the foaming torrent till she lost consciousness.

A searing pain in her lower back brought her round coughing and gasping. She felt herself being lifted up and out of the water, her arms and legs flailing helplessly in the air. Then she lost consciousness again.

"We thought we'd lost you" said Than, as he bent over to brush her tangled hair from her face. Sis felt his trembling hand holding hers.

"Sorry if I hurt you," said Zar Kala. "I had to grab you by the belt. You were spinning round like a jumping top eel. My beak is so sharp, I'm sorry."

"No one else could have saved you Aynjel, said Than, "only Zar Kala. He swam through the tidal wave alone. Three times we saw his huge frame thrown back by the massive wall of water, it was really terrifying. On the last dive he got through and brought you back to us." Turning to the giant turtle he said, "How can we ever repay you?"

"What happened to the others?" asked Sis.

"They're all safe" said Zar Kala, who was quite enjoying taking responsibility for others for the first time in his long life. "The marine turtles saved them. Lie still now, Than has called for the medicine Queen."

The crowd parted and an elderly lady, leaning heavily on a crooked walking cane pushed her way through and said sharply "All go away, I need peace to mend this Aynjel. Big turtle," she banged on Zar Karla's shell with her cane, "you sit here to shield her from the wind. Turn over Aynjel, carefully" said the Queen as she skilfully helped Sis and supported her neck and head. "Good job you're not big. I'm too old to mend big people" she chuckled. The Queen lifted the top of Sis' flying suit to reveal a deep wound made when the giant turtle grabbed her. She took in a sharp breath and screwed up her face at the sight of the wound.

"Could be worse" she said cheerily to Sis. "The cut's clean, but I will have to mend it and mend it well." She stood up and called out "Mella, bring me some water and fire and a frost wood blanket, and hurry. Lazy boy that Mella, but he enjoys mending people and is very keen to learn. He's just so slow" the Queen said impatiently.

Mella returned and started a fire with spark stones then poured the little remaining fresh water into a bowl and the Queen began carefully cleaning the wound. Fortunately, Sis could not see the long needles being heated in the fire, nor the twine that the Queen spun between her fingers and dipped into a dark-green paste. Opening her small bark bag, she took out two tablets wrapped in vine leaves. "Chew these Aynjel," she said and popped them into Sis' mouth. "They will help with the pain."

The Queen waited, stroking Sis' brow and singing gently to her. Like a lullaby it soothed Sis and she felt the ancient wisdom streaming from the Queen's warm fingers. Though her memory was hazy now, still her senses were strong. Her mind drifted back to the Doctor's surgery when she was off school with Flu and she felt again as if she was sleeping on her mother's arm in the waiting room. Such a wonderful feeling, warm and secure. It comforted her as she drifted into the world of dreams.

Another day passed before Sis woke up. She never knew of the arguments that had raged around her; about who should be her first guard and who the second. Monitors and Collectors, marine turtles and of course, Zar Kala all volunteered to stand watch over 'their Aynjel.' In the event all sat around together, willing and wishing her recovery.

Sis sat up, anxious for any news. "First you must eat," said the deputy warden who had taken over from her son to cook breakfast. A bark tray was placed on her lap and bowls of drink.

"Wow, that tastes good" said Sis sipping the tea.

"The turtles caught these for you" said the deputy warden as she presented a plate of succulent white fish. "I have taken the bones out, it's flower fish. The Queen said it's good for healing." Eating roasted fish for breakfast was a new experience for Sis - and a delightful one. Somehow the warden had also made bread from ground seaweed and grass seeds she had found in rock crevices. To the delight of the turtles Sis finished another plate of flower fish and two slices of seaweed bread as well as a final large bowl of moss tea, sweetened with honey.

Feeling absolutely 'bursting' with goodness, Sis raised herself on Zar Kala's flipper and took a few unsteady steps. "What's been happening Than?"

"Well, one thing's for sure, we'll need new maps" said Than . "Zar Kala took me for a ride, except I couldn't hold his hand and had to lash myself to his front flipper. I'd much rather fly with an Aynjel."

Sis felt her face flush as she looked into Than's eyes. "I don't know when this Aynjel will be strong enough to fly again," she answered.

Than continued. "Waldron Rise collapsed in a direct line to my home. The tidal wave swept over our Isle and on to the cliffs of separation. Zar Kala said the cliffs had been breached and the twin seas joined. When the tide is low you can now almost walk from here to my Isle. The marine Turtles are helping to build up the sea bed with rocks.

"Have they decided what they are going to call this new Island?" asked Sis.

"My mother proposed and every one agreed to…The Isle of Thanet."

"I'm so pleased" she said as she rested her head on his shoulder and thought again of the glass roads and the waiting silver Aynjels.

Sis looked on with satisfaction as his new found responsibilities brought a permanent smile to Zar Kala's face. He worked ceaselessly, ferrying goods and carrying on his back large rocks which he swam out with to drop into the gaps and soon, as the tide went out, there emerged a continuous, rocky pathway from one end of the Isle to the other… **The Isle of Thanet was born.**

One night, sometime later, Sis sat with Zar Kala watching the twin suns set. "Zar Kala" she began.

"Don't," he interrupted. "Don't say it, please. I've never had to say goodbye before and I don't like the way it feels. Goodbyes are no good."

"So what is good then?"

"Friends are good. Being together is best."

"Yes" said Sis "you're right. You are a trusting and loving friend." She laid her head against his huge cheek and felt a large turtle tear splashing onto her head.

"Will you say goodbye to Than and everyone else for me, and please thank the medicine Queen for my healing?" Zar Karla nodded slowly.

"Are you going to stay here for good?"

Zar Karla nodded again and murmured, "Please come back."

"I promise I will" answered Sis and placing her hand on his warm shell, pushed off up into the beckoning twilight.

Sis looked down to see the new Isle of Thanet fading into the evening mist below. The last glimmer of rose-coloured light from the second sun set reflected off the perma clouds as she burst through it into the eternal blackness of space, cheered by a group of cloud-bouncers and breeze-hoppers. Her strength had returned and she felt once again the ecstasy of star-flying. She swerved around large meteorite fields and raced any shooting star travelling in her direction. She flew with joy and expectation, longing to see her silver Aynjel friends wondering what roads the Vaspers had created, imagining the majestic sweep of their new known horizon.

Galaxies and star systems passed by until the lightening lower sky signalled she had reached the star deserts of Han and once more she set out across this featureless wilderness. The monotony was only broken by shoals of blossom fish that swam in close formation, turning as one and flashing first pink, then silver. When they moved away they became invisible then they turned again to reveal gleaming silver, then shining pink. They swam through the air following Sis and floated around her, like blossoms wind- lifted over a cherry orchard. Sis watched, fascinated to see their synchronised movements as they swept on into the darkness, like a long flowing ribbon.

When she spotted the faintest glow in the darkness ahead, her heart lifted and her pace quickened. There they were as promised. The crystal fires were still burning. Excitedly Sis swooped in to land on the pristine glass road and searched around. She listened but heard nothing. The whole road complex was deserted.

"Hello" Sis shouted. But no reply returned. She flew over the road edge and down along the blue trees. Their long roots swayed in the star-dust, their strong trunks stood straight and true. Above her all the branches had re grown and were full of new buds. Returning to the road she flew up and down, scanning around for signs of the Aynjels and Vaspers- but still nothing.

The Revenge of Lord Ri

Whether she saw or heard them first was of little consequence for as she turned Sis was wrapped up in heavy netting and dragged to the ground, struggling and shouting.

"Tie her well," the order was issued and two glass rocks were bound to her feet.

"Stand her up. I want to see this cowardly creature that ran away from the might of the southern Vaspers. "We've waited a long time for you, now I will have my revenge. Bring the prisoners down. I want every one of them to see the fate of any creature that dares to defy the Vaspers of the South".

He drew himself up, raised his spear and shouted "The only true fighters come from the south!" A great roar went up from the assembled warriors who stamped, banged their shield and spears together and let out blood-curdling battle screams.

Sis looked around her. The warriors were fully battle-dressed, their armour shining and their spears flaming. They looked terrifying. Most terrifying of all was Lord Ri himself. He stood head and shoulders above his men. He was massive. His cruel face was lined and twisted by deep battle scars. His mouth clamped in a permanent sneer and he continuously bit into his lips and blood trickled down his chin and onto his armour.

"Let him be the first witness to the Aynjel's shame." The King of the northern Vaspers was pushed through the crowd and made to kneel before the warriors.

"I am Lord Ri, King of the southern Vaspers and I rule this universe. This worthless thing is as dirt on my boot, not even worthy of my spear to end his pathetic life."

Lord Ri kicked the King to the ground. Sis could see that he had been beaten, his clothes were ragged, his body bruised and bloodstained.

"What think you now Queen Aynjel? Can you call this wretched thing before you, King? Bring in the prisoners, all of them." Sis was both relieved and sorry to see all the silver Aynjels with the warriors and a new group of older folk who she guessed must be the elders. All were bound, their clothes torn and hair ragged. They looked drawn and gaunt as if they had neither eaten nor slept.

Lord Ri walked proudly over to Sis, looked her in the eyes and slapped her face hard. A stinging pain numbed her face and she tasted the iron flavour of blood in her mouth. "Killing you will be a real pleasure, but you will be the last to feel the mercy of my spear, first you will watch every one of these unworthy creatures die screaming."

Sis felt faint, her body swayed, her head spun and tiny stars appeared before her.

"First you must give me the dream poison that this thief stole" and he lashed out his foot at the King again. "It's mine, give it to me." Lord Ri held his large dirty hand out under Sis's face and with the other hand grabbed her hair and lifted her off the ground. The heavy glass rocks tightened the chord which cut into her ankles. She couldn't help herself screaming out in pain.

"Oh" mocked Lord Ri. "Such a brave Aynjel!" and he held her up by the hair again and turned her around so all could see her. Sis fell awkwardly to her knees, the rope from her bound arms held her head upright as she looked up into the cruel face of Lord Ri. She could feel herself weakening, and part of her, for a split second, almost welcomed the thought of fainting as the only possible relief. But she fought it and willed herself to 'trust, trust' She had to find an answer, and she sought it staring deeply into his hateful eyes. Without blinking she held his eyes like a challenge. Lord Ri stared back. Sis's thoughts rushed around directionless as she struggled to visualise a plan, to picture something in her mind - anything! In reality she was too frightened to function and continued to stare into the dark pools of hatred as if mesmerised, just hoping and praying.

"Faith is born of trust" she said suddenly, in a confident voice. Lord Ri drew back, caught off-guard for one moment.

"What!" he roared and bent down to grab Sis by the throat.

"My Lord, my Lord," called his bodyguard who held him back and slowly released his hand encasing Sis' neck. "We need the dream-poison first. She is the only one who knows where it is. You are too wise a Lord to take your vengeance till it is time."

Lord Ri hated such flattery and wanted to run him through with his spear. But for once he resisted temptation, realising the guard had spoken the truth.

"I have hidden it in a place no eye has beheld, no hand has touched, no ear has heard."

"Stop your riddles" ordered Lord Ri and raised his hand threateningly. Then testing Sis' reactions held his spear point to the fallen King's throat. Sis instinctually closed her eyes. "Don't, don't. Stop it!

I will lead you there."

"Show me where it is on the map," he ordered as his men spread out all the star maps together.

"These navigation maps are not accurate and they end at the Sea of Separation. You will never find it with these."

"I have the entire southern fleet of war chariots under my command, nothing in all the twin universe realms can stop us" he boasted.

Sis was thinking now, and playing to Lord Ri's boastfulness. "Is that enough for such a long journey?"

"Five fully-manned Vasper war chariots can shake the very road to Hayvann."

"If I help you, will you spare the others?" asked Sis.

Lord Ri turned around and lashed Sis around the face again, sending her reeling to the floor. Her head hit the glass and she remained still. The bodyguards rushed to her and felt her pulse. "She is still alive my Lord, we beg you, do not harm her till the dream-poison is in your hands." Lord Ri, fumed, raised his spear and then held back again. He knew they were right, but that only made him despise them more.

"We leave at the second sunrise. Three war chariots with me, one to guard the star cloud the other remains here to guard the prisoners. I have spoken."

All the warriors knelt before him as he strode off down the road. Sis was carried into the nearest house and thrown on the floor. The King and several elders were pushed in after her. The door was closed and sentries posted immediately outside. The King rushed over to Sis and the elders stood around her.

"Did you find the Abyss, Aynjel?" he whispered into her ear. "Did you destroy the dream poison?" Sis made no reply.

"She is unconscious," observed the lady elder who took from a concealed pocket in her tattered dress a tiny bottle which she opened and wafted under Sis' nose. Sis rose with a start!

"What was that? I felt my head was exploding!"

"Smelling minerals from the mines of Zac, they are powerful enough to wake the dead," she laughed.

"Aynjel" repeated the King. "The Abyss - did you find it?"

"Yes, and I watched the molten rocks vaporize the phial. I saw it with my own eyes."

The King sat back down, desperately relieved. "You have done well. I am so sorry you came back to this shameful scene. The barbarian Ri ambushed the elders on their return and threatened to kill them all if we resisted. They searched everywhere for the dream-poison, and tormented the silver Aynjels till a young girl, to save her life, told them that you had taken it. They have waited here ever since. To Lord Ri, the dream-poison is a symbol of his power. He intends to use it to take over the whole circle of universes. My warriors and I have no weapons; we have been weakened, nearly starved. We are no match for his warriors. Lord Ri has promised them a star cluster each and all their riches. They are drunk with greed and will do anything he orders, even if that means slaughtering every living creature in a whole stellar segment."

The elders could not bear to imagine such horrors and turned away.

"Refusing to hear doesn't change the truth" said the King, "we cannot escape the facts. We have to believe we can overcome this evil or…" and he looked at each of the elders and said slowly "we are already dead".

Sis listened intently. This once proud warrior, though now imprisoned and his stature debased, spoke nobly and his words strengthened her.

"Yes" agreed Sis. "We must trust, we must believe. Only trusting will make us strong."

They all sat in a circle as Sis related the story of her epic journey in fine detail.

"We could really do with Zar Kala's help right now" observed the King. The southern Vaspers are very superstitious and never harm turtles, especially galaxy turtles. They believe they collect the spirits of fallen warriors and carry them across the universe to the 'land where dying stops' and warriors fight each other for eternity. They call it 'Hayvann'"

"It is hard to imagine such monsters believe in anything" added Sis.

"Only this" answered the King." It was their lust for combat that finally split our great tribe into the northern and southern Vaspers. We have been sworn enemies ever since"

It seemed a few life time's ago that Sis had sworn 'to be true to all worlds and to help people to become yet better.' She spoken those words sincerely then, now she felt helpless to put any of these words into practice. *To save the captives' lives she would have to conspire against the lives of the southern Vaspers.* She hated the choice. *It was no choice at all!*

"So" she asked the King, "We must become evil to destroy the greater evil?"

"Yes. Not much of a choice is it Aynjel? Before he died, my father, King Rezad of the united Vaspers told me that when I became King I would have to make awful choices. My only refuge was to act with wisdom and bravery, to believe and keep my heart pure.

From a King's heart I say this - 'I vow to protect all silver Aynjels and elders.'

We will find a way to disarm the war chariot left to watch us and then the star mist chariot above. The other three chariots I leave to you" said the King and he cradled Sis's shoulders with his massive arm, then looked down into her eyes, smiled and said – "I know now that together we can fight this evil."

"And I know," said Sis." With you by my side - we will win!"

The four war chariots left in formation, Sis alongside Lord Ri in the leading craft. On passing through the star cloud one craft steered off to guard all entrances to the glass roads and the other three roared on. Sis's mind had not stopped racing since her discussions with the elders and the King. She had several possible plans but whenever she thought about what needed to be done, she felt only revulsion.

She was sure she could depend on Zar Kala's help, but she could not risk putting the Isle of Thanet in harm's way. No, she would rely on the greatest natural evils to fight the terror of Lord Ri. And the greatest evils she knew were the Witch-Savages of Net Point, the Meteorite Marshes and the terrible Trench of Trevor. She would need all her wits about her now. Trust and imagination would be her guides. Imagination was a quality the war-mongering Vaspers would never understand. Even now they were singing war songs and totally ignoring the beauty of the aerial poppy fields that waved around them and stretched to every horizon.

Lord Ri untied the ropes around Sis's legs and wrists. "Don't think you can fly off Aynjel, the moment you leave you seal the death warrants of all the creatures of the glass road. "Draw me a route plan and don't leave anything out."

Sis picked up the dusty parchment and broken sticks of charcoal from the filthy floor of the chariot and started to draw. And it was as she noted down the landmarks that a plan crystallized in her mind. *She would highlight all the possible danger points and leave the Isle of Thanet off the map completely. Lord Ri would not shirk from facing challenges, his pride would not allow it. He was certain to make it a point of honour to take the most dangerous route.*

Lord Ri's route map

Star Deserts of Han

*

Twin Crystal Seas

*

The Trench of Trevor -- *Devil Fish*

*

Meteorite Marshes of Goddon -- *Marsh- witches*

 *

Fish Shaped Galaxy of Green stars

*

Tunnel of light

*

Net Point – *Witch-Savages*

*

Ribbun Plain

Dream Poison

Lord Ri grabbed the plan from Sis's hands. "That's my sort of map - straight, no avoiding danger and ever onward." He looked down proudly at the rows of flame - spears lining his chariot, then with a mad glint in his eyes roared "like true warriors we go, smashing down all who stand in our path. It is a good route map Aynjel. Now watch the Lord Ri tear up the skies."

He stood up proudly pointing his spear and shouted the challenge to the other chariots, "First to the twin crystal seas!"

Prisoners of the Glass Road

Planning an escape for the prisoners was a slow process. The first part involved acting frightened and obeying every command their captors gave so that gradually over time the warriors relaxed their total imprisonment and allowed the prisoners to socialise a little and carry out menial tasks.

The second part was the most dangerous. Many people, both elders and Aynjels had to be involved and the more who knew the more the King worried that they would be found out. The southern Vaspers placed little value on their own lives - how much less on their prisoners who they would not hesitate to kill. Nothing in the plan could go wrong. Every detail was rehearsed over and over again until the King was satisfied. The third part of the plan, which was conceived by the King himself, involved playing to the Vaspers' weaknesses of greed and pride.

Their weaknesses were to be their downfall and they began when hundreds of rhyme baskets, woven from finest glass thread, were prepared by the Aynjel artists, while the poet elders composed verses, lauding the bravery of the warrior that read them. They were written to make the reader feel that he was special; a more daring warrior than all the rest. Once these baskets were released and rolled down the road the Vaspers jostled with each other to catch as many as they could.

At first it was like a game to these warriors who were now bored by guard duty. Then as they read their 'own' poems they started to believe that the poems were special to them, that they themselves really were better than the others, and took to strutting around and looking down at each other as if the other were inferior. Gradually this behaviour turned more serious and fights began to break out.

This made the final part of the plan easier to put into action. The King himself would 'just happen' to be talking to some elders within earshot of one of the guards. The first chosen was a slovenly creature who spent his days eating, sleeping and sharpening his spear and, in between, swearing and spitting at anyone approaching him.

"We were lucky to hide the sun-diamond before these monsters came" the King said with his back to the warrior.

"Yes" replied the elder, "I would never have thought of hiding it in the blue tree-roots. Quite brilliant, none of these brutes would dare to climb down there."

They continued their conversation on other subjects. The warrior pretended he was sleeping as they walked on by, not moving until they were out of sight. Then he pulled himself up and waited to see if any other warrior could have overheard the King. *Good, he had been alone.* Then he went to the edge of the glass road and peered over into the blackness. He drew back in terror. The branches led down to the gnarled trunks and then the roots hung down, disappearing out of sight in the cloud mist. He liked his feet planted firmly on land *then he would have no fear of facing any warrior.* The sight of the bottomless blackness however, made him tremble with fear. He sat down and reasoned to himself. *I must plan this. I don't have to go now, I'll try to find out which tree holds the diamond. Besides - no one else knows, there's no rush.*

But there was, because the King and the elders continued to be 'accidentally overheard' where ever they went. Each time they waited until a warrior was alone and then planted a greed - seed. By the end of the day twelve of the fifteen warriors were secretly scheming how they could find this treasure and escape alone.

The wisdom of this plan was that none knew in which tree the diamond was supposedly hidden, and there were many hundreds of trees. They could not ask or threaten elders to find out, for fear of other warriors getting to hear 'their' secret. All twelve were thinking the same. All were unaware that the greed of each would be the undoing of them all. With so much fear and distrust growing in the Vasper ranks, the King merely had to sit back and watch.

And the second sun had barely set when they saw out of the window an untidy shadow tying a thick rope to a post and a warrior climbing down over the side of the road. He moved down, hand under hand, slowing his descent by curling the rope around his legs. The King watched through the glass road illumined by the blue branches and then the figure was lost in the darkness. Soon after another figure was seen to throw a rope over, this time from the opposite side of the road, but down through the same tree. As that shape melted into the root's darkness there was a clash of steel and angry curses.

This noise alerted the nearest sentry who rushed down the road and on seeing the two ropes and hearing the fight below thought only one thing. *They're stealing my diamond.* He carefully looked round then flashed his sword down, slicing the nearest rope, then ran over to the other side and slashed that too. He could hear the weakening cries as the warriors fell into oblivion but did not stop to listen. Instead he quickly untied both rope ends and flung them over the side. Three more warriors sought their prize that night. One after another their life supports were cut and they disappeared screaming.

By the time the guards took the roll call in the morning, six of the warriors were missing. Their first reaction was to blame the prisoners and they rushed over to the houses where they had been locked in for the night. All the locks were secure. They returned to hear the senior warrior screaming abuse at the others, threatening them with all kinds of torture when Lord Ri returned.

That day the prisoners were only allowed out to collect water and prepare a meal for the warriors. Search parties roamed the road while the chariot flew up to the star cloud to see if the ambush party had seen anything. They hadn't, and were too busy racing star beetles and then roasting them on their spears to pay any attention to what was happening below.

The King and elders were delighted their plan was going so well. Half of the twelve had gone already and time was on their side. That wasn't of course how the Vaspers saw it. Their usual confidence was gone. Distrust among them was obviously increasing, fanned by their intense suspicion of each other. Most especially the warrior who had cut the rope of the last treasure seeker - he was the most distraught of all. He believed he was the only one left alive who knew the secret hiding place of the diamond. It was so valuable he could buy three star clusters just for himself and raise an army to conquer as he willed. He decided there and then he had to find it that very night.

"Double sentries to be posted. No one sleeps tonight" bellowed the senior warrior.

And so it was their destruction came swiftly at their own hands. The senior warrior himself was one of the remaining treasure seekers. It was easy for him to move guards around and wait for his chance to climb down and claim what was rightfully his. He was horrified as he walked the road on inspection to find three ropes draped over the side. The ropes' vibrations indicating someone was climbing down on each. His razor-sharp dagger sliced through each in turn and then the knotted ends which he discarded into the dark. As he turned back he came face to face with two guards who, without blinking their eyes, stabbed him twice each and rolled his body over the edge.

They looked at each other threateningly, daggers drawn. "We can share", said the one with the scar across his eyes. *They both knew of the diamond.* "Half is better than nothing, isn't it?"

"Yes", said the other and he feigned to turn away. The scar faced warrior relaxed his stance and that was enough for the other to thrust his dagger into his chest.

"Here's a real scar for you" he sneered. "Half is never enough; never!" He twisted the blade out and stabbed him again. He was dead before he hit the floor.

The latest assassin struggled to lift his victim over the wall, the blood seeping down the gleaming glass. With a final effort the limp body dropped away into the darkness.

"Stop" shouted the three sentries who rushed down to the road. He turned and ran. There followed a whistling sound and three lines of fire as they launched their spears at the disappearing shadow. Two missed narrowly; the third found its mark killing him instantly and the flames setting fire to his clothes. They rushed up and rolled the body over.

"It's Raikal", one said, "I never had him marked as a traitor". The two other sentries spat at the body in disgust and dragging it to the side, heaved it over.

At that moment they were the only three remaining but they did not realise it. Nor did they notice the shadows moving as the King and his men crept around the back of the houses. As the three sentries walked up the hill the King's warriors unleashed a hail of glass rocks at them from above and hundreds of tiny glass balls rolling under their feet. They tumbled, slipped and crashed down on to the glass road – their shields, spears and swords flying into the air. Without mercy they were bundled alive over the wall. They screamed – and then they were gone.

The Northern warriors felt proud again and they did not need ordering by the King to prepare the chariot. Weapons were gathered, armour put on, two Aynjels were pulled on board and they screamed into the night sky, cheered from below by the freed Aynjels and elders.

Knowing how Lord Ri's warriors fought and where they would place their defenders, gave the King an advantage for the attack. Even though the Vaspers were probably drunk and sleeping, he could not take anything for granted. The King had but one chance to attack and finish them off. Everything depended on locating the ambush chariot without being seen, creating a diversion and then attacking them where they were most vulnerable.

"Are you sure you're strong enough to fly?" the King asked the two Aynjels.

"Yes, more than strong enough. Just hope the silver thread is long enough."

The King brought the chariot to a halt. The thick star cloud enveloped them in a clinging fog as they waited and listened. After a while they became disoriented, no longer certain of up or down, what was close, what distant. The moisture dampened all sound and dulled their polished armour and flame spears. Muffled voices and then coarse laughter filtered through the fog. Everyone strained to get a sense of the direction of the sounds. Again, voices and then the clang of metal were heard. Simultaneously, both the warriors and Aynjels pointed behind and above them. The King nodded and the two Aynjels flew up, letting the thread out behind them. They moved silently till they were directly below the ambush chariot then flew up on either side. They studied the positions of the lookouts, how the warriors were deployed and where their weapons were stored. Then pulling back on the thread they returned to the King's chariot to report on the warriors' casual state of readiness.

The silver Aynjels flew back through the clouds and took up position above the ambush chariot. They eased forward till they could just be seen through the mist and banged two glass rocks together. The warriors leapt into action in a flash, just as the King had said they would. With eyes peering menacingly into the fog they fired off two spears that flew past the Aynjels and burnt a path through the mist. The Aynjels chased after the spears and caught up with them. They were too heavy for them to throw back but that wasn't their plan, instead they carried them back up and dropped them. From that height the spears crashed down through the floor leaving gaping holes and cracks appearing across the front of the craft. As ordered the Aynjels then flew back to their original position, out of sight, and waited.

The flame spears lodged in the chariot and started to burn. While some warriors fought to extinguish the flames, others hurled their flaming spears into the mist. They then unleashed their exploding fire balls, which burst around the chariot, before they moved into 'kill-formation'. For this all the warriors faced outwards with their backs to each other. At the call of the lead warrior they sprang forward then launched their spears out into the mist. If any living creature was near, it could not survive this onslaught. The missiles radiating out like a deadly fan. The warriors waited for the screams of the injured enemy – none came. *Who were they fighting? Where was this enemy?* Their frustration grew and they called for the 'bound horn.' Two warriors blew down the tubes and a deep booming sound resonated into the star clouds. Any craft lying in the path of the sound would reflect it back and give its position away. No sound returned as the dying notes drifted into the mist.

"No craft around," shouted the lead lookout and the warriors stood down from battle-stations and busied themselves repairing the craft. If only they had blown the horn a few minutes later they would have picked up the King's chariot gathering speed and on a direct collision course with their ambush craft. It all happened so quickly. The King's chariot came out of the star cloud at full speed and rammed the southern Vasper chariot full in the side. The spears tore burning holes in the craft before the impact tipped it over completely. The crew were hurled into the clouds and were lost.

"Destroy it", ordered the King, "but wait for the Aynjels." Everyone shouted out to guide the Aynjels to the safety of the King's chariot. They arrived to everyone's relief, dropping gently from the clouds. "Now", said the King, "aim for the weakened middle section." A shower of flaming spears landed in a line from one side to the other. Fire-oil packs were hurled on top that caused the fires to explode. They watched as the red-hot sections buckled then split in two and spun down like large leaves. The two flame points illuminated the clouds briefly then disappeared into the void.

"Back to the glass road to prepare for your final battle." The King raised his sword aloft and roared, "To the death of Lord Ri."

The terrible Trench of Trevor

The attack chariots raced across the twin crystal seas with Lord Ri flying low to allow his warriors to practise shooting their ivy arrows at passing creatures. That meant any living thing that might be edible. The long slender arrows had five rows of pointed barbs set behind a needle point. The southern Vasper archers were incredibly accurate and very skilful in pulling in their prey on fine lines attached to the arrow shaft. What they fancied, they ate raw on the spot, whether it was fish, oily lavent birds or water melbons[1]. As the chariot swooped down amongst them, many were spiked by the ivy arrows, dragged in and then hung over the side with the other captured creatures like air-shrews and blow-lizards, in a sort of flying larder.

With little else to do, the warriors ate continuously, discarding half-eaten meat and fish over the floor of the chariot. The resulting smell of rotting flesh made Sis feel sick. The warriors, impervious to such concerns laughed at her. "You clean and we eat" they shouted at her.

When two spear-bearers in Lord Ri's chariot fell ill, poisoned by the fish and rancid meat, he forbade all warriors to eat anything but live food. The suffering of the poisoned warriors was of no concern to him, except that looking after them might slow him down. So he ordered them to be thrown overboard and the attack chariots sped on. Sis reported to Lord Ri that they were over the cliffs of separation and soon they would be approaching the Trench of Trevor.

"Don't fly too low here, the devil fish will catch you", said Sis seriously. Lord Ri and all his men roared with laughter, pointing at her. They could not stop laughing, especially when the King challenged his men. "Are any of you brave enough to fight a fish?"

---

[1] Melbons were lumbering creatures, something like a small flying walrus that lived on the surface of the sea. It was when a Melbon herd took off, slapping the surface with whirling furry wings that they were most vulnerable.

They rolled over the filthy bottom of the craft, clutching their sides with laughter.

"Leading Chariot, go down wait on the water and catch us some fresh fish. They won't hurt you," the King added sarcastically. "Other craft come to rest and check you weapons. Seven moon ring's rest for everyone!" Great cheers rang out.

Sis looked over the side and watched the leading chariot sweep down and settle on the surface of the Trench of Trevor. The sea was calm. One sun burned in the sky, another smaller sun was just setting. The warriors used their arrows, baited with slices of fish and sea bats and dangled them over the side into the dark water. From her vantage point above Sis could see curved shapes circling the craft, getting ever closer. The fishing party's vision, however, was cut off by the suns' glare reflected off the water. They could not see them coming. How many devil fish lunged out of the waters in the single ferocious attack, Sis could not count. She saw a foaming circle around the craft turning red, then large tails disappearing under the water. Sis had witnessed this alone. No one else had bothered to look around. She called out "Lord Ri, look at this." He caught the urgency in the tone of her voice and moved over to where Sis was still looking and peered over.

The whole crew of fifteen toughened warriors, 'proud killers all' had disappeared. All he could see was blood splashed over the chariot which rocked innocently in the growing swell and the red stained waters spreading around it. He drew back in utter disbelief, crouched down and stared into the distance. *Was this really happening? Had he been dream-poisoned?* He took out his knife and cut the back of his hand. It bled. He grabbed the nearest warrior and cut his arm too. He bled as well. *This was no dream!* His warrior heart screamed for revenge. His scheming cruel mind twisted and turned to escape the reality of this moment and look to the ultimate prize.

"Let the scale ropes down. Second chariot take up your defence" he called out suddenly. His craft was steered directly above the empty chariot. The second craft hovered lower and behind with all spears throwers at the ready. Two warriors were ordered down the ropes. They faced possible death below. Above, from the look on

Lord Ri's face and his raised spear they were certain of their fate if they refused. As they clambered down, their armour slung with every extra weapon they could find, they hesitated just above the watch deck, watching the movements of the rolling chariot to judge the best time to jump.

There was no need. They never made it to the chariot. Under the eyes of the spear-throwers, two devil fish lunged at the suspended warriors, snapped their cavernous mouths shut on their legs and dragged them below. It was so fast, so terrible, not one warrior had even moved. When their impulses returned a barrage of spears and arrows were fired into the sea - all to no avail. The dragon fish were deep below, storing their prey in the caves at the bottom of the Trench.

"Return to formation" shouted the Lord Ri and the second chariot, to the great relief of its crew, flew back up alongside. Now Lord Ri had to think, to somehow overcome the blinding emotion of rage that raced through his warrior veins. He paced up and down the chariot. No warrior dared to catch his eyes as he passed. One craft was lost completely with fifteen brave warriors. Both remaining chariots had lost two crew members each. *The only good thing about his position was*, he thought, *the guard and the ambush chariots were still waiting for his return to the Glass Road. At least he had them to rely on!* "Prepare to destroy the noble chariot" ordered Lord Ri in a commanding voice. "Drop the flame jars and burning oil, spare only three flame spears and light them well before they fly."

"Lord Ri, don't you want to avenge your men"?

"You are a child" snarled the King, "Don't interfere in matters of war," and he turned away from Sis.

"Wouldn't you at least want to kill some dragon fish?" He kept his back to Sis, thinking, considering.

"If you empty all the rotting fish and meat from your chariots, empty your larders and use it to cover the lost chariot, the dragon fish will be attracted to the fish oils and animal fats. Wait for them to come, then drop your fire and kill as many as you can."

"Wait" shouted Lord Ri to his men. "Clear every scrap of meat, fish, fats and oils from both chariots. Pull the larders in and pile everything together, now." Using their spears and knives, the

Vaspers scraped the foul mess into a heap, then pulled in the strings of the larder and threw on top the remains of rotting carcasses, legs, wings and entrails. From this disgusting and rotting pile, Sis watched the slime worms emerging and the swollen solar maggots rolling off onto the deck. "Take us down within range and cover the chariot with this fish food" ordered Lord Ri. The bloody gruel cascaded down onto the chariot.

The stench was so overpowering, even Lord Ri covered his nose and mouth (in his case with a rag that was just as dirty as the fish meal itself).

"Wait for the signal. Go on my command only. Light the flame spears"

Lord Ri looked down and saw the vicious dragon fish fighting each other around the downed craft, rolling over in the food, sucking the rotting flesh and picking off the maggots and slime worms.

"Now" Screamed Lord Ri. The burning oil was first to hit and splashed over the craft and onto the fishes' skin. Then the flame jars smashed into the deck and blue fames shot out. The spears hurled down with such hatred into the writhing mass of fish ignited everything into a fire ball that burst across the sea. Into this inferno the archers shot hundreds of barbed arrows. "Hold" shouted Lord Ri. They held fire waiting for the smoke to clear. The chariot, its decks burned through sank slowly leaving an oily pool littered with dead and dying fish- massive silver hunks twitching, mouths agape, odd fins moving.

"Archers kill them all" ordered Lord Ri. With such an opportunity to show off their skills the warrior bowmen picked off each injured fish and then aimed at the live dragon fish circling the carcasses menacingly. They too were despatched, each shot through the eyes. "Hold" shouted Lord Ri again and everyone waited and watched. Sis was anxious to share her insight. It seemed so clear now – a way to rid the sea of these killers. She hesitated.' *Why help Lord Ri whose downfall she was plotting*'? Then she realised *she could be removing the threat of the killer fish from the shores of Thanet.*

"Lord Ri' you can destroy them all," said Sis. This time he listened carefully to her suggestion then ordered his men to hold the chariots lower and further away from the smouldering mass floating below. By firing at a shallow angle on the cruising fish, the arrows and spears would cut gashes into their flesh rather than pierce their bodies. This way each injured dragon fish could still swim and would lay a trail of oil and blood for the pursuing fish to follow. The missiles flew down. At one moment a dragon fish was tearing flesh from another, then that fish itself was lanced by an arrow and it became the prey, pursued by a newly arrived dragon fish. The frenzied thrashing about sent out distress vibrations from one end of the trench to the other. The oil and blood spread the same message of death and mayhem across the frothing surface.

Lord Ri's eyes gleamed at the sight of the boiling water, spraying crimson foam. More fish arrived, streaming in from all directions to join the carnage. One by one they fell foul of the Vasper bowmen, their sliced flesh marking them out and changing them from the hunter into the hunted. "Hold your arrows" called Lord Ri. "Behold. See your warrior brothers are avenged."

They watched on. There was no such thing to a Vasper as too much killing, or too much suffering. It was impossible for them to tire of watching the mayhem and slaughter. And when the Snake eels came up from the deep and joined the killing, lashing out at everything with their poisonous fangs, the Vaspers cheered.

By nightfall the waters were dark red and still. None of the original shoals of dragon fish had survived. Like autumn leaves their bones drifted down, in layers, fluttering to their final rest in the bone wasteland below. The war chariots had left, flying high at Sis' suggestion, well above the perma clouds. As she drifted into sleep, she imagined Than and Zar Kala far below, building a new life on the Isle of Thanet.

The Witch-Savages

When the third brightest sunrise spread across the attack chariots, Sis stirred. She had no idea how long she had slept. The approach to the marshes of Goddon with four suns was a very confusing place to travel through. One sun was always setting or another rising while yet another burned in the highest orbit. She had been told by Zar Kala that creatures had adapted to survive here by sleeping for two beckons then keeping awake for four, then sleeping again for two beckons and keeping awake for four [2]. Certainly she felt disorientated, even just waking in the constantly changing light.

Sis took their bearings and realised they had already passed through the meteorite marshes of Goddon, without incident. Before them lay the splendid fish-shaped galaxy of green stars and the two attack chariots flew side by side at Y speed into the watery green light. Lord Ri stood proudly at the front, spear in hand, scanning the horizon. To his left the Spider star clouds danced and glowed as millions of green shooting stars were caught up, their light taken in by the web. He appeared not to even notice this wondrous phenomenon. Neither did he turn his gaze to the flocks of wandering Pearlies; giant galaxy birds, drifting and spiralling across the visible horizon on their migration from the Nefron belts. They soared with luminous tails trailing behind, rarely flapping their narrow wings.

Lord Ri climbed down and ordered his navigator to check their bearings. "Aynjel" he called out. "Come here and confirm our route."

"It is true and straight" answered Sis. "The Derwent galaxy approaches, we have to slow and watch out for the black star and bear under to the Tunnel of Light.

"Slowwn, why?" asked Lord Ri. "Don't play tricks with me."

"Was my warning of the dragon-fish a trick?" challenged Sis. Lord Ri chose not to reply. He had no answer but to agree and his

---

[2] How long a beckon was in earth time Zar Kala could not explain, but Sis guessed it must be about two hours in human time.

pride would never allow him to do that in front of warriors who held on to every word he uttered. Instead he turned away and stared emptily at the clouds of dull grey and black as the Derwent galaxy came upon them.

Sis could not see his face as he ordered 'slow to Wo speed.' She smiled to herself. *The Lord of the southern Vaspers might be merciless and lacking in all sensibility to the worlds around him, but he wasn't stupid. He would use anything and anybody and sacrifice even those close to him to hold the ultimate prize.* With the dream poison at his command he would rule with ultimate fear and would need no one but himself. He would share with no one – yet nothing would be refused to him. That was power. That was his destiny. It was Sis, with her keen Aynjel eyesight that spotted the star. She didn't in fact see it, as the star sucked in all the light and matter near it. She saw the circular swirl of dust and light around it being drawn into the blackness. Already the pull of the blackness was affecting the chariots which became more difficult to steer,

"Dive, dive" screamed Lord Ri, and he watched as his men strained to change course. The rocking waves of light that vibrated through the craft making them difficult to control until they entered the shelter of the light tunnel. The chariots dropped anchors which held in the tangled lily roots, then the craft landed with heavy grating sounds. The Vaspers, not given to washing, watched curiously as Sis cleaned her hands and face in the clear water. Then moving to the next pool she drank from a folded lily leaf. The Vaspers approached the other pools and jumped in fully clothed, splashing water over each other and rubbing their grimy skin with mud. Lord Ri ordered them out and stooped to wet his hands in the same black water. Then, plunging his head under, he drank noisily, wiped his eyes and then dried his hands on the nearest warrior's hair.

A loud shout rang out. The nearest lookout was frantically calling Lord Ri with exaggerated gestures. Even after his voice had failed he continued to jump up and down and wave, pointing dead ahead. A group of galaxy turtles were coming into feed on the lilies. Sis understood this, but the Vaspers stood frozen on the spot as the creatures flew over their heads and glided into the lily pools. Still the Vaspers could not move. *Was this an omen? Were they dead already and the turtle messengers had arrived to collect their souls?*

Or were they really here waiting, knowing that soon the Vaspers would die?

They were completely dumbstruck when Sis followed the turtles and sat next to them pulling out lilies to feed them. She stroked their heads affectionately and the touch of their leathery skin brought back fond memories of her giant friend. As Sis offered one a large swathe of lilies the turtle said "Thank you, who are you?"

"An Aynjel Queen from the glass roads sector, my name is Sis."
"Long ways from home aren't you Sis," said the turtle.

"Not by choice," She replied.

The turtle looked over to the warriors. "Their choice?" she asked knowingly.

"Yes, but please don't say anything. They are holding a whole sector as prisoner. If I don't help them find what they want, they have promised to kill everyone and believe me they will."

"Oh, I believe you, but you are safe with us" the turtle said. "The Vaspers, for all their cruelty, are frightened of us. They think we carry their spirits away to their 'Hayvann' where they fight for eternity."

"Yes I know" replied Sis.

"We will leave now. Watch, I will really give the Vaspers something to think about."

She issued a high pitched series of squeaks and the other eight turtles joined her. Each of them nodded their head to Sis then quickly turned and flew down the tunnel and into the blackness. Still the Vaspers stood and stared. Watching the turtles showing respect to Sis threw them into total confusion. *Galaxy turtles: 'Collectors of the spirits of warriors',' gate-keepers to the land where dying stops,' were bowing to a simple Aynjel?"* Lord Ri eventually gathered up enough courage to walk over to Sis. "Who are you really," he managed to say. "How do the turtles know you? Are you a spirit that has come to haunt us? Tell me" and he grabbed Sis roughly by the arms and shook her.

"I have never met them before, I swear. Go ask them if you don't believe me" she replied cleverly. Lost for words the Vasper Lord stormed away. The Southern Vaspers languished in confusion and disarray unaware that the King and his northern warriors were even now surging across the cliffs of separation. They were united in one common purpose - the destruction of Lord Ri and the renegade Vaspers.

A loud drum roll sounded, calling them to order. Lord Ri, standing high on the archer turret announced, "Battle orders follow. Five truest archers and three spearmen to the point chariot. We follow behind. At the crossing of the twin moons we leave. Now prepare." A sense of urgency returned to the Vaspers as they worked and for a while the turtles were forgotten. Not for long however for as the chariots pulled out of the tunnel of light the warriors could see the turtles flying in line above them and this unnerved both crews, and the craft slowed ."Don't stop, onwards at full speed" ordered Lord Ri, and he started to beat the nearest warrior to him as if it was his fault. The luckless warrior collapsed and for a moment Lord Ri's anger was appeased.

All their concentration was focussed on the ground below now. Net Point was approaching and the point chariot flew up higher as Lord Ri's chariot landed in the wastelands. At the mouth of the valley his fully armoured warriors strode out. They walked in pairs on high alert till they came to the nets of the Witch-Savages. Sis had explained how they attacked. The point chariot was to take the savages from behind while they were preoccupied with the warrior below. All was quiet, only the crunching sounds of warrior boots on discarded bones could be heard. Secretly Lord Ri felt relieved. He had fought many creatures in his time but had heard that nothing compared to the sheer cruelty of the Witch-Savages. For once he was glad to avoid unnecessary conflict and withdrew his men to prepare to cross the Ribbun plain.

Although Sis felt reassured by the circling turtles, she had no idea the King was hurtling to her rescue, otherwise she would have found some way to delay Lord Ri. As it was she had run out of ideas and was dreading the moment when Lord Ri finally found out the truth, that his treasured dream poison had disappeared into the Abyss.

Three suns blazed down on the Ribbun plain as they started to cross. The air was so clear and the light so pure, they could see for thirty Vasper bands, virtually to the horizon. It was becoming very hot for the armour clad warriors and when the leading craft spotted a lake below they signalled to stop. With Lord Ri waiting above, the point craft descended to fill their water bottles. Both the bowmen and spearmen left the craft carrying heavy skin bottles in each hand. Their weapons were left in the chariot as there was nothing around the flat desolate plain scape that could be a threat. On reaching the water they threw the skins in only to find the bags skidding across the soft sand. The water was a mirage!

"That's not possible" shouted the leading bowman in frustration. "Mirages are only seen on the ground from the ground. It's the hot air rising that looks like water. We saw this from above. It can't be a mirage. It must be some form of magic."

They cursed and shouted then turned back to their craft. Even from where they stood they could see their weapons had gone and nets at both ends of the chariot were dragging the craft away from them and into the sand. The warriors started to run, discarding the bottles, pulling off their heavy armour. They were catching up now and threw themselves onto the nets, using their weight to slow the craft down till it ground to a halt.

The trap was sprung. From out of the sand flew the Witch Savages who circled around the warriors now held squirming in sticky nets. They taunted them, lashing out with claws that ripped their clothes and flesh together. The unarmed and immobilised warriors fought the Savages with bare hands and terrible screams. Then suddenly the Savages stood back making weird cackling sounds and mockingly putting on the Vasper's war helmets and taunting them lashed out again and again with sharp claws. The warriors looked on in horror as their own weapons were raised in the Savage's claws and rained down on them...

Lord Ri's shouted curse caught the Savages' attention and they looked up from their bloody feasting. The last thing they saw were the oil- filled balls, trailing flames as they poured down. In the next instant a fireball erupted engulfing them all. The death cries of the Witch-Savages rose to Lord Ri's chariot then receded. An odd Witch-Savage moved, a few charred shapes crawled and then all was still. When the smoke cleared only a blackened mass marked the terrible spot in the sand.

On their return none of the surviving Vaspers spoke. Their despair was heightened when they saw a raft of turtles floating above the tunnel entrance. Then the muttering started "Omens".... "We're doomed!"..."They are waiting for us."

Lord Ri kept his back to his men. He could hear their whispers; he felt their unease and sensed their fighting spirit was gone. *Anyway he didn't need them,* he reasoned to himself. *The prize was near and it mattered little how many warrior lives were spent. All that mattered was the dream poison, and with it everything was his.*

"Anchors down" he called and the last remaining chariot scraped along the tunnel floor.

"Make firm" he roared and pushed his way through the weary warriors, dragging Sis behind him.

Under the glare of the tunnel lights, Lord Ri's skin turned yellow. His eyes darted around menacingly then Sis saw a new madness in his stare – a fixed look with mouth twitching. His hand clenched onto his sword handle and he started shaking uncontrollably as his knuckles turned white. He began to mumble to himself, something unintelligible and one of the warriors approached and asked "Are you well my Lord".

Sis was flung to the floor as Lord Ri grabbed the man by the throat.

"Do you want me well or do you want me ill? Eh" he snarled and pushed the warrior away. "Here's your medicine – you traitor!" He swung his sword and cut deep into the warrior's side, exactly between his plates of armour. As he withdrew his sword he twisted the blade with a skilful 'kill cut' that sliced into his body. The warrior died eyes wide and questioning. "Any more traitors?" roared Lord Ri.

It took some time before the other warriors felt safe enough to approach and remove the body. Eventually they crept up slowly and dragged him away to the end of the tunnel, closed his eyes and rolled him out. Lord Ri continued to rant and rave, walking around in circles. Sometimes in deep conversations with himself, sometimes arguing with imaginary people further away, he would run after them shouting and threatening any shadows that crossed him. Sis slowly and very carefully moved up to the chariot and hid behind it just as Lord Ri picked up a bow and began firing at the drifting turtles.

"This is insanity. Stop!" shouted a warrior who could bear it no more." You kill a turtle and you damn us all, my Lord, please stop." The last word had barely left his lips before Lord Ri's arrow pierced his throat. The warriors were to leave him where he fell.

Lord Ri had gone mad. He was possessed by some Galactic demons. He'd lost all control. He'd lost command! He wandered aimlessly down the tunnel, arms held high, shouting at the lights, oblivious of what was unfolding behind him. The King's chariot had crashed into and slid across the tunnel floor. With the King leading, the northern Vaspers poured out smashing into and crushing the first three Ri warriors underfoot. Most of the remaining Vaspers, though demoralised, fought bravely, but were eventually overpowered and silenced by the northern Vasper spears. The very last of the renegades fell in a shower of deadly ivy arrows. The King took Sis by the hand. "It is well Queen Aynjel. Your friends are safe, all safe. I gave you my oath, now it is fulfilled." The relief on Sis' face spoke to the King's heart. No more words were needed. He smiled and turned to walk away. "Be careful" Sis called after him. "Lord Ri is totally insane and a madman is doubly dangerous."

The King picked up a bow and shield and two extra throwing knives which he slipped into his boots and strode towards the ranting Lord Ri, who was now cursing the stars for not talking to him and shooting arrows at them. The King banged his bow on the shield and Lord Ri spun around, firing two arrows together. The shield did not offer full length protection and the King instinctively fended off the highest arrow. The lowest pierced his calf and went straight through. The King could see that Lord Ri only had one arrow left. He had six, and shot two along the floor to bounce up at ankle height, under his shin armour. One struck and split the bone. Lord Ri, roared in pain, braced himself against the tunnel wall and let his last arrow fly. His madness had not affected his superb marshal skill and the arrow bounced off the tunnel side to cut into the King's shoulder blade. The heavy leather armour plates took some of the impact but the barbs of the ivy arrow split his flesh and numbed his arm.

The injured warriors rushed at each other screaming. The King's right arm hanging loosely down, he now held his sword in his weaker hand. The insanity of Lord Ri, gave him a distinct advantage. He was blocked off from pain as he smashed his sword down again and again forcing the King to the floor. The King fell onto his injured shoulder, his sword clattered across the floor. His left hand moved down swiftly to the knife in his boot, as Lord Ri's killing blow descended. The King rolled away, the sword cutting through his sleeves. Despite the terrible pain, he rolled over again quickly. Lord Ri chasing him repeatedly hacked at the King with his sword from all angles. Then he took a two handed hold on his sword and drew back to thrust it into the King. The King saw this opening and twisted round to throw the knife at his chest. As Lord Ri staggered and clutched at the blade piercing his armour, the King swiftly reached for the other throwing knife and with all his strength hurled it. The force drilled the blade deep into Lord Ri's temple. He crashed stiffly to the floor. Dead at last!

His warriors helped their hero King to his feet. Sis collected water from the lily pool and ran over to tend his wounds. The southern Vasper bodies were thrown out of the tunnel under the watchful eyes of the circling turtles and just as the King's men were collecting Lord Ri's body, Sis called out. "No, I made him a promise to lead him to the dream poison, and Aynjel Queens must keep their word." The King nodded his approval. Lord Ri's body was lashed to his chariot and the direction set for the Abyss sector. It moved out of the tunnel, gathering speed and glowing in the blackness to shrink to a pinpoint of light. Out of sight beyond the Ribbun plain, the funeral chariot approached the Abyss, tipped downwards and exploded in the boiling rock. Sis had kept her promise.

"Tala, Tala."

Sis entered the veil. Meaning and time from the Ancients' Kingdom faded from her understanding. Then there was a light that grew brighter in her mind and stored memories flooded into her as she crossed over. Sitting on the rock beside her was Tala. Sis tried to speak but Tala put her finger to her lips and placed the sunlight crystal in Sis' hands.

"Hold it to your heart, close your eyes" said Tala. The crystal glowed then went out.

"It's done. Welcome back" said Tala and the two girls embraced.

"I had so much to tell you, only my memory isn't clear."

"So it must be, said Tala. I watched everything, saw and heard everything just like you. It was a wonderful journey and every memory is now safe in your crystal. It is yours to enjoy wherever you want and a road for your return. You do want to go back again, don't you?"

"My heart aches to return. Only, I don't know why" said Sis.

"This is how it has to be. Each of your journeys will be stored in your sunlight crystal and I will keep it safe for you. You have experienced so much. It would be impossible to keep all these memories in your young mind and still live a normal life with your family. No, each journey you take is kept as a complete memory in your crystal, yours to re-live whenever you wish. The realm of the Guardian and Angels is your safe-zone Sis. It will protect you and always provide the crossing place from your home through to your chosen veil. I will always be your guide and companion in this realm right up to the veil."

"You mean I will have no memories of my journey when I get home?" asked Sis.

"You will know you have travelled. You will feel the happiness and sadness you encountered. That is all. More would be unfair to you. You have no one you can share this with in your human world. No one can ever know your secrets or the veils will be closed to you Sis. Remember you promised to be true to all worlds and," Tala continued in a gentle tone, "Isn't the Promise of the Heart the strongest promise in the universe?" "Yes, of course." answered Sis.

Tala smiled and with a twinkle in her eye said "I think I prefer you in a golden star flying suit to that night dress." Sis knew she knew what Tala meant, or at least she knew she thought she knew.........

Tala smiled at the confused expression on Sis's face.

"Sleep well, Queen Aynjel" she said softly.

The summer holidays drew to a close. The arrival of September brought stronger winds and across the Isle the subtle changes in leaf colour were already discernible.

"I'm glad you washed that transfer off your hand before school" said her mother at breakfast. Simone did not understand. The three butterflies glowed as bright as ever. When later in her classroom Sis sat down with her friends, hands flat on the table in front of her, no one said anything. No one, except Simone herself could see them. "*Cool,*" she chuckled to herself.

There were other changes too. She found she could concentrate for longer periods in her class. She started handing in her homework on time and even began to enjoy her lessons more - particularly history and geography. At home she began noticing the different birds that visited the tables in the back garden and like her Dad saved extra bread and rice to add to the seeds, nuts and fat balls put out every day 'now winter was coming'.

It was Christmas morning when her Dad called her. "Look at that Simone, poor thing's got a crooked leg." Simone looked out and there stood a young herring gull, longer from beak to tail than the table itself. It looked enormous and sent the robin, house sparrows and starlings diving for cover. It stood strongly on its left leg. Its right dangled down with its webbed foot rolled back into a fist. Not that it stopped him eating. He cleared the table then flew off.

"I know him" said Simone. "Swear I do. I've seen him on the beach Dad."

"Yes, maybe you have. He probably caught his leg in some discarded netting or wire. It's amazing how well birds adapt to survive. I haven't seen him around here before though. Maybe you should give him a name if you think he's special."

Simone ran over possible names in her mind. Then she thought of the names of colours and tried to remember the shade of brown of the feathers on his back. Then she remembered. "That's it! I'll call him……Rufous."

The Terrible War of the Witches

It was New Year's Day on the Isle of Thanet. Sis had promised herself that on the first daylight minute of 2005, she would cross the veil again. She sat up on her bed and watched the skyline to the east. At last! Golden streaks of light strained through the dull grey sky and she dived back under the covers. "Tala", she called softly and placed her finger on the blue butterfly.

"Happy New Year Sis," said Tala as she greeted her.

"And to you too Tala," replied Sis. "How did you know it was New Year? I thought you were outside our time."

"Don't forget, we record everything and now your New Year here is January 1st. Of course, it wasn't always like that. In earlier human times New Year was celebrated in Thanet on the 21st March, the first day of spring. A special time when nature comes alive. Come – let's go to the map room".

They stood before the map of the Kingdom of the Witches and Tala slowly turned the wheel.

"Tala, you told me that this age began with the dark and terrible war of the Witches" suggested Sis. Tala stopped turning the wheel but continued to stare into the map without speaking.

"What's wrong, Tala?"

"You are free to choose, Sis. I am here only to guide you."

"Then why do you look so worried? Tell me, please. I've never seen you look like this."

"The truth is," she paused as if rehearsing the best words to use. "I don't know if you are ready to face the horrors that start this Kingdom. I know it's not my place to express opinions but I can't help feeling frightened for you."

"It seems," said Sis, you are becoming more human and maybe I am becoming a little more angelic." Tala smiled and turned back to the map.

"There," she pointed, "and its close too – the veil hangs before the cave entrance on the cliffs of North Foreland." They flew along the chalk caverns and stopped at a small opening onto the cliff face. "This is your entrance Sis. I will wait for you here". Tala took both of Sis's hands in hers and in a serious tone said, "Nothing I say can prepare you for this Kingdom. You must hold in your heart all our love to strengthen you, and trust."

Sis walked to the edge and through the veil and found herself flying over the dark waves towards a large ship moving off shore. Her arms outspread, she glided effortlessly over the sea, lifted by the wind channelled between the waves. She felt weightless yet strong and began turning and twisting this way and that until she was above the ship and drifted down to hold onto the highest mast. Below her she saw rows of Grey-robed witches chained to the deck, pulling on large oars and being whipped by three Black robes who walked up and down the boat thrashing any witch whose energy was failing. Two large sails billowed below her feet. These, with the churning oars drove the ship forward.

Then she saw her. On the bow stood the largest witch of all. She was dressed entirely in dull black and holding up a golden sword roared out "Faster, faster". The whips cracked across the rowers who strained on the heavy oars. Some collapsed and were thrown overboard, but still the whips cracked relentlessly, bruising and splitting the flesh beneath the slave's soiled tunics.

What sort of ship was this? A slave ship? She felt weak with fear and disgust and clung onto the mast as if it was life itself.

"Withdraw oars, Net-throwers prepare", came the order from the bow. The wretched slaves pulled in the oars and collapsed, coughing and moaning. Black-robed witches stood along each side as they approached a group of small boats. Each boat had two Fisher-witches in it who were taking turns to dive into the sea and bring up small fish on short stabbing spears. A torch burned brightly on each boat which blinded them from seeing the ship's approach. The witches' ship ploughed into the fishing fleet, splintering the small craft under its bow. The nets were thrown, engulfing boats and creatures together, dragging them under.

"Bring on the Swimmer-witches," rang the command and a group of seal-like creatures hobbled and slid across the deck. Each took two sharp hooks in their clawed flippers and dived over. Sis could see the paths of silvery bubbles streaking away from the ship at lightning speed. It was too dark to make the shapes out under water, but their presence was registered by the screams of the Fishers as hooks tore into their flimsy craft and pulled them under.

"Empty the nets, Straggler searchers ready," ordered the Black robe leader. The throwers wound their nets in, shaking out the remains of the drowned fishermen. The Straggler searchers pushed past to replace them – peering into the gloom for any sign of survivors. The call for 'quiet' went up and a hushed silence fell on the ship. Sometimes a searcher would hold a torch out or throw a burning brand into the air to illumine the scene. A few Fishers were seen and if not despatched by the hooks of the swimmers, became target practice for the ship's knife throwers. Soon all was quiet. It was done. The Swimmer-witches crawled back on board to report their kill to the chief counter. To this was added the net throwers' tally, the bow lookouts' score and the searchers' victims.

"A good catch, worthy of you great Ceear," said the chief counter reporting to the Black-robe leader.

"How many?" demanded Ceear rudely, "just tell me the number" and her eyes flashed murderously at the counter.

"Thirty-eight Fishers destroyed Great Ceear".

"Not enough, never enough," ranted Ceear and she lifted her helmet to brush her filthy hands through her matted hair. "Take my killing cloak from me, there will be no more good deaths tonight. Mark the kill on the mast, signal the other ships and make for shore."

Her dresser carefully collected Ceear's war helmet, metal cloak and sword and stored them below. Sis watched the Black-robe leader as she stared, snarling into the moonless night. Everything she wore was black. Her metallic nails and sharp filed teeth were black: contrasting strangely with her dazzling eyes of aquamarine blue. Her skin was tight and colourless except for her large shapely lips which were coloured bright crimson. When she stood still and expressionless she looked as if she was wearing her own painted death mask.

Sis remained hidden above, clinging to the mast. Below, the rowers strained as the oars splashed into the dark rippled sea.

"Anchor down" ordered Ceear and she walked down the centre of the ship to receive reports from the other ships now anchored each side. The leaders from each ship clambered aboard and a tally meeting was called.

"Our kill was twenty-seven", said the first boastfully, his single eye glinting red.

"Thirty-three", reported the second.

"Our tally, eighteen", added the third Black-robe leader solemnly.

Ceear was pleased. Again, her ship had the leading kill and her place in the fleet was assured. *It was her destiny*, she thought, *to be the greatest killer on the seas. The woman everyone would fear. The war champion whose very life brought death.* She swelled with pride. "Mark on the mast: group kill 116, now disperse! We meet again at next nightfall off Cliffs End to finish the sandbar Fishers. Then all the land and seas around Thanet will be ours."

As the leaders departed, Ceear called back the chief counter. "I want more kills, let the Swimmer-witches out early before the others arrive, and get me fresh rowers. These Grey-robes and all their 'goodness talk' – throw them all into the sea."

"Great Ceear, would that I could, I fear these are the last rowers we have. All the rest died at the oars or were drowned" answered the chief counter nervously.

Ceear's nostrils flared, her mouth twisted in anger as she turned round and held a gutting knife to the counter's throat. "Replace them! Men, women, strong children – I don't care. Send out a raiding party over the Isle now. We are at war!"

The terrified counter slunk away and ordered all the slaves to be dumped overboard and he watched without pity as they were unceremoniously heaved over the side into the shallows. In the darkness Sis was relieved to see that all the slaves managed to scramble ashore then collapse exhausted on the sand. The raiding party assembled with nets and wooden staves, then jumped down into the water and waded ashore.

'They can't fly' said Sis to herself in amazement. *Black-robe witches can't fly!* She waited until the guards settled down for the

night then took off back to the shore. The darkness soon swallowed up the ship behind her as she flew up and over the Isle.

Sis followed the raiding party. It was easy as they walked slowly, picking their way in the darkness towards a village along the coast. Their torches were put out as they quietly moved in pairs to encircle the village which nestled on the cliff top.

The attack, when it came, was swift and skilful. Nets flew in the darkness, staves crashed down on unsuspecting heads and houses were ransacked as the Black-robes swarmed through the streets. No-one escaped.

"Only the strong", came the shout and the overwhelmed Grey robes were tied together and marched off back to the ship. Any attempt to delay the Black-robes or to plead for the freedom of their loved ones was dealt with violently. Fifty young men and women left the village leaving behind them seven older Grey robes, lying injured or unconscious.

Sis watched on; shocked at the savage cruelty shown by the Black-robes as they dragged their newly enslaved prisoners away. When they were out of sight, she glided down and searched the houses, guided by the crying of children and the moaning of the injured. She gave what help she could and waited with them for the morning to come.

"That's the second time the Black-robes have robbed us of our loved ones. Now we're not enough left to rebuild our village. We're finished", sobbed an elderly lady. "I've lost my husband and two brothers, now my son and daughter have been taken. I don't want to live any more" and she threw herself down onto the wet clay path and struck the ground over and over again, then hammered her fist on her head. "No more. No more!" she shrieked. Sis knelt down and took her in her arms, brushed her grey hair from her muddied face and whispered, "There will be no more, I promise you."

The Grey-robe stared up at Sis. "Who are you? Where have you come from? Why are you kind to me? Just leave me, please leave me."

"I won't leave you" promised Sis and she continued to hold her, gently rocking her in her arms until her crying slowed. "What's your name?" asked Sis," tell me about your village."

"I am Adah and this village is Broad Cliff stairs. We are only farmers, simple folk. Not bred for war like the Black-robes. They use us as slaves to row their killing ships. They came from the north four sun-cycles ago. They have destroyed so many communities and now seek to wipe out all fisher folk from Thanet. They want the seas to themselves, the hateful creatures!" "Is there no one to stand up to them?" asked Sis.

"There were only ever the Cave-witches and the Ground runners. The Cave-witches used to attack the killing ships, flying out at night from their caves in North Foreland. In time they were overwhelmed by the sheer number of Black-robes who blocked up their caves. We still don't know if any survived."

"And what happened to the Ground-runners?" Sis asked.

"No-one's sure. They used to live at the edge of the Island in marshland. They were the only witches that could run on all fours and were so light and fast the Black-robes could never catch them. But they were few in number even then and after the great marsh fires they've rarely been seen. It's possible they escaped but their marsh home is now destroyed and they can't return till the reeds grow back."

"Who are you really?" called out an elderly Grey-robed witch who struggled over on his walking stick to meet Sis. A chair was brought out for him and Sis could hear his bones creak and crack as he sat down and sighed. "You're not from here, why should you care about us?" Then staring deep into Sis's eyes, repeated "Who are you really?"

"I've come from deep within the caves of North Foreland", answered Sis. All eyes fixed on her. Yet no Grey-robe spoke.

"You come from the caves yet you are not a Cave-witch. Your gown is of silver and your hair silver-white. Show me your hands," requested the old man. Sis held her hands out. For the first time she became aware of herself. Her skin was soft silver that shimmered in the morning light. Her fingernails deep pewter grey, flashing into gleaming silvers as she turned them.

"That's the sign, that's the sign!" gasped the old man. "The Warrior-Witch has come. Look, see her nails. All the fire-stories tell of the coming of the Warrior Witch in the 'Time of Death' to protect us. She will come with gleaming fingernails and the stain of the blue butterfly. Look!" He pointed. Sis glanced down again. The blue butterfly key was glowing brightly on her silver skin.

Everyone saw it and believed.

The coming of the Warrior-Witch

A strange sense of excitement and purpose coursed through Sis's veins. It was as if she was being strengthened from within and her mind sharpened. Though she was not moving she felt as if she was passing through yet another veil - all the time gathering new memories and new knowledge. She sensed her abilities were increasing. Crossing from this witch world into another she gained new wisdom and insights from the ancient realms. She could not understand these changes but it was impossible to deny them. Then it happened. In a brilliant flash of light that illumined her whole being - Sis was transformed into the Silver Warrior-Witch.

As she stood up she could see some of the freed slaves struggling up the hill to their left, and great shouts of joy from children and parents alike who rushed down to support them and help them up into the village.

She spoke with real confidence now and announced to the gathering Grey-robes, "We must unite all the witches of Thanet to destroy the evil of the Black-robe slavers. Send out messengers across the Island. There will be a War Council, here at noon."

While the Grey-robe elders prepared for the meeting, Sis sat listening to the stories of Thanet from the old man. There had been several invasions in the past, but nothing as devastating as the Black-robe slavers. He feared the Island could never recover. So many witches had been destroyed or were missing. No one knew if they were in hiding or already dead. "It was a beautiful Island once", remarked the old man.

"And it shall be again. I swear to you on the blue mark on my warrior's hand. We must believe in our cause and trust. Now we must prepare."

Sis flew off to North Foreland and hovered at the cliff face, searching for openings, calling out for the Cave-witches. Up and down she flew until she saw a movement in the shadows of a small cave entrance. Staring into the darkness she called out, "I am the Warrior-Witch, come to destroy the Black-robe evil. Who among you will help me?"

Her call echoed into the cave network and she waited and listened. No sound came back. Again, this time louder, she repeated her call.

"How do we know you speak truly? A voice echoed from the shadows. "We await the coming of the 'Warrior-Witch' but she will come with a sign."

"Then see this", said Sis and she plunged her hand into the opening. The butterfly glowed blue, her nails flashed in the dark. She heard gasps of astonishment from within the cave and the grinding sound of rocks being rolled aside.

"Come in. Our hearts greet you", said the first Cave-witch who stretched out his hand to welcome Sis. These witches were bigger than the Grey-robes and had long shining wings held behind them. Their piercing eyes glowed yellow in the darkness.

"Light a torch for our honoured guest", came the order from behind the group and a young man, taller than the rest, stepped forward. "You have been promised in all our ancestor tales. We had given up believing and have lived here in sadness, now your coming brings us hope." As the torch lit up the cave, Sis admired the Cave-witches. Their clothes were deep blue, like silk velvet. Their skin, a shining blue-black and their hair long, wavy and grey.

"I have been told that you are brave fighters who battled long with the slave ships. I come to tell you that you have the place of honour by my side in the final battle that is coming."

"My title is Storra," said the tall young man. "I, Storra, and all the Cave-witches pledge our lives to you. Ours will be the honour to be by your side."

"Then meet us, Storra, on the beach by Broad Cliff Stairs at noon. We will draw up battle plans there."

On Sis's return she found the beach busy with activity. Word had spread around the Island and representatives were arriving from all directions. There were Fishers and the Grey-robes who were all proudly wearing their best clothes as the hosts of the War Council. A few Ground-runners sped up and down the shoreline, groups of Pine-witches with their sharpened spears practised their throwing skills across the sand. Down the cliff, the small Spider witches rolled, as Sis saw Storra flying in.

A Fisher-witch stepped into the water and blew a strange whistle, turning his head around as he blew five times to each part of the horizon. The birds flocked in and settled around him on the sand. The biggest, the Great Black-Backed Gulls were given the sea watch and flew off on heavy wing beats. The Herring Gulls were to patrol the approaches and the beach. The smaller, more buoyant Black-Headed Gulls, assigned to patrol around the marsh edges.

"That's Jonn the fisher. He talks to the birds," said Storra. "Birds have sharper eyes than any witch, they will be our guards. They see everything and will report back to him."

"Please ask him to join the meeting," requested Sis as she walked back to the crowd gathered around the tables.

"I know this" Sis began "that at night fall the Black-robes will assemble off Cliffs End to destroy the sandbar Fishers. And I know too that their leader Ceear will be there before the other slave ships and will have her Swimmer-witches already in the water. She has boasted she wants the best kill. We have little time left."

"We pledge a hundred bell ties of invisible thread", said the Spider- witch, "no hand can break its hold".

"Good" said Sis "I can see many uses for that already." The old Grey-robe noted this down on a large sheet of parchment which he stretched out across the table. Sis looked over his shoulder as he wrote. Then she suddenly stood up. "No witch tribe can stand alone against the Black-robe evil. We need to chart the strengths of each witch groups and everyone's skill with weapons. If we all work as one, plan as one then, together we become an army. And I, the Warrior-witch shall lead you." There were loud cheers and hammering on the table. Then every witch joined in shouting "The army of Thanet, The army of Thanet!"

The old Grey-robe immediately started drawing up a chart, recording every useful detail as the witches spoke. The Pine-witch, a tall green figure, stood up. "Every man, woman and child carries two spears, our community is ready." A cheer broke out.

The Ground-runner stood up on her hind legs. "Our crowd has gathered. We are as fleet as the wind, ready to serve you Warrior witch."

"And you Storra, how many Cave-witches fly with you?" asked Sis.

"Every living one, twenty in all, but we have few weapons", he said.

Sis turned to Jonn, "You know the tides. How can they be read to our advantage?" Jonn took out a small net and fumbled with the knotted twine as if calculating.

"If we can get the slave ships to come deep into the bay, they would get stranded on the sands as the tide began to wane – around two hours after mid night If only we could keep them there for long enough…"

"We have to, we just have to. We have no ships of our own," stressed Sis. Our biggest challenge is how to deal with the Black robes' Swimming-witches. I've seen how they operate and they are fast and deadly and they can hide underwater."

"Well, only the otter swims faster" said Jonn, "but I don't see any here."

"We need them" insisted Sis. "Can't you call them?"

"I could send a message with the gulls, but otters keep to themselves and anyway, we've had so many fights with them,

always over fish. They won't listen to me."

Sis sat back and looked over the chart. A plan was forming in her warrior mind – a plan of battle.

She stood up and said loudly, "It won't work without the otters. Where are they? I will go myself."

"Probably lazing on the sandbars now, fly into the sun, you won't miss them."

Sis flew across the island to where the cliffs sloped down to the sandy shore of the bay.

There, on a partially submerged sand spit, wallowed the otters. She landed amongst them. A raised eyelid was the only recognition they gave her, before they returned to snoozing.

"Who is your leader?" asked Sis. Her question remained unanswered. "I've found a new river where the salmon run", announced Sis. This did get a response! The largest otter, a dark grey male with black spots, curled his lips to show his sharp teeth. "Salmon eh?" now that could be tempting."

"We need your help to fight the Black-robes. They're coming here to kill the Fishers tonight."

"We should be helping *them,* not you", said the otter sourly. "Fishers take our food, we'd be better off without them" and he turned to lie down again.

"And when the Fishers are gone and the Black-robes want all the fish for themselves, they will come after you – then you will be alone with no one to help you. You are so selfish. Don't you see! Unless you join the witches' Army of Thanet against our common enemy, you have no future." The otters remained quiet. Sis stamped in dire frustration. The vibrations in the sand woke a few up, for a moment, and then they settled down again.

Angry and disappointed Sis returned to the meeting. "They're not coming", she announced. "We'll have to do without them."

"But how do we tackle the Swimmer-witches? We can't swim," said the Pine witch. "Maybe we can use nets" suggested Sis. "Anyway, let's concentrate on the battle."

"We have pooled our knowledge of the Black-robes," said Storra and handed Sis a parchment. Sis took this and the Greyrobe's chart over to a side table and sat reviewing them with Storra.

Witch Tribe	Weapons	Capabilities /Skills
Grey-robes (stone grey)	Fighting sticks, swords, good archers.	Strong bodied, courageous individuals, skilled sling shots, good swimmers.
Cave-witches (deep blue)	Swords, spears, excellent archers.	Sharp eyesight, experienced warriors – Thanet's sole flying witches.
Pine-witches (dark green)	Double pine-spears, killing staves.	Fast movers and practised tree climbers. Good at woodcraft and concealment.
Fisher-Witches (dull grey)	Short stabbing spears, gutting knives.	Good swimmers, skilled boatmen, tenacious fighters.
Ground-runners (mottled green/beige)	Flat bladed slashing swords, knee knives, needle spikes.	Smallest but fastest witches running on all fours. Hide in low undergrowth – use surprise attack and ambush. Savage fighters.
Black-robes (black uniform)	*Four killer ships* Heavily armoured, hardened warriors. Skilled in archery, spears, swords, knives and unarmed combat.	Merciless killers, dedicated to destroying all Thanet witches. Swim but cannot fly.
Swimmer-witches (seal grey)	Ripping hooks, razor claws.	Cannot fight on land. Fastest underwater witches, deadly hunters.

She called across to the assembled witches. "While I prepare the battle plans choose an escort to take the children to safety in the centre of the Island. They should leave soon to reach the caves before nightfall."

Sis studied the parchments in detail and began to sketch out a map. She had many questions for Storra. She wanted to know everything about the Black-robes. Were they a disciplined force? What were their weaknesses? How skilled were their warriors? Slowly, very slowly, a plan was evolving in Sis's mind. She now understood that the Black robes were most vulnerable on land. Somehow she had to get them to abandon their ships. One thing was now certain in her mind; *the price of failure was too horrible to contemplate. She had to trust and believe and she had to get all the Thanet witches to trust too and to believe in her plan. For this she must lead by example.*

The meeting was called to order. Sis rose and addressed the gathered fighters. Each group was told to elect one leader to report to Jonn. Only messages from Jonn to be accepted as true.

"Fishermen, float all your boats close to the shore and at night fall fire your torches and swim back to the beach to join the Pine witches along the shore line. A little further north, a joint group of Grey and Fisher witches will hide below the rocks at Cliffs End, to cut off any attempt at retreat. Along the whole length of the bay the Grey-robes will light large fires and keep them burning for the torch spears. We need to draw all the killer ships into the shallow bay until the tide leaves them on the quick sands. Then the Ground-runners will attack across the sands and the Cave-witches from the sky. We will destroy them. Go now, prepare for the longest night of your lives! We meet at twilight on the sands. The old Grey-robe looked up at Sis and asked "What of the Swimmer witches?"

Sis shook her head slowly. "I honestly don't know", she admitted. "I really don't know."

High tide saw the otters dispersing from the flooding sand bar and small fishing craft being anchored in an arc close to the shore. No gulls had reported sightings, each witch group waited, ready in their allotted place. The Spider-witches continued to spin, coils and coils of web as Sis flew from one group to another and the excitement and anticipation grew. Everyone waited and watched the sky darken then they heard Sis's voice calling "Storra stay close, if anything happens to me, you take command."

"Please take this, it will protect you" said Storra and he handed her a glowing blue sword. Sis took it and held it in two hands.

"It's beautiful, what is it made of?"

"A rare metal mined in the caves many generations ago. It is light as a feather and sharper than the rays of the sun. It has never been carried into battle before. Perhaps it was made for this night. There" he said, "a blade worthy of a Warrior Queen." He bowed to Sis and left to prepare his fighters.

The first gulls reported Ceear's ship rounding the headland and the message was winged to the waiting fighters. *It begins,* Sis said to herself and as twilight descended Sis ordered the boat torches to be lit.

They watched the slave ship approach, slowing for a moment to let off the Swimmer-witches and then picking up speed towards the small boats. Then Sis saw the outlines of three large gulls overhead and the message came, "three Black-robe ships approaching from Cliffs End."

"Roll up the sails", shouted Ceear. "Hold oars" and the Black robes scrambled up the rigging to gather in and lash the sails.

"Go!" ordered Sis and six Cave-witches flew out, a web coil in each hand. They flew around and around wrapping the sails and Black-robed witches to the beam with the invisible thread. Their cries were ignored by Ceear till, impatient for their return, she glanced up and saw her crew members festooned helplessly, unable to move, choking.

Her attention switched to the small craft ahead and she shouted orders for the oar slaves, "fast ahead". The oars moved back a fraction then came to a juddering halt, throwing the slave drivers across the deck. The whips cracked across the rowers but strain as they might the oars would not move. Ceear stamped on the rowers as she stumbled across the deck to look over the side. The oars were fixed, immovable. She screamed with rage. In the dim light the threads weaving the oars together on both sides of the ship could not be seen, nor could the Cave-witches who were skimming across the water returning to the beach.

"That slowed her up", observed Sis. "Light the fires all along the beach". Ceear scowled at the fires, imagining them to be fishing villagers and vowed to wipe them all out on sea or land.

"Free the oars", she roared." Untie the slaves, get them overboard, now. Kill anyone who tries to escape." It took the slaves a while to cut through the web ropes and free the oars. By the time they had finished and were scrambling back on board the other ships arrived and raised their sails alongside. Unseen, the Cave-witches wrapped up the sails and the rigging crews of the other ships then flew back to the beach.

"Killing speed", Ceear ordered as her ship crashed into the first boat, then the second. She could hear the crisp 'ripping' sound as the Swimmer-witches' hooks smashed into the fishing craft, pulling them under. Her killing passion rose and she ordered the net throwers to prepare and all the time her ship was drawing closer and closer to the shore.

"Fires out", Sis shouted and the Grey-robes doused the flames. "Bring down the Pine-witches with torches burning. Scatter the Ground-runners with torches-everywhere!"

The crew of all four slave ships looked around in bewilderment. A long line of torches processed down the coast line towards the bay. Before them, flames raced along the shore, criss-crossing the sand dunes, leaving a blur of light. Then the screams started and Swimmer-witches broke surface, waving and pleading for help. The water boiled as otters rolled among them, biting into flesh and flashing away. Again and again the Swimmer-witches were attacked with such power and speed. They thrashed around in blind panic. Above, the Cave-witches watched then flew back to Sis to report the otters' appearance. News travelled along the line of waiting witches and a relieved cheer sounded for the otters.

Ceear stormed to the bow. "Signal the outer ships to beach to the west and east. We'll cut these Fishers to pieces. Throw the nets" she roared as she drew her massive sword and waved it in the air. The gulls soared above the fleet, calling the ship movements back to Jonn. Sis dispersed half the Pine-witches to the east and ordered the other to hold the west beach with a few Grey robes. The Cave-witches were split into three support groups: to the east, to the west and behind the Grey-robes. The Ground-runners waited at the front.

"Pull in the nets", ordered Ceear, and she waited to see her first kills dragged on board. The nets were heaved over and crashed onto the deck. "Count them", she roared. No answer came. The counter trembled with fear as the injured Swimmer- witches writhed in the dripping nets. Ceear rushed forward and stared in disbelief. *No Fishers. No Fishers!* She lashed out with her sword, slashing into the injured Swimmers till blood ran across the decks. "You have failed me. You have disgraced me." Then turning to the throwers ordered the Swimmer-witches to be ditched overboard. "Let none back." Ignoring the screams of the Swimmers falling prey to the darting otters, she called for the rowers to stop. "No torches. No sound."

Ceear glared towards the shoreline, listening for any sign. The death cries of the Swimmer-witches ceased leaving only the calls of the circling herring gulls and the gentle lapping of the waves against the ship. She sensed there were strange forces arrayed against her this night. She felt it in her blood. *If necessary she was prepared to wait till daylight and go ashore to kill the Fishers herself.* Her head swam with hatred. *She would wait for the outer ships to attack then take all the glory for herself.*

Now that the sea was safe, groups of Grey-robes waded out in the darkness on either side of the western ship as it ground into the beach with a dull roaring sound. As the Black-robes streamed off they were cut down by a hail of bone sticks and knives from Fishers. The next wave stormed onto the shore chasing the Grey robes who ran back into a gully between the sand dunes. As the Black-robes followed screaming battle oaths, the Ground-runners sprang from behind running between their legs with spider web netting. The Black-robes tripped and stumbled, swearing at the threads they could not see. Then the Grey robes turned and ran back, their bone stabbing spears ending the lives of the cowering Black-robes.

The cry went up from the ship as the guards jumped down and raced to the sand dunes. They too were cut down, this time by the Cave-witches, who flew out of the night with swords raised. It happened so swiftly, not one guard even had time to raise his weapon in defence before they all crashed into the sand, dying.

The Grey-robes clambered up the sides of the ship and wrenched out the chain anchors holding the slave rowers and helped them ashore. A Cave-witch flew swiftly to report back to Sis. "Keep the middle slave ships busy, keep them on edge. I'm going to help the Pine-witches". Storra with five of his best archers flew around the two middle ships, firing odd arrows from differing directions. The Black-robes responded by throwing spears and firing arrows into the night's blackness. But they were just wasting weapons on assailants they could not see - and it went on.

To the east the witches from the second ship stormed ashore and searched the horizon for the Fisher's fires. All was dark, very dark as they moved slowly up the beach. The first attack came from the Ground-runners who charged out from behind the grass hillocks and wielding sharp, flat blades, hacked into the witch's legs. Those hit, crashed to the sand in agony and were left behind as the main force charged over the sand dunes and into the hawthorn bushes. There was only one clear path leading inland that was not crossed by tight Spider web rope hung just at ankle height and above at shoulder level. As the last Black-robe passed through the bramble entrance that too was sealed with bands of web stretched tightly. They were now encircled.

The Black-robes saw the glow as torch spears were lit around them and watched in terror as the missiles rained down amongst them. Still the Pine-witches remained hidden. Then the gulls came, wheeling and screaming out of the blackness in their thousands. Ghostly grey forms swooping and pecking at the Black-robe's eyes. Then just as suddenly they disappeared.

Sis, the Warrior-witch, led the flight of the Cave-witches. Screaming down low and fast with swords flashing they sliced into the Black-robes and were gone back into the night in an instance. Without a second thought the fallen Black-robes were abandoned as the rest charged off in all directions screaming for blood. They shouted and cursed and crashed down caught in the Spider-witch webs. As they thrashed around helplessly the spears of the Pine witches despatched them one by one, while all around the Ground runners searched for any stragglers.

Back on the water line Sis watched the slave ship roll gently in the waves. It's rowing chains hung empty, dead Black-robes floated face down in the shallows around the ship. *The Thanet witches had done well,* thought Sis, *yet it was far from over.* She called for Storra and handing him a rolled parchment said "find a survivor and give him a boat to deliver this to the evil Ceear." The wounded witch was thrown into a fishing boat and pushed out towards Ceear's ship. Sis called for everyone to regroup behind the gorse covered dunes, out of sight from the sea.

A grapple rope was flung into the boat as it approached and was dragged to the ship. The wounded witch was helped aboard and carried to Ceear. With shaking hands he presented the scroll then screwed his eyes shut as Ceear read:

Post this on your mast

Black-robes 121...*a good kill.*

Fishers 0..............even better!

The terrible rage Ceear experienced was beyond any normal form of expression. She shook, she trembled, she stamped and raising her eyes to the stars let out a scream that carried across the bay. All the released slaves heard this awful sound and pictured the monster howling, and were filled with fear.

"We must wear them down", ordered Sis. "I want the fastest runners with torches on the beach now. Grey-robes collect all weapons and bring them here. Cave-witches prepare your attack. You must be accurate, we cannot harm a single slave.

On seeing the runners on the beach the Black-robes unleashed a flurry of arrows, over and over again. Torches were put out, the arrows collected, and the torches lit again and carried through the darkness in weaving patterns. More arrows flew till the air was full of their swishing sound, but all fell short and were collected to fill the arrow pouches of the Cave-witches, who, bows in hand now took off. They flew behind the killing ships, picking each target carefully. Their arrows loosed they flew back out of range. Below them, Black-robes crashed dead onto the ships' decks, some splashed into the sea and they continued to fall as the cave-witch arrows flew with deadly accuracy.

The second ship tried to break away and move off shore. Ceear had it lashed to hers and rushing onto the second ship struck the leader down in front of his men. It was a vicious thrust of her sword straight through his heart. "So die all cowards" yelled Ceear. "Now I want every Fisher dead by dawn. Move in"

The oars splashed down as the slaves heaved on the oars. Both ships moved forward momentarily only to grind to a halt.

"Why are we stopping?" screamed Ceear.

"We're on the bottom" the steersman shouted.

"Row harder - get us off" and she looked over the side to see the oar blades skidding across rippled sand bars now appearing under the receding tide. "Untie the slaves. Bring them forward". The hapless slaves were made to stand around the ship as a living shield.

"Bring your slaves too. Line them up in front" he ordered the second ships' crew." Let's see if the Fishers' have nerve enough to kill their own."

Sis looked on with growing sadness and bitterness too, that the evil Black-robes could be so cowardly as to use innocent slaves to hide behind. This was not in her plan. She called a meeting of all groups, who gathered around her. The sky was just beginning to lighten and already a pink hue was spreading across the horizon.

"Get the Ground-runners, Pine and Grey robes to form a circle around the ships. Let them see you but stay out of bow range on the sands" ordered Sis and she watched as the group moved out into the gloom splashing through shallow pools.

"How many Black-robes left Jonn?" asked Sis.

"The gulls count fifty in the second ship and about the same in the lead killer"

"That can't be right", said Sis. "Ceear's ship is bigger with nearly twice the crew of the others. Where are they?" Everyone froze and listened intently when from above and behind came shrill cries as a flock of black-headed gulls wheeled overhead.

"They're behind us!" shouted Jonn in alarm as the Black-robes smashed through the undergrowth with weapons clanging and fell upon the group. The battle that raged saw many witches fall. At first it was chaos. The Black-robes swept through the group lunging and slashing with swords and short spears. Some Grey robes rolled away under the bushes; others, alongside the Pine witches were cut down where they stood. The cries of pain and terror ringing out above the sounds of clashing steel brought a smile to the dripping mouth of Ceear, who believed fortune to be now turning in her favour.

When reinforcements arrived from the beach they could make no immediate impact. The Black-robes fought, killed and died intertwined with their sworn enemies in close combat. There was no clear target for fear of hitting their own, so bows discarded, the Pine, Grey-robes and Fishers charged into the mayhem with swords and daggers poised. Yet again the Ground-runners more than proved their worth. Keeping low they slunk, weasel-like between the fighters' legs, aiming quick, vicious slashes across the knees of the Black-robes who crumbled to the ground in agony. The call came "Dive. Down. Down" and those that heard threw themselves forward just as arrows hissed above them. The Cave witches had waited for this moment. Having chosen their prey and become accustomed to the dim light accurately let loose a flight of arrows that pierced the Black-robes' helmets with a sickening 'cracking' sound. A few Black-robes ran into the bushes, pursued by a group of Fishers, who hounded them into a sand dune and onto the waiting spears of the injured Pine-witches. Their revenge was swift as they lanced the Black-robes running straight at them. The gulls were sent to search the scrubland for survivors. There were none.

"Call the fighters together" called Sis." Grey-robes to tend the wounded, Pine-witches help move the wounded back to the forest edge then return quickly. Cave-witches go with the gulls and survey the Island and sea all around. We cannot stand another surprise attack. What are our casualties?" she asked Storra and Jonn as they stood together.

"We've suffered two dead and six injured from the Cave witches" said Storra."I know the Ground-runners lost three and the Pine-witches have seven dead and ten injured; some very badly". "And you Jonn?"

"We lost five Fishers but the Grey-robes lost at least thirteen in that last attack. I'm afraid they may have more injured."

Sis looked down at the sand beneath her feet. It caught the early morning light. As she raised her head she could see clearly across the bay. Dawn had come and gone and she hadn't noticed. The other witch leaders joined to form a circle and one by one their eyes fixed on Sis, waiting for guidance, waiting for the call to action.

Sis jumped up. "We must finish this now before the tide frees their killing ships but we must protect the slaves. The key is to destroy Ceear. With her gone we can match the Black-robes. That way lays victory and freedom for Thanet."

Storra rose slowly. "Give me with this task and I will not fail". Then taking out an arrow kissed its flight feathers. "For the heart of the monster Ceear" he shouted then held out the arrow for all to see.

Sis stepped forward and placing her hand on his shoulder said, "Go with the blessing of all Thanet - and may your ancestors guide you Storra."

The sun was drying out the sand into hard ripples as the Thanet witch army closed in. On the beach a line of Pine-witches marched forward just out of range of the Black-robe archers. Cave-witches flew across drawing more arrows from the ships. This went on till all their arrows were wasted and Ceear called for spears at the ready. Behind the ship Storra hovered with bow drawn - its string taunt against his cheek. He waited.

Around the stranded ships the circle of Pine and Fisher witches closed in as Sis called "archers ready" and took off. Flashing past each ship she shouted for the slaves to "Jump now!" The slaves could see the encircling archers and jumped down to the sand and rolled under the curves of the wide bows, pressing themselves against the barnacled timbers. The arrows rained down on the Black-robes who collapsed and fell overboard onto the sand.

"Shields up" called Ceear and she moved back from the bow.

"Ceear" cursed Storra. The Black-robe leader was out in the open now. For a split second her sparkling eyes caught the glint of the arrow point before it struck her, piercing her armour and tearing into her chest. She stood, mouth agape, looking down in utter disbelief. She saw the arrow shaft dripping blood then as she went to look up the second arrow smashed through her helmet into her forehead. She stood, dead. Then crashed like a felled pine into the pile of slave chains.

The archers now closed in from all sides, raking the ships with the Black-robe's own arrows. "The great Black-robe Witch is dead" shouted the slave master. "Flee for your lives." On hearing this they threw themselves over the sides and ran mindlessly across the sands in all directions. There was no escape from the charging Thanet witches who surrounded them, or from their lethal barrage of spears and throwing sticks which cut them down. Ground runners slashed at the legs of any Black-robe escaping, bringing them down and rushing past to leave them at the mercy of the following Pine-witch spears.

Suddenly a group of six Black-robes broke free and ran towards Sis as she bent over to help an injured grey robe. With shields held tightly together they burst through the line of defenders straight at her. Sis sprang into the air above them and then brought her sword slicing down into one, then two black helmets. She spun in the air as the swords followed her, cutting the air around her with vicious whistling sounds. In one movement she landed and ducking down low thrust her sword up into a Black-robe's belly. Again she sprang up and the swords followed her as she landed behind them. First one, then another Black-robe charged at her. She fended off the first blow and slipped to the side. The second lunged as Sis twisted away and brought her sword around into the first attacker's side. Then she swung her sword back to cleave clean through the second witch's sword and into his neck. Seeing this, the last Black robe roared and turned, raising his sword to strike at the helpless Grey robe still lying injured. In an instant Sis took her sword by the point and hurled it at his back. It hit squarely between the shoulder blades and tore through his chest. He collapsed lifeless onto the sand…. *Now it is finished.*

The bonfire of bad memories

The final death moans of the Black-robes drifted away on the rising wind as Sis called the Council together for the last time. "Thanet is now free. The terror has gone. It must be marked by a symbol for all to see, all to believe," she announced. "I know you have all suffered but I ask this. A fire to be built, higher than the cliffs and all the Black-robes burned in their ships. There shall be no graves, just the blackened soil to mark their end."

And so it was that on the sand dunes a huge bonfire was built. Four killing ships were broken up. Fallen trees were dragged across the island and hauled on top of the dead Black-robes. Their clothes and weapons were scattered on top. Small clumps of tinder brush, dried reeds and straw were pushed into every crevice and each witch group brought a sheet of parchment naming their dead. The names of each of the fallen witches were read aloud. Then the sheets were rolled up and pushed into the timber stacks.

When it was time, Sis led Adah to the foot of the massive pile. "I promised you on the beach at Broad Cliff stairs there would be no more Black-robe slavery. I have kept my promise Adah. Now close your eyes and hold out your hands". Stepping from out of the crowd her daughter took her mother's left hand tenderly. Her son emerged from behind to clasp her right hand.

"Can it be true? Have you both returned from the slave ships?" She turned to look up at her freed children and cried uncontrollably. They hugged their mother, weeping with joy.

"Bring the flame," Sis ordered. A torch was brought forward and offered to Adah. "Come burn the past, burn our sadness that we might all begin anew." Adah's face glowed with pride as she plunged it into the pile. There was a roar as a pillar of flame exploded, lighting up the bay.

Throughout the night the Island celebrated. New friendships were forged, old enmities and misunderstandings forgotten. There was a sense of a new coming together of every inhabitant and every creature. On the tide line the fishermen fed fish to the otters that showed off, spinning and darting through the waves - heroes all. Daylight came and the fire burned on.

Through the early morning chill of the sea breeze, Storra walked alone across the sands. Before him, driven deep into a fallen tree trunk was the sword he had given Sis. He bent down to pull it free. The leather-bound handle still held the warmth from the Warrior-Witch's hand. When he wrapped his fingers around it the metal blade glowed and he felt all of her strength and courage flowing into him. He looked up into the empty sky and then turned back, a re-born leader. In that loneliest of moments – the Age of Healing began.

*

Sis flew through the early morning light and then raced faster and faster up into the endless darkness. She flew with a purpose, as if shedding her role as the Warrior-Witch and cleansing her heart of the horrors of battle. Here, in the pure limitlessness of space, her memories of the ravages of war were burned away and her innocence returned. Freed now from that age of pain she turned back again to Thanet. She flew down, twisting through strange bands of colour: all blue, from the palest silver blue to the darkest shade of midnight. Then the air cleared and the earth rushed towards her......

Great Hunt Day

Sis strolled along the muddy river bank with a group of excited Witch- traders. As they neared the village where the river forked, they were met with a gaudy wall of banners all announcing 'Great Hunt Day market.' It was a noisy and untidy village, or at least what she could see of it, beneath the swaying banners that clothed every house, tree and cart. Even the big horse-dogs harnessed to sledge wagons, carried drapes proclaiming Great Hunt Day market. *She had certainly chanced upon a special day - that was for sure.*

The square before her was cluttered with benches and tables being set up for the market. The trader witches she had travelled with were now arguing and pushing among themselves, all trying to have their stall set up at the front, leaving little room for anyone to walk by. As Sis wandered through this chaos she was nearly pushed over as two men in green uniforms suddenly grabbed a Witch trader who was standing next to her.

"She's wearing gold," said one.

The other roughly grabbed her around the shoulders and threw her to the floor. "You dirty hag. You know the law. You want to bring unluck to our village?" He bent down and ripped the gold necklace off the trader's neck then grabbed her wrists, pulling up each of her sleeves to check for bracelets.

"She got any more?" the first man asked.

No. No more. Just the usual dirty silver." As he stood up he deliberately trod on the trader's ankle and she cried out in pain. Both men started to laugh and turned away into the crowd.

Sis was dumbfounded. She was angry, firstly at herself – not having the courage to challenge the bullies, and secondly at all the traders around. None had stopped working or gave any appearance of even noticing what had just happened. Ignoring the woman who was still laying in the mud they either stepped over her or walked round her as if she was a pile of dirt to be avoided. Sis knelt down to help the trader up and re-arranged her clothes. "Who were they?" Asked Sis.

"Village elders, they hate all Witch traders and have tried to get us banned from the Hunt market. But the Healing witch won't allow it. She makes most of her money on this one day."

"Well, what about your gold necklace, can't you get it back?"

"No. Traders are forbidden to wear gold in the village. It's an old law, it's my own fault, and I forgot to hide it." "That doesn't make sense," said Sis.

"Little in this sad village does" explained the trader. "Come on, or we'll miss a space to set up the stall."

To their left the children of the village played with the trader's children. They ran and laughed and splashed through the reeds that lined the river bank. Then grabbed odd banners and tied them to branches which they dragged around the trees, carving perfect circles in the mud and waterlogged meadows.

The sky suddenly darkened and a bell was struck loudly on the hill above the village. Down flew a formation of Hunting-witches, dressed in bright red cloaks, which landed in the field opposite Sis.

"Who leads the hunt" called out a serious looking witch, who was draped in a black lace cloak. She stepped out dramatically from the crowd and bellowed, "Give me my knowledge due."

"I give you this knowledge. I have been chosen to lead the hunt. I am the Medicine-witch of Mar. My request of you is to ring the great Cant bell to let the hunt begin."

Her request was granted and the bell struck. With the tolling still ringing through the air the witches flew off. In front of them, sometimes running, sometimes flying for short distances raced a group of Fang-witches sniffing the floor as they went. Sis watched them till the bright red cloaks disappeared over the hill top and the snapping snarls of the Fang-witches died away then she turned back to watch the market growing. Most witches had settled down now and were busy laying out their wares in an extraordinary mix of colours, shapes and smells.

"You aren't from these parts are you witch girl?" said the smiling Witch- trader, who had managed to clean most of the mud from her clothes. "I'm grateful for your kindliness. "Here, have a drink" and she offered Sis a dark blue liquid in a wooden spoon.

Sis drank a little. It was smooth at first but then turned lumpy in her mouth making it hard to swallow. When she did manage to swallow, it burned her stomach.

"It will do you good, got rock- lizard liver in it. Girl of your age needs all the goodness she can get, after all, as they say - *there's no such thing as too much medicine.*"

Sis grimaced and asked the trader the price of her goods.

"Well everyone's using rats' tails this hunt. It was decided to use them as barter counters because this spring we had a real plague of them. Last market we used bull rush stems and one year, when I was a girl like you, we used daisy petals. Anyway, doesn't matter, we all count them up at the end and swap medicines to whatever price they have increased to. Today, to start, there's ten rat tails to every dried bat".

"Oh! I see" said Sis, still totally confused.

"If you've got no barter yourself you can help me. Anyway, my sister's turned ill and I'm by myself. Can you imagine on the busiest day of late spring going ill? I told her checked badger glands weren't any good - far too common to be good medicine".

"I'll help if I can but you'll have to explain the prices to me" said Sis.

"Right, let me introduce myself first, my name is Adgit. You can call me Adg," said the Trader-witch now warming to Sis and very grateful for the unexpected help. "I'll call you Girlie. See - we sell on the old and trusted medicine principle of *common can't cure, rare heals.*"

"So the rarer something is the better it is for you?" asked Sis.

"Exactly", smiled Adg. "You wait till the hunt returns. Sometimes the prices go sky high. Do you know, I once saw the last tree hog in the whole of Thanet caught by the hunt and it went for 500 bats - amazing?"

Adg then went through her stock of drinks and potions, dried creatures, charms and an odd assortment of animal, fish and bird parts. Sis, struggling to understand the weird logic rehearsed her understanding out loud for Adg.

"So the fewer there are of anything, the more expensive it is. If it is more expensive then it must be good for you, so you keep buying it till there's only one left and that last one is the very best possible medicine".

"That's it, exactly" said Adg.

"But that means that things become extinct" said Sis in alarm. "Lost for ever- that can't be right?"

"Yes of course it is, that's how healing works. Things only start healing when they are rare. It gives them special power. When they are all gone the Medicine-witch names other things to hunt and so they too become scarce and good for healing and up goes their value. If we have a good day we might sell off a lot of something and increase its value. Anything you see that we have stocks of, sell it for one or two rat's tails. Get rid of it."

"Do you mind if I just sell what you have lots of and leave the rarer things to you?" asked Sis.

"That's fine," agreed Adg" then when the hunt returns we'll go and watch the Medicine-witch of Mar name new healings. It's so exciting to hear of new things that will do you good."

The market was crowded now and business was hectic. The pile of rats' tails grew in Sis's bartering basket and Adg looked across and smiled her approval. Before buying anything the customers would ask 'what is it good for?' and 'will it be rare soon? Adg had drawn up a list of ailments and the best medicines. Soon Sis was calling out the 'cures' to the crowds with such enthusiasm that Adg's stall became a magnet of interest. Witches flocked to Sis and the growing crowd's noise and activity attracted others. By mid-day Adg's stall was empty. She stood with her arm around Girlie and thanked her profusely. Never before had she sold out all her stock before the Hunt's return. She had to keep looking at the two enormous baskets of rat tails to convince her it was true.

"You really are a marvel, Girlie. Now we can be the first to the medicine ring and sit right at the front for the sale. Come on, let's get something to eat while we're waiting." They sat eating and talking. Gradually the ring began to fill up with different witches, conversing intensely, exchanging 'dead things' and all the while she overheard the most important question repeated, "*Is it rare?*" "Want a Seer's tale, young witch?"

"Want a what?" asked Sis. The woman had appeared out of the crowd and now stood so close to her she could feel her breath on her skin. Her face was young and her eyes bright yet she had wrapped a red shawl around her head like the elder witches who seemed to be following her.

"How much a tale then?" interrupted Adg.

"For her or you, old crone?" cackled the woman, her eyes squinting against the sunlight.

"It's for Girlie here. Come on – a special price. It's her first time and she ain't mothered yet."

"Twenty bats, no less. Not a single wing less." The Seer almost spat out the words. Adge nodded her agreement and moved round the bench for the Seer to sit opposite Sis.

"Give me your hand. Close your eyes and keep them closed," the Seer ordered.

Sis relaxed, wondering how this woman, who was pretending to be older than she was, could possibly have the wisdom to tell her fortune. She felt a sharp pain in her left wrist and flinched involuntarily but managed to keep her eyes closed. Next a cool liquid was poured over her right hand.

"Don't move or you'll spoil the reading," said the Seer irritably. "Now, when I tell you –open your eyes and look deeply into mine. Not up, nor down, nor side to side. Only deep into my eyes. Do you understand?"

"Yes," replied Sis, who was now quite curious about what would happen next.

"Open your eyes!"

The mid-day sun dazzled Sis's eyes but she did what she had been asked and focused on the Seer's eyes. "Look deep, deep" she said and with a barely perceptible movement brought a small cup up to her lips and slurped the liquid. Sis could hear the noise of her sucking and rolling the liquid around in her mouth. Then the Seer suddenly turned her head and spat the blood onto the floor. Finally she licked her lips, tasting the last droplets knowingly.

"Mmhhh," she moaned. "Satin blood Girlie – good and all. Smooth and sweet as your babe will be. Strong and true as his heart'll be. He'll be a healer for sure."

Sis had not moved. She felt as if she was in a trance and slowly lowering her head her eyes fell upon her bloodied wrist, wrapped round with a thin cloth from which her blood dripped onto the soil below. Then the shock hit her and twisted through her body. Her stomach churned and her hands began to tremble. Even though she was sitting her legs felt weak. "That's disgusting!" she shouted. Drinking blood to tell the future – ah! That's sick!"

"There, there Girlie," said Adg to comfort her as she cradled her arm around Sis's shoulders. "Don't go on so. How else can the Seer tell your future without tasting your blood? See, it's stopped bleeding." Adg lifted Sis's wrist and turned it gently. "There won't even be a mark left by the full moon."

"Never seen a Seer working before, have you," asked the woman.

"No" admitted Sis. "Sorry I shouted."

"And what did my eyes show you? Sis thought for a while as a crowd gathered around expectantly.

"I saw stars and I was flying between them when I heard a voice telling me I belonged on the earth and suddenly I was back again. I was in a beautiful forest with ferns as tall as pines and I was floating down a wide river holding on to the sun like a giant floating ball."

"Was that all you visioned?" asked the Seer.

"No. An army of angry horsemen were chasing me on both sides of the river. There were thousands of them and their heads were on fire. They we screaming at me for stealing their sun. I managed to roll the sun into a cavern under a waterfall and hid till all the horsemen had passed – that was all."

The Seers young face lightened into a smile. Adg looked on at Girlie with real pride and the gathered traders sighed as if relieved by the story. Sis looked around her at the wreath of admiring faces then back to the Seer. She took Sis's hand and spoke in a gentle, almost loving tone. "You will have many tests and trials in your life

–it will not be an easy way for you. But as strong as your blood is, so will your fortitude be. You will bear a son, a servant to his tribe, a healer to the body and spirit. This is your future, your life – immutable."

One by one the gathered witches stretched forward to touch Sis's hand and as suddenly as she had at first appeared, the Seer melted back into the crowd.

The Medicine-witch of Mar

"Who are they, Adg?" asked Sis, as she pointed to a group who sat apart.

"Ah! They're Amie witches, always desperately seeking new and rare healings. They've just arrived from the south. They fly up to Thanet every summer then disappear in the autumn. Can't stand our cold winters. Some say they are very rich, I've never talked to them myself".

"And that lady witch over there wasn't she the one who started the Hunt?"

"Oh yes, she's the elected 'Great Hunt Day marshal'. She starts and declares finished the hunt. Funny, all the village Witches really think this is an important job, just for one day. Us outsiders thinks it's daft, dressing up in black lace and speaking in a silly language - but it is all part of the Hunt tradition now. Listen, I can hear the Fang-witches. The Hunt's coming".

These words trickled through the crowd and everyone stood up to hear the Cant bell 'toll the return.' They watched in hushed silence as the Hunting-witches landed in the ring. The Fang witches, with blood-stained fur around their mouths, were led away snapping and snarling. The Hunt's kill was then ceremoniously piled in the centre of the ring to gasps from the crowds.

The Medicine-witch of Mar stepped forward and dramatically bowed as she handed the Hunt gift to the marshal. She accepted the blood-spattered bundle of fur and called out in her loudest voice "Let the Cant bell toll. The Hunt is finished." The bell rang and cheering broke out around the ring as the Hunting-witches raised the Medicine- witch onto their shoulders. Round and round they paraded her till the marshal as her final act announced "From this Hunt may my words travel. I declare the Medicine-witch of Mar will name new healings this day."

Her moment of glory finished, the marshal melted into the crowds. Unseen she slipped behind a tree and removed her formal lace clothing and dressed in her normal green gown. These beautiful lace clothes she had made herself could never be worn again; just as she could never be marshal again. She quickly wrapped them around a stone and closing her eyes threw them into the river. *May my healing last longer than my fame* she whispered sadly, then she bent down to wash her dirty hands in the shallows. Back to being ordinary again, she re-arranged her clothing and returned unnoticed into the market throng.

Back in the ring the crowd fell silent. Sis watched as the Medicine-witch of Mar walked along the line of creatures now laid out before her. She inspected each corpse, weighed some in her hand as she sniffed them and broke other pieces off to taste the skin, blood, fur or feather. Other dead things were held up to the sun and turned in her hand as she studied their shapes and the way the shadows fell across their limbs. No observation, no sense reading was left out. It seemed to Sis to be extremely complicated and she struggled to understand how healing properties were being assessed. *It simply did not make sense at all.*

Having completed her thorough inspection, the Medicine-witch raised both hands and called out. "The measures have been taken. I will return" and she strode out of the ring as the excited crowd cheered her.

Turning to Adg Sis asked "What now?"

"The hunters meet to drink together from the bullion, a giant goblet filled with blood taken from the Woolly Rampard. A Rampard is the biggest creature there's ever been in Thanet. A few are kept just for this ceremony. For some reason they have never been judged as good for healing. Strange that, since they are so rare," explained Adg. For the first time Sis saw a look of bewilderment on the trader's face.

"Look", exclaimed Adg as she began joining in with the hand clapping. "It's the Children's-tellers. You'll like this." Into the ring bounded three small witches dressed in dull brown clothes with large fur hats on. The two with black curly beards held up a big banner while the other gestured for the children to come closer.

"This is where the children learn, you watch," said Adg. "The grey bearded witch has taught healing at all the meetings I have ever been to." Taking a long stick, Grey-beard began pointing out the different sections of the body on a crude diagram drawn on the banner. Sis tried hard to listen and understand but was not able to grasp much of the explanation. When he had finished and the children clapped with glee, she turned to Adg and asked her to explain.

"Don't you know anything about your body Girlie? You really ought. You'll only ever have one, pays to look after it." She rummaged in her bag and pulled out a scrap of parchment and a piece of charcoal for Sis. "Here, get this down. Put simply your body is made up of four sections.

1.   **Shell.** That's the outside cover, you know: skin, hair, nails and eyes.

2.   **Blood.** This is most important of all as it carries all your life juices.

3.   **Frame.** Bones mostly, but all the string and muscle inside that help you move.

4.   **Flowings.** These are the most difficult to explain but include your heart, lungs, liver and other dark slivery things only the Medicine-witches can really understand. Surely you've heard witches say 'My flowings feel a bit sore today' or 'I don't feel my flowings are running well.'"

"Can't say I have", answered Sis in complete honesty.

"Then good job you have me to teach you and learn you will my girl. One day you will be a mother and it's a mother's duty to make sure their children learn, not just about healing but body sections too." She was going to continue but as the ring cleared, a horn blew to signal the start of the sale.

Adg sat up, transfixed as the Medicine-witch of Mar returned and announced, "We begin naming. We begin valuing. We begin setting the rare."

"And what is our truth, say?" she asked of the crowd.

"Common can't cure, rare heals", everyone repeated in unison.

The Medicine-witch smiled broadly and announced "We begin with the rare and end with the rarest".

She bent down and picked up a small nest. "In here is a whole family of scarrion warblers, two parents and four chicks. All the other nests were carefully destroyed by the hunt. I declare that nest and birds boiled together will cure all ailments of the shell and frame. Who will bid? There's not a mix as fresh as this anywhere on the Island."

"I've never heard of scarrion warblers", said Adg in a hushed voice. "They must be very, very good for you". The bidding stopped at 50 dried bats. "Oh, maybe they weren't so good for healing after all" Adg said disappointedly.

There followed a list of animals which were declared 'good for healing' and some fish and plants too. When the Medicine-witch lifted up a small turtle and described it as 'rare and excellent for the blood,' Sis felt sick and turned away. This was the prize the Amie-witches had waited for. They dominated the bidding, throwing bat after bat on the floor till they were piled high. It was theirs for 400 bats. "Our blood needs warming in this cold place" the first Amie said as he collected their prize. Then taking out a knife from his silver belt he hit the shell and then held it to his ear. "Not been dead long, let's have it quick" and while the crowd watched they crushed the shell and carved the flesh up with rapid strokes. Sis turned back as they greedily devoured the raw flesh on the spot. The broken shell was discarded as another Amie stood up and bellowed to the crowd "I will give 800 bats for the next turtle."

"See what I mean Girlie? What amazing medicine. It's doubled in price. The beaches will be full of hunters tonight." Sis had no answer.

"Before the rarest", the Medicine-witch continued, "I now give warning and show things hunted but not proved good for health. The following can be killed for sport – never used for healing". The murmuring chatter died away instantly at this announcement and everyone strained to listen. Adg hurriedly pulled out a charcoal stick and pushing it into Sis's hand said "Get this down, here, use this reed parchment scrap. It's just as important to learn this."

The Medicine-witch disdainfully raised a long pole on which were impaled a string of animals and birds. She pointed to each in turn and warned of its harm. The list began: "The pole rat, the giant-muck worm, the pale owl, the checked badger (at this Adg poked Sis on the arm-"told you so"), the double-tailed lizard, the pygmy-slush pig and, finally, the spitting pus spider." All the traders nervously ran over their remaining stock in their minds, just in case they had any of the banned things. *Someone seeing they had even one and it would ruin their business permanently.*

"Now for the best healing of all; so rare I have never before set eyes on its like. I have judged it fair and I now declare it 'the finest remedy for all ailments.'"

Adg gasped. "Nothing has ever been declared a remedy for all ailments. What could it be?"

"Good for shell, blood, frame and flowings" said the Medicine witch of Mar. Then she paused, enjoying the excited expectation of the crowd that was hanging on her every word. She bent down and with a flourish pulled from a sack a plump black and white bird and held it above her head. It had a large flat beak, striped with yellow, red and grey and orange webbed feet that dangled down as she swung the lifeless form around for all to see. The audience were dumbstruck. It was not like any bird they had ever seen before.

Adg sighed, "How can you put a value on that?"

"Where did the hunters catch it?" asked the largest of the Amie witches, trying to hide his obvious excitement.

"The Fang- witches chased it down along the beach at Foreness. We think it was pushed on shore by the strong winds. So, what am I bid?" Within seconds the bidding reached fever pitch, with bats being slammed down in piles all around the ring and the price racing up from hundreds into thousands.

"Way out of my range," confessed Adg sadly as she looked on, eyes darting around trying to guess the next bidder.

The Amies, alarmed at such strong competition, huddled together, arguing anxiously until the Medicine-witch called out. "I have a bid for 3,200 bats, anymore?"

"4,000!" screamed the Amies at the top of their voices.

They waited in a breathless silence then the announcement came, "Sold to the Amies. The greatest healing is yours." The Amies were absolutely beside themselves. They had the rarest healing in the history of Thanet. It could cure anything. They were aware of course that bird healing was traditionally boiled and taken as a soup but they could not wait. They set about cutting the bird up on the ground into equal shares then ate it raw, feathers and all!

It tasted awful - but then the best medicine usually did.

The crowd around the ring began to disperse. Adg's eyes shone. "There Girlie, now you've seen it all. I reckon my flowings must be near boiling after that, let's go and get some calming." She held Sis' arm and led her down a path between the trees to a grassy opening. Here, in the dappled sunlight various witches were standing around three stalls. The first was offering 'rubbing healing'. The banner proclaimed 'calm your flowings' and listed the various treatments on offer.

"What does this do, Adg?" asked Sis.

"Ah! This is new healing, comes from the mainland over the sea. It treats the shell but it is said the goodness soaks through to your followings." Sis looked up to read the rubbings available. There was maggot juice, shredded toads' eyes with mint and blood of the spotted mole with oak apple. The mole's blood was five times more expensive than the others!

"Come on Girlie". Adg turned to the Rubbing-witch and handing over a wad of rats' tails said "two treatments of spotted moles' blood and oak apple."

They were asked to lie down on woven reed mats as the Rubber pulled up her wide sleeves and washed her hands in a silver bowl. Her assistant pulled up Sis's and Adg's sleeves and tunics and prepared their skin with gentle stroking and fanning with blue muslin. Treatment began with the Rubbing-witch pouring a crimson liquid into the palm of her hand and applying it to the patients' skin with slow, rhythmic strokes along their arms and legs. As she worked, warming and smoothing the skin she hummed in a monotonous tone. Then a second coating of moles' blood was applied, this time using a thick brush made from jebbits tails, to stroke the goodness under the skin. Adg opened her eyes and turned to Sis. "Can't you just feel how expensive this is? My flowings are settling already."

"Now lay still" said the Rubbing-witch. "You must allow all the healing to be taken up by your followings. Close your eyes." She covered them with shawls and left to attend to new customers. A short while later the assistant brought them a drink of bark and lime mould to 'cleanse the channels for their flowings'. They adjusted their clothing and slowly stood up, then walked out into the afternoon sunshine. The warmth of the sun on her skin brought a smile to Sis's face. "Thank you, Adg", she said. "I feel so relaxed. In fact my edges feel really clear."

"I've not heard that expression before", said Adg.

"You know it's like when you touch a cloth or metal on your teeth and you get that intense feeling in your nerves and you say "It puts my teeth on edge?"

"Yes" said Adg.

"Well" explained Sis, "the expression comes from that, only it's for your whole body and your feelings."

"You mean like the 'flowings' of your body and mind? I like that Girlie," smiled Adg. "Reckon I can use that to sell a lot more healing medicines." She looked back to the banner listing the treatments. "One thing's for sure, your edges certainly wouldn't have been feeling as clear as this with the cheaper maggots or toads' eyes. No rare healing in them for sure" she told Sis reassuringly.

The next stand they came to appeared to be even more popular. There was a line of customers, queuing up quietly without the usual jostling. "Look" said Adg pointing to the queue "'Newies', all of them. They may look happy now but you wait, there will be a lot of them very unhappy if they don't get the mark."

"What mark?"

"Like that" said Adg, nodding towards a grinning witch emerging from behind the screen with a bright yellow circle painted on her forehead. "Newies are renowned in these parts," continued Adg. "They only value new things and discard anything older than two moons. I've never seen one content for more than a day. You see, someone is always finding something new or inventing something which they 'simply have to have.'"

"So what's going on here?"

149

"Started last week by a healer from the Kelvin hills area, it's a judgement mark. They call it the 'over brimming circle' and it is completely new to Thanet."

"What's that got to do with healing?" returned Sis.

"Oh, everything, you see only the rich witches can afford to eat well and only the really very, *very* rich can over eat. If you are judged by the Kelvin healer to be 'over brimming' he prescribes a special reducing potion which is extremely expensive. You also receive the yellow mark so all the other witches know immediately they see you that you are so rich and you have overeaten so much that only the rarest healing potions can help you."

"But most of them look pale and thin, far from over brimming", ventured Sis.

"Newies are very thin. Their flowings are in constant dangling. They are always seeking out the new, never satisfied with what they already have. I'm sure none of them eat properly, certainly they don't take traditional healing seriously."

The Newies emerged, those with the yellow foreheads were smiling, those without were despondent and went straight back to the end of the queue to be judged again. Watching the group lining up again Adg said "I reckon they are thinking how much more they can pay to the Kelvin healer to buy a yellow mark, and I reckon too, that no Newie will ever bother to actually take the special reducing potion. Anyway, this business will only last another moon then close like all the others. Then the Newies will be off chasing something different, something new."

"No Girlie," Adg said smiling as Sis stared at the last stall. "No Newie will try that. It's an ancient healing idea and even our generation don't believe in it anymore. When it first began it was called 'frame strengthening'."

"Looks like frame breaking to me," said Sis who started laughing.

"You aren't wrong there Girlie, let's watch a while".

They sat in the shade opposite the giant beech tree. On the floor was a black mark, on which stood the patient with his back to the long thick branch. To the side stood a line of young male witches dressed in their finest 'healing greens,' talking and joking. The branch was pulled back by two massive Farm witches who, to the shout of 'strong frame' let go the branch which flew back hitting the patient squarely across the back. Some were knocked off their feet to the jeers and giggles of the girls looking on. Others, who managed to brace themselves against the impact, stood tall and delighted the girls who ran up to congratulate them. The really brave went back to be 'frame strengthened' a second time and if they were still standing afterwards received a string of flowers and the prize of a kiss from the girls. No one ever went up a third time. "They seem to enjoy it," observed Sis.

"They certainly do" answered Adg. "Can't imagine how many bottles of retch juice they will use on their bruises tonight though." They walked off laughing together. The sun was beginning to set on a very special day as Sis said goodbye to Adg.

"Sure you won't come back to my village for some newt's foot soup. My sister made it?"

"No thank you. I really have to go". Sis felt she was being drawn away again. A strong urge to fly welled up inside her as she waited impatiently for Adg to walk back behind the trees. When at last she was out of sight Sis ran down the hill and dived into the air; speeding up into the waking star clouds.

Frozen to a Star

Maybe there really had been some healing in the spotted mole's blood after all. Maybe she was just delighted to be flying again after walking on the ground for so long. Whichever it was, Sis simply burned with energy. She chose a star, thought of a number and raced towards it. As she flew she counted. Her feet touched down on the frozen star on the count of five hundred and two.

"Missed by two", she shouted out into the frozen atmosphere, "Wow! This is cold" and went to jump up but her feet stuck firmly to the ice sheet. She tried again but could not lift them and now her fingers felt numb and her whole body stiffened. A dull, deep ache filled her limbs and her breathing became shallow. Her hair became solid and her eyes froze over. No movement was possible. She barely sensed her consciousness waning before there was nothing.

"Did you see that flash Elaz?"

"No. Where do you mean?"

"By the frozen star, could be a screamer, let's have a look", suggested Qel. The two witches streamed together landing next to Sis in a shower of silver sparks.

Elaz looked at Sis' frozen form. "Why, she's a star flyer. I thought such creatures were myths from cycles past."

"Is she still with life?" asked Qel who began rummaging through his catching things for anything useful.

"What was she doing out here with no ice-layers on? It's far too dangerous. Even her breathing has frozen. Quick", said Elaz, "empty your catcher sling and wrap it around her. We have to get her warming started." Qel wrapped the large sling round and round Sis, while Elaz cradled Sis's head with her arms and held her, breathing first on her face then blowing her warm breath onto Sis's lips.

"How many warming sticks do we have left" he asked.

"Only one and we can't wait" said Elaz as she blew on Sis's lips again and the ice began to soften on her skin. "Start it now Qel, before we lose her". Qel ripped the crisp cover from the cylinder, pulled open the catcher sling and tied the warming stick over Sis's stomach, then quickly wrapped her around again. "Come round the other side, we need your body warmth too. Hurry!" pleaded Elaz.

They huddled together sharing warmth, willing Sis to wake. Slowly the ice began to melt over her hair. "Cover her head, use anything" said Elaz. "I think she's started warming. Qel took off his warming neck band to stretch over Sis's hair and looked into her pale face searching for the slightest sign of movement. He thought he saw an eye lid flicker but couldn't be sure, maybe he was just wish – dreaming. He glanced over to Elaz and for the first time noticed her face taut with anxiety.

"How long do you think we have left?" he asked her.

"Till the warming stick dies and no more or we'll freeze over too. We've been on this ice far too long already and my feet are beginning to numb. Just watch the ice skin. We can't risk getting our boots stuck."

"No, but we can leave hers, why not?" exclaimed Qel as he knelt down and began fumbling with Sis's boots. "They're frozen solid, I'll have to cut them off". He took his long flamer blade from his boot and began to cut down the side of each boot. "Should be enough, we'll pull together, now!" Elaz and Qel grasped hands around the bundled body of Sis and squeezing her between them, leapt up from the ice. It was agonising, breaking the hold of the ice. Their bodies shuddered and strained together till they felt Sis's feet slip free from her boots and they began to ascend.

"Don't let me go" gasped Elaz. "I've no strength."

"Hold on, we're nearly out of the cold field" called Qel and he closed his eyes, desperately fighting the cold and fatigue that now gripped his shaking body. He began to sense Elaz's strength returning as their movements became easier. He pushed forward and they started to gather speed towards the planet of Joon. The rest of the journey was a blur in their minds. They hung on to Sis and flew and thought of nothing else.

Their landing on Joon's pink sand wastes lacked all their usual precision and skill. They simply crashed down and rolled over together and laid still, warming under the blue sunlight. Elaz was the first to stir and she rolled over to hold Sis's hand. It moved and held hers. "You're alive! Qel, she's alive".

Qel scrambled to his feet and helped Elaz unwrap the catcher sling. "Don't take it off completely yet," said Elaz, "she's still shivering, she could be in shock." They knelt on either side, warming Sis's hands. Her eyes fluttered and then blinked in the strong blue light. They saw her lips move, then she lost consciousness again.

The blue sun's rays were lengthening before Sis moved again. Both Qel and Elaz woke with a start and looked down on Sis's face. "What happened to me?" she asked.

"You were caught on an ice star, nearly froze to death" said Elaz. "If Qel hadn't seen your flash, well… we're happy he did".

"I can remember flying and racing to a star, then", she hesitated,

"then nothing."

"Where did you come from?" asked Qel. "Were you alone?"

"Yes" said Sis. "I said goodbye to the Medicine-witches and flew away. Then cold, such terrible cold."

"You said Medicine-witches? You mean like the witches hundreds of cycles ago who are supposed to have eaten animals and birds for healing? I think you must be ice-dreaming" Qel said kindly and he looked over to Elaz with a knowing smile. "You have had a terrifying shock. Here take a sip of this water."

Sis looked up at Qel. He was gentle in his expression. His skin was smooth and a pale mauve colour. His smile beamed kindness. His long hair, like Elaz's, was a deep brown and fell across his broad shoulders. She turned to look at Elaz who still held her hand and began tenderly stroking Sis's brow. Her gentle face shone with compassion and kindness sparkled in her black eyes. Her skin was mauve too yet even smoother, *what wonderful witches are these* she thought to herself.

"We are Dawn-witches from an island far, far away" answered Elaz.

"You read my mind?

"No. No need" explained Elaz. "I listened to your heart."

Sis looked deeply into Elaz's eyes and whispered "Where all is possible, all is secure"

"What do you mean" asked Qel. "I didn't read those words in your heart."

"No?" asked Sis," maybe they were hidden too deep. I only just understood them for the first time myself."

"Qel and Elaz both smiled at this idea and slowly helped Sis to her feet.

"Sorry about your boots, I am afraid they're stuck on a star" Qel said jokingly.

At this Sis threw her arms first around Qel, and then embraced Elaz. "I owe you both my life. How can I ever repay you?"

"Your happiness is our delight, we are both honoured" said Elaz." Now we have to find our way back home. Neither of us has ever flown this sector before. We came here because we were told it was good for flamers." "Not that we found any", added Qel disappointedly.

"And what's a flamer?"

"They're tiny shooting stars in rare and beautiful colours. If you catch them before they burn up and put them in a zaron catching box, they stop burning, explained Qel.

"And then" Elaz continued excitedly, "you can open the box later and they fly out and fill the skies with wondrous lights. We had planned a celebration for the first day of spring on our isle. Spring is what the Dawn-witch Queen calls 'the blossom coming'

time. We really wanted it to be special."

Sis became silent and thoughtful, peering into the flashing sky. "Hold on, slow down!" called Qel. "Even I can't read that fast. Your mind is racing like a writhing star burst."

"I'm trying to remember my past, something to help us get our bearings. Perhaps if I could read your memories of where you have travelled from, I could make sense of where we are?"

"You can try. I will close my eyes and imagine all the routes we took before we spotted you", said Elaz. Sis stood next to her and concentrated, waiting for some insight but nothing came to her. Her mind remained blank.

"Sorry, it's not happening. I can't do it", she admitted.

"Don't worry, we should have known better. It's a Thanet gift we are born with" explained Qel.

"What? Say that again, asked Sis." Did you say Thanet?"

"Yes, that's where we live. That's our Island. The home of the Dawn-witches" explained Elaz.

"You know it, don't you?" said Qel. "Yet your mind pictures seem dark and sad. It is like you are seeing back in time". He stared at Sis. "Please tell us, who are you? Have you really been to Thanet in the past? Is all this possible? Are you really a star flyer?"

"My Kingdom name is Sis. Yes, I can star fly and have travelled across all galactic sectors. I fought in the War of the Witches, traded with the Medicine-witches and heard the Cant bell ring out on the Great Hunt Day."

"These legends you speak of Sis, they're lost in the dim of time. We've only ever known peace and beauty on our Isle and we live by a simple witch code." Elaz and Qel stood stiffly to attention and recited:

"Night closes on the nightjar's wings
And the silver dawn awakes
Live well, Live true
Serve old, Serve new"

"This is all we have ever known" explained Elaz. "We are taught from childhood by the Dawn-witch Queen that true happiness is only to be found in service to others."

Sis listened spell bound and in a flash the Guardian's words returned to her. 'The second Kingdom… ends in the peaceful and very beautiful Dawn-witch era.' *This was a new beauty* she realized

- *a beauty of the spirit, a beauty of pure hearts*. She had received the gift of a new understanding. *"Thank you Guardian."*

"Why are you smiling so, Sis?" asked Qel. "I read your heart and it is full of wonder."

"Trust, trust", she repeated. Then taking them each by the hand said "Close your eyes, we're going home."

Flying the Twilight Path

The Dawn-witch Queen herself greeted Sis's arrival. She was escorted into a soft lit dressing chamber where a warm bath was prepared. Delicately perfumed oils were added to the water and scented candles arranged around her. Smiling Dawn-witch maidens sang to her as they combed her hair and delighted in helping her choose from wondrous silvern gowns that decorated one whole side of the chamber. There were so many and *all beautiful.* Sis took ages to choose. When eventually she was led back to the Queen she found Qel and Elaz waiting for her dressed in the palest blue and lemon robes. "What beautiful colours" gasped Sis?

"Please take a seat. You are our honoured guest. First let us eat then we shall talk" said the Queen.

"Thank you your majesty".

The Queen smiled graciously at Sis's courteous tone. "Come", she said, "Elaz, Qel, you must be hungry too. Please join our special guest."

They all sat down on deep pearl cushions around a low table. In the centre were plates of cooked foods surrounded by baskets of breads, fresh herbs, fruits, nuts, seeds and flower petals. The Queen served the first course and poured sparkling juice into silver cups. Sis ate with a passion, desperately trying not to rush as she saw that Elaz and Qel were picking slowly and delicately at their food and chewing carefully.

"Don't you worry about us" said the Queen kindly. "We've had countless cycles to perfect eating styles, please don't slow down for us, eat and enjoy your meal."

Sis smiled, a little embarrassed at her haste, then relaxed and continued. *The food was good, very good.*

"Everything you see before you is grown in our own gardens and picked fresh each morning. Was it to your liking, Sis?" asked the Queen.

"It was wonderful, quite delicious. Thank you."

The Queen continued, "You know many cycles ago one of my ancestors studied food and healing from all the known wisdoms and collected plants and seeds enough to establish five gardens. He developed a way of living off only things grown in the earth and forbade the eating of any creatures. He was a great one for the ancient ideas of balance and harmony in the body. And even now we are still learning new things every day."

"My son and daughter told me you had star flown here before and you know of the dark times. Can this be true?"

"Yes your majesty."

"Then you must fly through passing time itself. Amazing!" said the Queen.

Sis looked over to Qel and Elaz. "Your son and daughter saved my life. That is more amazing to me. In the expanse of the empty galaxy they found me. That is like spotting one grain of sand in a star desert."

The Queen looked at her children with great pride. "Close your eyes then, let me read your memories." Elaz and Qel closed their eyes and relaxed their minds. "They were guided! I saw them suddenly change direction for no reason. They did not even notice it themselves. They suddenly flew off to where Qel saw your flash as you entered the ice star mist" announced the Queen, visibly shaken by her insight. "There can be no doubt that some force guided them to you."

She moved across and sat down in front of Sis and taking hold of her hands stared deeply into her eyes. "There are strange and wonderful forces guarding you Sis. I feel their strength through your hands. I see their protecting auras around you." She sat back speechless. Qel and Elaz shared in their mother's amazed silence and looked at Sis with new eyes. When the Queen eventually spoke all she could say was "You truly honour us Sis". Then gathering her thoughts together asked "And how can we best help you?"

"Most of all I would like to fly out on the twilight path and return on the path of dawn. Elaz has told me so much about it. It is the wonder of your Isle."

"It will be our pleasure to escort you. We will all go together. Now you must rest till evening time for we will be awake throughout the night. Rest well Sis", said the Queen, as she took her leave. "Elaz will show you to a sleep chamber."

As the evening deepened and a cooling breeze came from the sea they left the Queen's Palace together and flew to the centre of the Island. From where they alighted the sea could be seen on three sides. In ages past this was called 'Look- out point'" said the Queen. "Now we call it – Contemplation hill, where you can enjoy the silver of sun rise and the gold of sun set from this same spot."

They swept down the slope and entered a sheltered orchard. Here the air was warmer and still.

"Are they there Qel?" the Queen enquired.

"Yes, come quietly."

They moved silently to the trunk of an old cherry tree and Qel pointed to the lowest branch. "Look Sis, they've just started," he whispered. In the gloomy shadows a group of tiny squirrel-like creatures scampered back and forth plucking the blossom petals and dropping them to the floor. They worked ceaselessly till the ground was carpeted. Then they ran down and with delicate movements picked up each white or pink petal separately and carried it into a hole beneath the tree roots. Elaz, couldn't resist, she picked a bunch of blossom and held it in the palm of her hand on the grass. The creatures climbed up her hand and plucked the petals off one by one and then walked down her fingers with their prize. Sis watched enchanted - almost afraid to breathe lest she should frighten them away. Then with all the blossoms collected they scurried quickly down the hole and the activity was over.

The group retreated quietly. "What were they?" whispered Sis.

"We call them Blossom-thieves, aren't they a delight?" answered Elaz. "They only come above ground when the blossom flowers. For the rest of the sun's cycle they are never seen. Did you notice that the white of their fur matched the white blossom exactly? And their eyes matched the colour of the pink petals? They really are the shyest creatures that have ever been found on the island. I'm so pleased we managed to see them. Let's leave them and go to the stream."

"You'll need patience here" said the Queen. "Sometimes we sit up all night, watching and waiting. It's so exciting, thinking we might actually see a new creature for the first time. Get comfortable Sis". They settled down to wait in silence as their four dark shapes were absorbed into the shadows. Sis lost all sense of time and took to closing her eyes to listen to the sounds of the night all around her.

Qel leant across slowly and whispered to her, "Whatever you do, try not to make any sudden movements" and he motioned with his eyes towards her foot. Her eyes moved down to a shape, a form sitting by her foot. She strained to make it out then it moved and lifted up a paw to scratch its neck. It was a moth cat, so perfectly camouflaged that when it remained motionless it was invisible even to Sis's sensitive sight. Then it walked along Sis's calf to sit on her knee and settled down, licking its fur and cleaning its tiny paws. Without moving her head she looked around. There was another, rubbing its head against Qel's boot and a little further behind two kittens rolled over playing on the Queen's hand. Then, as if by some pre-arranged signal, they all walked off towards the stream and melted into the night.

Elaz searched in her pocket and took out some nuts and dried fruits which she shared out. Sis copied the Queen and lay down with her hand stretched out in front of her flat on the ground. Soon there came rustlings in the undergrowth around them and odd movements that were impossible to follow. She distinctly felt the brush of a tail against her wrist and tiny clawed paws pulling the nuts from her hand, *so close, they are so close.*

Then she saw them, first the dwarf stoat with its black tipped tail and then a strange rat-like creature sat on her hand together. They nibbled the nuts and chewed the fruit, every now and then stopping to sniff the air and look around them. Sis could feel each individual claw as they scampered across her palm. When they had finished eating they started carrying the nuts away, one at a time to some hidden store. Back and forth they came until the nuts were finished. Finally the rat–like creature licked the fruit skins off Sis's hands, and then shuffling and sniffing slowly along her arm turned off into the shadows and was gone.

Sis waited till the others moved and asked "what was that animal Elaz?"

"Was its fur dark or light?"

"Difficult to make out in the dark" answered Sis, "But I did see big black spots all the way down its back, I saw that very clearly– it was so close."

"Really, what about its tail?" asked Qel excitedly.

"It didn't have a tail at all" said Sis "and its nose was long and it had very large eyes. It even had long eyelashes!"

"That's it" said Elaz rather too loudly, sending creatures scampering through the leaf litter. "Sorry, didn't mean to shout, but it must be, mustn't it Qel?"

"Can't really be anything else from Sis's description?"

"No it can't" said the Queen excitedly. "I saw it too as it ran away. No mistake. We've found the Spotted-charm shrew!"

The Queen rushed over to Sis, kissed her on both cheeks and embraced her warmly. "What a wonderful night this is. You've really brought us luck Sis. We've searched for this splendid creature since I was a girl. I remember so many nights I spent with my Father, hidden in the dark watching and waiting, season after season. Do you know this is the first time it has actually been seen in forty sun cycles! If only he had lived to see it. When everyone else said the spotted charm shrew had died out, my Father alone continued the search, he never gave up believing. Yes, it is a wonderful night."

The Queen stood silently, looking away into the silver band of moonlight that swept from the sea across her Island. She remembered her father, his wisdom, patience and endless kindness. How he had loved all the creatures of Thanet. *If only he had been here tonight, what joy it would have brought to his heart*. At that moment she was not thinking as a Queen. She was a young girl missing her father and the pain brought tears streaming from her eyes."

"What's wrong mother? Please don't be sad" said Elaz as she held her mother's hands and kissed her delicately on the cheek.

"Forgive me, please. Sometimes we cry from happiness. Sometimes, when we miss those that we have loved, it is as if our very hearts are breaking. This is such a wonderful, wonderful night. Come, we should celebrate."

"Shall we show Sis how to fly the moonlight path? Suggested the Queen." Qel and Elaz looked across at each other in astonishment then back to their Mother. They had never seen her so joyful.

"Come on, let's become children again, just for tonight. Let's all fly back in time. Your Queen invites you."

"What's the moonlight path Qel?" Sis asked as the Queen and Elaz walked on hand in hand down to the beach.

"It's the maiden flight of all Dawn-witches. It's like a 'coming of age' ritual for all girls and boys on their eleventh birthday. Each child has to select an older companion to fly with them and witness them 'Touching the Moon' and to watch as they return to sprinkle moon dust over the sea as they make their life wishes. For a child of eleven it really is the journey of a lifetime. For some Dawn witches it is the longest journey they will ever make".

They stood ready in pairs on the shore line. "Qel, you go with Sis first. Elaz and I will follow" suggested the Queen.

Qel, bowing in an exaggerated manner and sweeping his hand to the ground said "No - after you your majesty."

The Queen laughed and launched into the air alongside her daughter. Turning back Elaz called to her brother "Catch us if you can!" Sis smiled at the child-like excitement in Qel's face as they raced after his mother and sister.

"Watch out for the moonbeams Sis" called Qel. "The challenge is to fly in-between them. On the way back we can slide down them, you wouldn't believe the speed you can reach!"

The Queen and Elaz were superb flyers. They swerved in and out of the moonbeams with such effortless grace. It was beautiful to watch. Sometimes they slowed to dance around a clump of moon beams and then, as Qel and Sis approached closer, they would shoot off in a shower of sparks.

Qel was content to follow behind with Sis. Sometimes they caught up to see the Queen's ageless smile irradiating the darkness and Elaz spinning and twirling in sheer delight as she relived the wonder of her childhood. *Yes* thought Sis *this really was a wonderful night!*

They were coming closer now and the reflected light from the moon was dazzling. Sis called to Qel "How can we see where we're going now, the light is blinding Qel?"

"Ah! That's the Dawn-witch secret. We can see with our eyes closed. Don't let go of my hand and I'll guide you." He looked across "Go on, close your eyes." And she did. And it felt strange but at the same time liberating. She could feel the rush of speed against her body now as all her senses heightened. *I can even feel Qel's heartbeat through his hand* she thought, *and it was racing!* This was a new kind of flying, a new kind of trust and Sis loved every moment. Then they slowed, turned and finally dropped down to the surface of the Moon. Her eyes still tightly closed she bent down and picked up a handful of dust.

"Ready?" asked Qel. "Let's find a double moon beam." Sis felt his strong hand pulling her upwards and they gathered speed till Qel shouted "you can open your eyes now Sis." As her eyes became accustomed to the light she saw before them a wide band of moon beams, leading down to Earth. The Queen and Elaz were already there waiting for them.

"I've found two double moon beams for us Sis. We'll all go down together" said the Queen "and don't forget to hold onto your star dust. We're going down feet first, lie back and keep your hands in by your sides. Let's ride the moon beams!"

They started together and fell down and down. As Qel had said rightly, Sis couldn't believe the speed. The difference here was she had no control. She simply let go and rode down the moon beam. It was fast, furious and totally exhilarating. She tried to look over to the others but she was accelerating so quickly now she was unable to move her head. So she just gave in to the absolute thrill and found herself screaming with excitement. They were all screaming, just like children at the fun fair.

Sis lost all idea of time. Unable to think, she was enraptured by the sheer speed until finally, as the moon beam began to fade, her speed slowed. It was like waking up from a very deep sleep and it took time for her to gather her senses, then Qel took her hand. The Queen called out "children, make your 'life wish' and sprinkle your moon dust." They all opened their hands together and the dust trickled down into the sea. "May all your wishes come true?"

They flew, hand in hand back to the beach like a silver bracelet drenched in moon light. As they landed the wind died and the night suddenly became very still. The tide was high now and the sand spit almost covered. "I've been here before" said Sis, as all the memories of the Black-robe war flooded her mind. The Queen, Elaz and Qel read her heart and shared them too. Instinctively they put their hands to their eyes as if to shut out the horrific scenes before them.

"Stop, stop, I can't stand it" cried Elaz. "It is too terrible. It can't be true. No! Stop. Please". The Queen with tears streaming down her cheeks embraced her daughter, holding her protectively to her breast. Qel stood staring into the night sky shaking with despair.

Sis broke the agonising silence. "I am so sorry you had to see that. It's this place. This is where it happened and it all came back to me" and she scanned the sand bar, half expecting to see the otters.

"You have nothing to regret Sis," said the Queen. The sacrifices made by those ancient witches made our world possible. We owe them a debt that can never be repaid. It is right and just that we should be reminded." They stood silently with their heads bowed, each in their own way paying homage to their ancestors.

"Look Elaz, it's your gull" said the Queen. Elaz lifted her arm and the bird landed and settled unsteadily on its left leg. Under the pearlescent light Sis watched Elaz gently stroke the bird's head as its yellow eyes stared back at her. Seeing the gull seemed somehow to intensify Elaz's sadness and she began to cry.

The Queen looked on and fighting back her own tears explained to Sis. "Elaz rescued the gull from the claws of a Dang cat when it was only a few week's old. Its damaged left leg never really healed.

It has flown back to her, wherever she is on the island, every night since. All the birds and creatures on our Isle seem to know we would never harm them and many are quite tame, but nothing like this. There is a special bond between Elaz and her gull that I cannot explain, it's just wonderful."

The bird became restless and took off on silent wings, gliding along the tide line. It seemed the gull had carried away some of Elaz's sadness. As she looked up and her soft smile returned, she announced, "It's nightjar time."

"Yes" said Qel. "The night has passed so very quickly. Let's walk this way." They followed him and stopped in a fern filled hollow behind the first sand dune. Sis could see the darting shapes against the sky and hear the churring calls all around.

"Let Sis go" suggested Elaz. "She's never seen the 'night closing on the nightjar's wing'.

"Come Sis, lie here with your head against this grass tussock. Lie still, it's almost time," said the Queen.

The sky began to lighten to the east as two birds flew down together and settled, side by side on Sis's chest. Their eyes half-closed they folded their legs beneath them and nestled down. She held her breath, feeling their brooding warmth as they lay motionless on her and the dawn's first rays reached their flecked feathers. The sun crept slowly across each subtle marking, bringing their plumage alive in fawns, greys, russets and cinnamon shades. Then with the sun reaching beyond them they rose and lifted off on long scything wings, floated over the dunes and were gone.

"Night closes," announced the Queen, "and the silver dawn awakes."

*

"Sis, you're shaking. Please, sit down" said Tala. "Don't cry, you're back safely with us now".

"Oh Tala, It really feels as if my heart and mind are bursting."

"It's little wonder Sis. We saw everything and the Guardian sent this new moon crystal for you to store the memories of your 'crossing over'. Sis took the pale blue crystal in her hands and gazed aimlessly out of the cave entrance. After a long silence she turned and asked "what really happened to me Tala?"

"You crossed over through a second veil and truly 'became' the Warrior-witch. I was so frightened for you because for all our knowledge and wisdom we could not have helped you. We were powerless. From behind the second veil you could not even call my name. You were utterly alone. Come now, take the moon crystal to your heart that it might hold your memories from beyond the second veil."

The crystal flickered brightly. There was a flash and then a glow that died away gradually like the dying embers of a fire. "Now the sun crystal" said Tala. Sis took it and held it against her heart and closed her eyes. These memories left her gently and the crystal glimmered slowly like soft candlelight.

"You know Sis, we record all history, every wonder, every moment. Now you have witnessed this too and more. You have become part of the history of a world - a Kingdom removed from your own. There is a great mystery in this which even the Guardian cannot explain."

Tala looked into Sis's face. It was young and fresh again and her eyes were glinting. *Yes, Sis had come back to her.*

"Time to go Sis, your home is waiting...Happy New Year.

The Divided Kingdom

The first week of March 2005 brought heavy snow falls to Thanet. For days the sky was a uniform dull grey and the icy wind from the east chilled the Island. For the first time in a number of years the county of Kent bore the brunt of the UK's severe weather, which now swept in from mainland Europe. The good news for children was that many schools closed for a few days. Simone had thought she was really suffering bravely when she arrived at school and was immediately sent home because the air temperature dropped to minus 2 degrees. Until, that was, she received a phone call the same night from her friend who was visiting her sister in Canada where it was minus 25 degrees! *On hearing that, winter in Thanet didn't seem so bad after all.*

Home again, and looking out of her bedroom window, Simone watched the cars skidding around the corner however slowly they were driven. The snow on the road gradually turned a dirty grey as it was churned up by the traffic and the neighbours swept the snow off their paths into discoloured heaps on the kerb side. Lines of deep footprints along the pavement traced the postman's route from house to house and on the opposite side of the road an elderly lady walked her old dog. The animal, wrapped in its makeshift overcoat hobbled through the cold leaving irregularly patterned paw prints behind. A little later with the snow falling thickly the footprints were covered and the road was painted white, just for a moment. Then the buses came along and the road was churned into slush again and new footprints appeared. No matter how much it snowed it seemed as if nature could never catch up and complete its white blanket. In the back garden, however, it was a very different world!

Simone came downstairs to gaze upon the brilliant white that covered the garden. She sat in her Dad's comfortable leather chair by the window wrapped cosily in her dressing gown to enjoy the wonderland before her, which was somehow all the more special because she was alone. The snow was thick, quiet and pure. No prints to spoil its completeness, only giant flakes fluttering down endlessly. The thick carpet that covered the grass and lay heavily on the trees positively glowed. Sometimes a thin branch would be bent down by the weight of the snow, that slid off and like a tiny avalanche crashed silently to the floor as the branch sprang back. She opened the window and stretched out to catch the enormous snowflakes that now cascaded down and saw Rufous on the garden wall. He was standing on one leg, the other nervously trailing in the air as he were balancing. She rushed back into the kitchen and grabbed a few slices of bread. It was wholemeal multi- grain, her Dad's favourite. *Only the best for Rufous!*

Rufous was already waiting on the ground in front of the window, hopping in the deep snow when she returned. She broke the bread into small chunks and flicked it out. With only one strong leg the bird found it difficult to turn, so Simone aimed the bread to fall in front of him. He moved closer and closer picking up the bread till he was almost under her extended arm. He ate quickly and constantly looked up at Simone, not nervously, but as if he was checking she was still there. Then he stopped eating and moved away, looked back at her and took off with powerful wing beats towards the sea.

Simone watched him disappear over the rooftops, closed the window and sat back down. Seeing Rufous again had stirred up so many memories. He was after all the closest physical link she would ever have to the realm of the Angels. Her heart suddenly yearned to return. Her right hand moved across to the yellow butterfly and she called "Tala, Tala…."

"How long has it been, Sis?" Tala asked, as she greeted her friend.

"So long I've really lost count. Do you remember?"

"Yes, it's sixty three days, five hours and forty two of your minutes – exactly! Answered Tala."

Sis laughed and embraced her friend. "I've missed you so much."

"Me too, I was watching you feeding your bird and willing you to come through to us. Did you notice how close he came; he had absolutely no fear of you. He knows you're special too – that's why he entrusted you with the Dawn witch's bracelet. He's a very intelligent gull that Rufous. Oh! I'm so happy you're here Sis."

Tala took her hand and once again Sis revelled in the joy of flying. In the map room Tala turned the wheel to reveal The Divided Kingdom. It was spread out before her eyes like a live tapestry. "Where can I begin" asked Sis, "I see so many places in so many worlds?"

"You have to start somewhere and for your first journey Sis - I know just the place. Trust me", said Tala "now close your eyes and open your heart."

Meeting the Singers Or 'Insults over the fence'

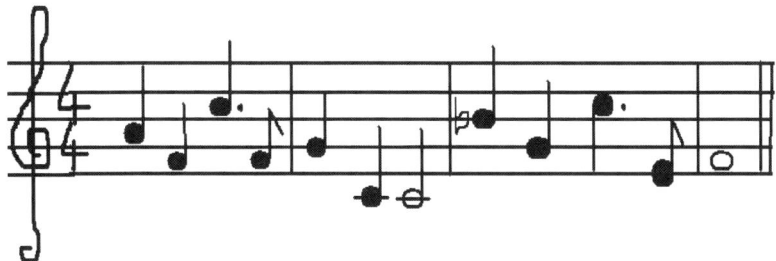

"Well?" said the dapper man who stood blocking Sis's path. "Have you no response to make?" Sis looked aghast. She had been walking down a narrow street when suddenly this man had jumped out in front of her. He had raised his blue feathered hat in greeting, bowed and sung loudly as if aiming the song directly at her.

"Well?" He asked again.

Still Sis had no idea what he was asking her or indeed why he had jumped out and sung at her. "Sorry" she said, "I don't understand."

The man went red in the face and shook his arms angrily. "I've never met such disrespect in all my life. That, young lady, was my finest greeting song. I can see it is totally wasted on you and to think, I just drank my last singing oil to perfect my sound. It's outrageous!" With this he buttoned up the collar of his long blue coat, spun round on his heels theatrically and marched off. She watched him go, then he stopped suddenly as if considering something and marched straight back to face Sis and - sung at her again!

"Well?" he smirked smugly and waited.............. So Sis sang back!

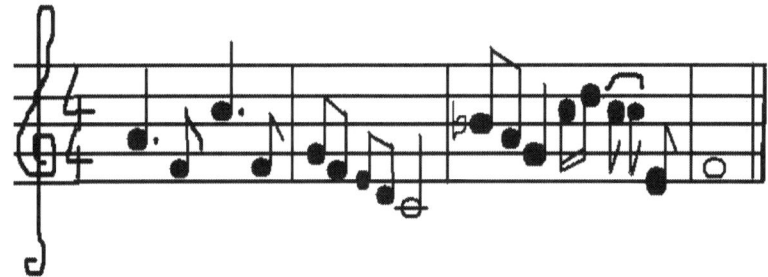

"Oh! My" he said. "I salute you. Whatever singing oil do you use? That was magnificent – and by a girl!" "It was only a very simple tune" said Sis.

"No, no, no. It's the sound that is important, the pure beautiful sound that carries the words. Come with me, I have to show you to my wife, she won't believe it! Come, come there's a wind picking up and you have to protect your voice".

They walked together through narrow winding streets between rickety painted houses. Every now and then someone would jump out and sing or shout at them, but he was in too much of a hurry to respond with more than an approving nod or smile.

"Here's my house. I would like to sing you a welcome but my oil's dry. If you don't mind we'll skip the ceremonials and I'll speak the welcome instead, 'please do come in' this is my wife Gem".

"Hello. My name is Sis. It's very kind of you to invite me to your home".

"You're welcome. I'm Gem and my husband here is Li," she replied.

"Please Miss Sis; sing for my wife- show her your sound". Sis sang a short melody she knew.

"See, see Gem?" Li asked excitedly "and with absolutely no voice oil at all."

"Yes, an amazing sound, so pure. Maybe you could teach an old woman like me?"

"I'm still learning myself," confessed Sis. "Singing is my greatest pleasure - I just love it."

"What a quaint idea" said Li. "Imagine Gem, me singing for pleasure? I'd soon lose my lead in the 'insult' rankings."

"You certainly would" replied Gem. "And I can't see anyone paying you to sing 'nicely' over the fence!" Li just laughed at his wife's suggestion..... *The very idea!*

Turning to Sis Gem explained "It's not easy staying at the top here in the West, there's so much jealousy of Li's position as the lead Insult Singer. Why" she said, quickly changing the subject, "I clear forgot to offer you a drink. I'm so sorry. I'll bring a gargle of course but would you prefer a throat cleanser or a warm rinse, we have both?"

"Whichever you are having is fine, thanks."

Sis sat opposite Li enjoying the comforting warmth of the raging log fire. She looked around the room and noticed that apart from a few decorative pots, some with dried flowers in, the room was dominated by a large map on the wall facing her. "May I ask a question? I only arrived here this morning and everything is new to me."

"Yes of course" replied Li, "If you will excuse me talking and not singing. At home we speak simple and save our energy for the shouting and singing outside." He saw the confused expression on Sis's face and asked "Don't you know anything about West Thanet then Sis?"

No, I've never been here before."

"Ah! A real first time stranger, that's not common these days. Even with the fence dividing the island folk move around quite a lot now. It's not like it used to be. In fact recently Gem and I have crossed over to the East a few times, mostly as Western representatives to the peace meetings" he smiled proudly. "And we take every opportunity we can to go to the animal village in the South. Of course the creatures don't understand insult singing and they get nervous if you practise shouting at them, but some of the animals, especially the owls, have such incredible hearing they can spot a note that is one in a thousand sour - unbelievable eh? Yes, it is excellent practice, singing to them".

Sis's head was beginning to spin with all these strange ideas, when thankfully Gem returned with a tray of drinks. First the gargle was taken noisily and spat out into the big yellow jar by the fire. Sis just copied her hosts' actions. Then a raspberry coloured warm rinse which, she was relieved to see, was sipped slowly and swallowed.

"I was just telling Sis about the West, she is a real first time stranger."

"Then tell her straight and simple. There's plenty here to confuse the poor girl without us helping," said Gem."

"Alright Gem" Li answered defensively, "Save your anger for the Tapers. They're the real enemy, not me." Gem smiled apologetically. She hadn't meant to sound so harsh. She absentmindedly pulled on the white cuff of her blue velvet dress and wished she hadn't snapped at her husband, especially in front of a guest, and a first time stranger at that.

"Easiest way to explain is to look at the map." He rose from his chair and continued, "Here Sis, come over and have a look."

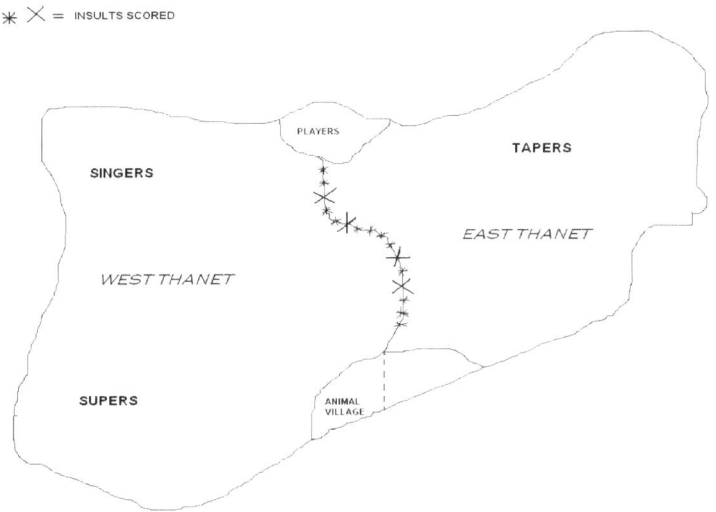

THE DIVIDED ISLE OF THANET

"Well here's our island. In the west here," he pointed, "our group, the Singers live side by side with the Supers. In the East there," he stabbed his finger at the map, "live the Tapers – all by themselves."

"Who would want to live with those …?" cursed Gem.

Li continued, moving his finger down the map - "The animal village here has many different creatures including, some believe, Celfytes. Folk used to call them Fairies in olden times. The village really is a little world of its own, certainly worth a visit while you're here and," he added, "it is the only place on the island where the fence has been broken down so you can roam around freely. Animals can't be confined; every time the fence was repaired they trampled it down again. Now it's just left and no one bothers."

"It's not as if you'd meet a Taper there anyway," said Gem. "Don't think they like animals much, they don't stand still long enough for the Tapers to measure them."

"Oh I don't know, replied Li, I reckon they measure everything on the Isle, can't help themselves. After all, they've got nothing more useful to do."

"Yes, and that's a fact," agreed Gem.

"What's that Players' area at the top there?" asked Sis "it looks like it's on the other side of the fence."

"Ah, yes that's a special place. Players don't belong to a group - sadly they can't take sides because they like everyone. So their area is respected as a sanctuary. In fact shouting and singing insults have been forbidden there for generations and the Supers think the whole area is so unlucky they never go near it anyway."

"Yes, added Gem," and it's the only place the Tapers can't take their stupid measuring tapes with them, so you rarely see a Taper there either."

Li looked back to the map, then to Sis and then back to the map again and waited. Neither he nor Gem spoke anymore. There was an empty silence. *They're waiting for me to say something… what?* Sis looked back at the map then asked "What are all those star marks on the fence?" Li's smile told Sis that her guess had, thankfully, been right.

"Can I explain to Sis?" asked Gem.

"Yes, please do. Come on Sis, sit here and get comfortable." He sat down too, looking Very pleased with himself. He unbuttoned his coat and nonchalantly threw his hat onto a chair in the corner before pouring another rinse for Sis.

"I mark these stars on Li's map every time he appears publicly to sing insults over the fence. The larger red stars are for the times when he has actually got the men Tapers so angry that they turned away or the women started to cry – they both count the same. See here, if you look closely there's not a meeting place where he hasn't sung insults over the wall. When it's been too cold or wet to sing properly, he's shouted them instead. Quite a record eh?" She looked at Li proudly. Li was grinning from ear to ear.

"In West Thanet we're proud of our way of life and traditions, we don't need measuring to order our lives, we believe we should be free. The Tapers have tried for generations to make us like them." She shook her head and sighed sadly before continuing. "You know, Sis There's an old Singer couplet:-

A Taper till seven is a child from heaven.

A Taper at eight measures Hell's gate."

"There's truth in that too," interrupted Li. "It is so sad to see what happens to them when they start Taper school. From the moment the measuring tapes are hung round their necks during the 'becoming ceremony' on their first day it's as if their spirits and imaginations are ripped from them. Then their lifetime drudgery begins." Gem sighed. "Yes the first day of the Taper's school is Li's busiest day of the whole cycle. Sad but true", she shook her head despairingly. "Folks here get so angry. They write insults and pay Li to sing them at the Tapers over the fence outside the schools. Hundreds of Singers turn out to watch. That's when Li's strong voice gives him a real advantage. He's the only Singer that can always be heard clearly above all the noise and jeers." She looked at Li again affectionately. "Yes indeed, folks trust him. They know that any insult he throws across the fence will always reach the Taper's ears and be heard by all their Singer neighbours on this side too. He's not cheap - but he is the best."

"Well," said Sis "it's better than fighting each other and at least words can't kill."

"Oh! We've had many wars during the last hundred cycles," Gem explained, "but all the killing got us nowhere so the fence was built to keep us apart. Now instead of throwing spears we throw insults. Nothing's really changed."

"Tell you what Sis, there's a torchlight meeting at the fence tonight and I'm performing in the dark. It's the first time it's ever been done. A very rich Singer is paying for everything to celebrate his son's seventh birthday. Why don't you come along and watch?"

"Thank you, I will if I can."

"You'll have to excuse me now Sis, I have to go and work on the insults for the party tonight. The Father has particularly asked for the insults to be, in his words, 'full of venom and hatred'. He's quite a distinguished man in his own profession, anyway - he's paying" Li said with a grin.

Gem walked Sis to the door. "You know Sis, with a voice like yours I reckon you could become a top insult singer and," she added with a chuckle, "a girl singing insults would scare the hell out of those cowardly Tapers!"

The Supers of West Thanet

Sis continued down the street, passing small stalls selling voice oil, throat cleansers and rinses. A young woman called out to her "Hey Missy, you better look after your lovely skin. Try this, only arrived this morning." She held out two small dishes, one in each hand. "Go on, try some."

"What is it?"

"The very finest lotion. This is for your face, this for your hands. It keeps your skin supple, ready for those times when you have to shout a lot."

"No thank you, but can you tell me where there's a place I could stay for the night?"

"Ah! A first time stranger, thought I hadn't seen you around before. Well, when you do need singing oil, you know where to come now, don't you? Right, somewhere to stay." She pointed. "Down the path by the orange pond, there's a big wooden house with a white door. You can't miss it. It's a Supers' house so you won't get much service but it will be very, very clean."

"Thank you" said Sis and she strolled on down by the pond where she sat and watched. Her body wasn't tired but her mind was. *This was a very confusing place.*

The lawns around the pond thronged with people. Opposite was the wooden house with a white door and there seemed to be a number of people streaming in and then walking out. Others got as far as the door, turned round back to the pond side, lifted their right leg then repeated their movements. Back and forth they went, over and over again. *These must be Supers.* They looked quite different from the dapper Singers who all wore blue and all wore hats. The Supers wore identical clothes, more like a uniform: orange tunics, wide orange trousers and brightly polished black shoes with silver buckles on both sides. The men had their hair cut short whilst the women wore theirs long in a single plait. As a group walked close by Sis noticed that they all had a hanging earring, shaped and painted like an eye. And then she realised something else. For the whole time she had been watching, not one orange-clad Super had remained still or stopped doing anything. They were all in constant motion, rehearsing the same actions; repeatedly brushing away imaginary flies with a long feather.

"Here, want some?" It was the young woman from the voice- oil stall who came and sat next to Sis on the grass. She had a basket of breads and what looked to Sis to be a collection of small pies and cheeses.

"Thanks, I'm really hungry." The girls sat eating together, enjoying each other's company.

"My name's Delfie, what's yours?"

"Sis."

"And what do you think of West Thanet Sis?"

"It's certainly interesting. To be honest, everything here is so different it's given me a real headache."

"That's being honest all right," Delfie said laughing. "It's all normal to me, I was born here but I have to admit I get a headache sometimes too, trying to understand life on the East side."

"Oh Yes, Gem and Li told me about the Tapers."

"You met them, did you? Li's the top ranked Insult Singer. He sometimes buys his voicing oils from me. My Dad's dedicated to singing too, and both my brothers, but they're not in Li's league. Sometimes when they are all practising at home my Mum and I run down here for some peace and 'Super watching."

"Do you know why they all dress identically Delfie?"

"Probably because they believe it would be unlucky not to - who knows? Their real name is the Superstitious tribe, called 'Supers' for short. They all wear the earring to ward off 'the evil eye.' That means anyone who might wish them harm. The reason they continuously repeat actions is to prevent any 'bad edges' getting into their life-space."

"Yes, I saw some women going in and out of the door repeatedly, agreed Sis.

As they chatted a Super walked right up to them, shook his head and warned them. "You girls be careful, sitting in two's with one basket is very unlucky and when you finish that bread leave two pieces, not more mind, and both throw a piece over your left shoulder. That will keep the Wingars away, it works every time. "And", he continued, "Don't sit too long on this wet grass - you'll be sorry." He clapped his hands twice, hopped on his left foot and touched his eye earring and went back down the slope. That took some time as he, took two steps forward, one back, shook his head, brushed his sleeves then took two steps forward again.

"What a complicated life they lead" said Sis.

"It certainly is" agreed Delfie. "Come on let's see if there is a room for you."

They made their way to the Supers' house, past groups of children who called out to them "don't walk too much on the left, the grass isn't flat there, hop over it." Another young girl skipped over to them saying "take this flower and sleep with it under your left shoulder and the Taper curses will never get in- promise."

The front door was wide open so the girls walked inside. "Careful, the floor's wet, mind you don't slip. A wet floor's a Wingars' trap for the unwary" said the lady super as a kind of greeting.

"Do you have a room for my friend?" asked Delfie.

"Can't come in without an eye" she replied, staring at Sis's ears "too unlucky. No telling what Wingars would find their way in.

She ain't from the East is she?"

"No, she's a visitor and what if she had an eye earring?"

The super started counting on her fingers. "Sorry, no. Just put clean sheets on all the empty beds. Have to be left empty till dawn to let the cleanliness sink through then we'll turn them for luck and then, of course she can have a bed." "When's that?" asked Sis.

"Morrow evening" replied the Super. Come back then. Now mind your heads and please step out backwards and here, put this mustard seed in your pockets till night fall. I've heard the Taper's ghosts are flying at sunset so don't walk backwards less than twenty three steps – just to be safe."

The girls wandered back up to where they had sat on the grass. Delfie jokingly picked up a pinch of discarded breadcrumbs and said to Sis in a passable Super's accent "You be careful my girl. Put two crumbs up your nose, hop on your right foot backwards for eighteen paces then run into the pond and stand on your head. That will keep the melling wurthars away for weeks – guaranteed."

They both rolled over laughing. Then Sis sat up and asked "Delfie what on earth's a Wingar?"

"Ah, those Supers are frightened of everything! They're even frightened of being frightened. They believe the Tapers breed bad spirits and send them over the fence each night. These spirits, they call Wingars, are supposed to creep into your room at night when you are sleeping and bury themselves in your dreams. And once they're in - you can't ever get them out!" "What a horrible thought" said Sis?

"Yes and imagine how those poor Super children feel, hearing all these terrifying things every day. Do you know I've yet to see one smile" added Delfie sadly.

"No wonder. Poor things, their lives must be a misery. At least the Taper children have seven years of normal childhood before they have to go to school" said Sis.

Delfie looked down. Her expression grew more serious as she asked "So Li told you about the Tapers then?"

"Yes. He and his wife really hate them. He keeps a record of every time he's insulted them - he's very proud of it."

"Well he would be. He hates the Tapers for a living. That's how he gets his money. I wouldn't believe everything he told you though Sis."

"What do you mean?"

"The Taper school is strict, and Taper parents really push their children to do well in their examinations but that's only because they want them to be successful. Without qualifications in measuring they won't be able to get a job when they leave school. But they love their children and want only the best for them. Can you imagine how frightening it must be for a seven year old, on their first day at school, having to walk past crowds of Singers screaming horrible things at them over the fence?"

"How do you know all this Delfie?"

Can you keep a secret?" Sis moved over closer to Delfie and carefully scanned their surroundings. *There was no one near.*

"My best friend's from East Thanet. Her name's Attar. We grew up together and played every day when my family and hers lived near the fence. She's the sweetest and kindest girl you've ever met. We moved away just before she started school but we still meet secretly, usually in animal village, its safe there. How stupid is it to think you can love a friend for years, grow up together then when you're seven, suddenly you have to start hating each other. We made a pact before I moved away that we would never stop being friends. That was over six cycles ago and in all that time we've kept our promise."

Sis's face flushed with admiration for this brave girl. "Do your parent's know?"

Delfie smiled. "Can you keep another secret Sis?"

"I promise. I would never break your trust Delfie."

"Well, Attar's mother and mine are best friends too."

"That's wonderful" said Sis. Then she started to laugh." Imagine old Li's face if he saw them walking together. He wouldn't know who to sing insults at first"!"

"Brilliant. That I would pay to see," said Delfie.

When I was very young I had a bad illness and the Singer doctors could not make me better. My family had given up hope, till one day my mother was walking along the fence crying and praying to her forefathers for help. She was desperate. She hadn't eaten or slept for days and was so delirious that she suddenly collapsed against a broken pane of the fence, fell through, and rolled down the hill into a small valley. She could not have known that it was in East Thanet!

Many years later she told me the story. Attar's mother had found her and hidden her in her house. She had seen my mother across the fence many times and even knew our house, so she sent her husband through the fence at night to tell my father and give her word that she would protect my mother. For two days and nights she nursed her, never leaving her side. When my mother's strength returned and she told Attar's mother about my illness, she immediately called her Doctor.

My mother always recalls how kind that doctor was. How he listened to her giving every detail of my illness, how he comforted her and promised he would do everything in his power to save me. That same night he crossed the fence and secretly made his way to my house. My Father was exhausted from watching over me and he did not wake when the doctor came. He gave me some ancient Taper medicine and wrapped my body in special leaves. Throughout the night he sat with me, watching over me and praying.

When the dawn came my Father was woken by my crying. He told me years later that the sight of the Taper doctor holding me so tenderly in his arms and reciting the sweetest prayers, melted his heart and he had felt so ashamed for all the years he had mistrusted the Tapers.

The doctor refused to take any reward. He told my Father that healing is of two kinds; the physical and the spiritual. "Both were necessary for treating the whole person" he said. Then as he was leaving he turned to my Father and said "there is one thing you can do for me."

"Anything, my father answered.

"Please don't let this precious child be ruined by hatred as our generation is. Let her grow to be a pure and free spirit."

On his way back he was attacked by a group of drunken Singers 'for being on their side' and thrown back over the fence. Somehow he made it back to Attar's mother's house before collapsing, but he was an old man and could not survive the beating that the Singers had metered out. He died shortly after. So you see my Mother and I both owe our lives to the bravery of the Tapers. An old man, who I was too young to remember, gave his life to save me. And now in return I'm supposed to hate them and ridicule them!! How can I?"

Delfie burst into angry tears and fell into Sis's arms sobbing.

Tears streamed down Sis's face too, and then she whispered "You are a pure and free spirit Delfie. I'm sure the Doctor is very proud of you."

Delfie wiped her eyes and turning to Sis asked "Do you really believe that? The Singers all say that when you die there's nothing, so you had better enjoy this life while you're here. Honestly Sis, and I've never told anyone this, I know in my heart that this isn't true. I know there is another world after this and when we die that's where our spirits and love go." Delfie paused and looked into Sis's eyes before she continued. "If ever I am sad when I go to sleep I have a dream-and it is always the same. I am lying in bed ill. I see a thick mist that slowly turns into a pure light and an old man appears sitting next to me. He holds my hand and his lips move as if he is speaking but there is no sound. I cannot see his face very clearly but I can feel his smile and it warms me as if

I'm standing under the summer sun. And when I wake up in the morning I feel a strange happiness that lasts all day."

"How wonderful Delfie, you are so lucky. Yes, I do believe the Doctor watches over you from the other world and he is proud of you - very proud."

The girls sat together in an intimate silence, united by so many shared secrets. Then Delfie said "It's getting late now Sis, why don't you come and stay at my house and you can meet another Singer family. I'm sure my Mother won't mind?"

"Thank you, are you sure?"

"Of course, listen I've just remembered, our family have got a pass for the Peace meeting at the Tapers hall tomorrow and we're allowed to bring one guest. Please say you'll come. I'm hoping Attar will be there with her parents, I'd love you to meet them."

Sis was woken up by the household gargling. For one moment she had no idea where she was, until Delfie came into the room.

"Sorry about the noise, the men are oiling up, they're all performing this afternoon. They've been selected to sing at the beginning of the reception for the Peace Meeting. Breakfast's ready, come down."

Delfie's family were very hospitable. It was unusual for them to have guests for breakfast and with all the questions they threw at Sis it was a very noisy but enjoyable meal. They plied her with plates of breads, cheese and pears and cup after cup of worse snip tea.

"Well Sis" said Delfie's Dad. "Do you still feel a first time stranger?"

"Not any more. You've really made me feel part of your family. Thank you."

"We're very pleased to have you stay" said Delfie's Mother "Have you ever been to East Thanet?" "No I haven't" Sis replied.

"Well please make sure you stay close to Delfie and don't lose this". She bent forward and pinned a red ribbon on Sis's dress, then handed out the remaining ribbons to the rest of the family. "This is your pass, it will be checked at the fence and you'll need it again to get into Taper hall."

"We won't have to worry about the fence check Mother we're going by boat" announced Delfie excitedly.

"Will we all fit in?" asked her mother.

"Yes, Dad's borrowed Uncle's boat, it's more than big enough and Sis and I can sit at the front and look out for Celfytes."

"That's my girl" said her Father as he kissed her head affectionately. "She never stops dreaming and hoping. You really will have to be very lucky though Sis to find a Celfyte. Do you know I've been travelling the rivers for 34 cycles and I've never seen one!"

"Ah but you don't know where to look Dad" said Delfie with a teasing smile. "And we might be lucky this time if Yot and Yat can paddle quietly enough not to scare them away" said Delfie, cheekily raising her eyebrows at her brothers.

"Come on Sis, Delfie," said her mother, "help me clear up now and get ready. We need to make a picnic for on the way. Let the boys rest for a while they will need all their energy to row us. It's a long way there and back in one day. Come on girls, we don't want to be late for the reception." She turned to Delfie and with a glint in her eyes added "I wonder who else will be there?"

They moved steadily up stream. Sis and Delfie watching every bank side movement for the tell-tale sign of a Celfyte.

"You have to watch under the bank where the brambles hang over. The story goes they nest in small holes right below the thickest vegetation" explained Delfie.

"How big are they?" asked Sis.

"I reckon a little smaller than those sparrows on the bush there," she pointed. "Celfytes are said to be like beautiful miniature Players with small wings and they can change into any colour. They have even been known to land on your hand to take bread, can you imagine that?"

"Have you got any bread Delfie?"

"Just this, shall we try?"

"Of course" replied Sis and both girls held their arms out just above the water and watched and waited. Later as they rounded a bend in the shadows of some matted bulrushes Sis suddenly turned her head and speaking out of the corner of her mouth called "Delfie, Delfie look!"

Sis could see every fine detail. Its fluorescent outline looked as if it was painted in faint neon light. The creature sat on Sis's thumb and with tiny hands picked at the fragments of bread. Its wings were folded back, its legs hung down and its tiny feet rested on Sis's palm.

"What kind of creature are you?" she breathed gently.

"I am a Celfyte" the creature replied. Sis was surprised at how a tiny creature could have such a strong voice. It was both high-pitched yet gentle to the ear.

"Where do you come from?" asked Sis.

"Our whole nation came from the Minla Kingdom, a world which is hidden behind the second universe. It was a beautiful world until the fire rains came. Then we had to flee before our world was devoured by flames from the sky."

Sis gazed in amazement. "How long have you been here on the island?" she asked.

"Measured in your time," said the Celfyte, "for 900 cycles of your sun. But the journey here across the galaxies took many Celfyte generations. Now at last we are at peace here and we are content." The creature continued to explain as Sis looked at Delfie. "Who were you talking to?" Delfie asked.

Sis nodded towards her hand, "the Celfyte."

"Where, I can't see it?"

"It's alright" said the Celfyte, "I have changed my reflection and the others can't see me. It's our only protection." She flew up onto Sis's shoulder. Sis lifted her hand and Delfie turned round to continue watching her own hand skimming the water.

"There are many of us all over the Island now, along every stream and river or shaded dell. Few creatures know where to find us because we only open our reflection to those whose hearts are pure and who can keep our secret."

"I will keep your secret" said Sis.

"No need to say it. It is in your heart as clear as daylight for me to read. Just as I see in your eyes that you have flown the twilight path. We see everything" replied the Celfyte. "And by the way, we change the volume of our voices to suit whoever we are talking to. I can speak much louder if you like?" Sis could not believe what she heard. She was shocked. But before she could gather her thoughts the Celfyte opened her wings and flew on upstream, disappearing around the bend. Sis closed her eyes to store the magic in her mind.

"Sis, are you awake? We're here now" Delfie called. "Look there's Taper hall over there on the hill and the Players have come down to meet us."

"You girls can stay here to see the Players if you like, I'll go with the men folk" said Delfie's mother. "Meet you at the Taper hall mid-day and please, don't be late."

By the time Sis and Delfie had tied up the boat and climbed onto the landing stage there were Players everywhere. The girls danced in circles around them, the boys hung by their feet from branches and called "come and play". They were all smiles, giggling constantly, then the girls started climbing up the trees and the boys dropped down to form a circle, hand in hand, running faster and faster till they got dizzy and fell to the floor laughing.

"They seem so happy Delphie, are they always like this?"

"Yes, always. They simply never stop playing", then addressing a group of Players Delphie knelt down and asked, "Would you like to meet my new friend, she's never met Players before?"

"Oh, yes" and turning to Sis asked her "What's your name. Have you come to play?"

Sis looked down fascinated. Both boys and girls were of similar height and barely came up to her waist. All wore yellow and white striped clothes. The girls had shorts and blouses, the boys' longer shorts and jerkins. All had one yellow and one white sock.

"Hello. My name is Sis. I am so happy to meet you and I would love to have time to play with you, but right now we have to go to a meeting. If we have time we will try to see you on our way back."

"Stand up slowly and don't stop smiling, Sis. Now turn round and don't look back."

Sis did as Delphie had asked and when they had walked out of earshot Delphie explained.

"Players are so considerate and never like to displease any one. Once you said you couldn't play right now they were so disappointed and some had started to cry, that is why I said keep smiling so they thought you hadn't seen their sadness. Such sensitive, loving creatures…

"Indeed," said Sis." Such pure souls." She paused, looked up and said "It's nearly mid-day. Your Mother will be wondering where we've got to. Come on…"

Measured by the Tapers

Finding the Taper hall was easy enough, actually getting into the Peace meeting was another matter! Ever since the first Peace meeting was organised it was the Supers who had been put in charge of organising the security for the event. They had expressed many anxieties about the dangers of so many people meeting together. They feared the opportunities it offered for Wingars and other loathsome spirits to creep in so they refused to take part unless they could be solely responsible for checking all visitors. As neither the Singers nor the Tapers could be bothered their request had been granted immediately.

There were three barriers that all visitors had to pass through. First was the security check. Here their ribbons were checked, their left thumb measured and their names recorded in four different books. They then had to swear an oath that they would not insult or attempt to deny in any way others the right to speak and declare their beliefs openly. Then it was on to the Super's edge-clearing arch.

Up until now Delfie and Sis had managed to keep a straight face but this was too much for them and they began giggling uncontrollably. They were made to walk through a foot bath 'to cleanse their shoes of Wingar seeds', then to stoop under a low archway made from woven mistle-toe and rosemary 'to clear their edges of any bad feelings.' They nearly tripped over coming out of the arch they were laughing so much.

"This is a serious meeting and you are expected to take it seriously. We are seeking peace here today. It's not a time for playing" said the lady Super who was hopping on one leg as she sprinkled more dried rosemary leaves over their shoes. Then she stopped hopping and took out a sheet of card to perform the last check - fanning the girl's hair to clear any lingering Wingar shadows. At last they were through!

Sis and Delfie entered the grand hall and were almost deafened by the noise. It was packed. Singers were warming up producing all manner of sounds which filtered through the crowds from every side.

"Look Sis, there's the Tapers. Come and see," suggested Delfie.

The girls pushed their way past a line of Supers who were warning their audience of all kinds of impending dangers facing both East and West Thanet and offering charms and weird remedies to protect them. Sis noticed Delfie's mother standing in the main singing section, arm in arm with a Taper lady. Seeing their obvious happiness together Sis guessed it must be Attar's mother and called across "We won't be long we are just going over to see the Tapers."

Suddenly they found themselves surrounded by Tapers of all ages looking them up and down, consulting tables in small red books they took from their pockets. Just as all the Singers wore blue and all the Supers dressed in orange so too the Tapers dressed identically to each other. They each wore a white shirt, black waistcoat and striped grey trousers; men and women alike. All had measuring tapes hanging around their necks, even the little children who were playing on the floor measuring peoples' feet.

"Stand still. You want an accurate measurement don't you?" scolded a distinguished looking Taper who held out his hand towards Sis. If anything he was a little shorter than the other adult Tapers but he held himself erect as if he was trying to stretch himself to be taller. He alone had golden buttons on his waistcoat and golden tips to his measuring tape which hung not around his neck like everyone else, but was slung nonchalantly over his shoulder.

"This is Master Taper, Sis" said Delfie. "Master, this is my new friend Sis."

"Yes, yes, I'll see to the helloes once you're measured." He then stepped back and announced proudly and in a very loud voice "Exactly five and three quarters", he paused as the crowd around quietened in expectation. "Five and three quarter – weasels!"

"Can you believe that? He's using animal measures. That is clever, very clever" said a young Taper standing next to Delfie.

"No wonder he's the Master" added another in an admiring tone.

"Wait" called the Master in a somewhat boastful manner. "Or, a whisker over one and a half badgers or", he paused again, "twelve and three quarter common shrews."

"One more Master, please, just one more" called a jolly faced woman who actually wore three measuring tapes around her neck and carried another two in her hand.

The Master closed his eyes, looked up then announced "the final measure I give you is nine and a half moles." Loud applause echoed around the hall as Sis looked across at Delfie waiting for some kind of explanation.

Instead the Master stepped up to Sis and asked her haughtily, "ever been measured better? I doubt it. There's fifteen cycles' study and a lifetime of research behind my measuring."

"I know my height" Sis replied confidently, "it's one hundred and forty six centimetres."

"What nonsense is that? Centipedes more like" scoffed the Master. "And for your information, young lady, insects are excluded from all measuring tables .Didn't you know?"

"No. How could I? But insects have up to six legs and therefore Centipedes are not……"

"Oh Bah! The master interrupted quite rudely and turned round to address his more adoring followers.

"Please Miss, can I measure you? I've just started my last cycle at school and I need to practise on new people for my project," a young student asked Sis shyly.

"And what subjects do you study in school?" she asked him.

"Oh, every subject you can possibly imagine. The first three cycles we take 'things to measure', and then there's the difficult three cycles on 'recording measurements' and finally, four cycles on 'advanced measuring'. If you manage to pass the final examination you might be chosen to take the advanced course run by the Master himself, 'measuring odd shapes.' That would make my parent's so proud."

"Alright, agreed Sis, "but only if you measure us together at the same time." Sis pulled on Delfie's arm and they both started to giggle. For one moment he lost his composure as the two girls smiled teasingly at him and he felt his face blushing. *He had to concentrate!*

He began his measuring in earnest, feverishly noting down figures in his book. He was conscious of many envious eyes on him. '*What an honour* he thought. *To be publicly measuring two girls at once and in front of the Master.*' He fought back his nervousness and tried as best he could to look serious and professional.

Both girls found it difficult to stand very still, they were giggling so much. Everyone else stared fascinated as the student worked. They looked on as if this was the most important thing in the entire world.

Sis sensed that the Master Taper was becoming a little unsettled. After all, *everyone's attention was now focused on his student and not him - and he had been invited as the guest of honour to give the key speech. He had to turn this situation around.* "Friends, friends" he announced. "You all know the school motto 'If a thing is worth measuring it's worth measuring accurately'. Well, in my life's work I have always striven for greater perfection and have lived by my own rule: 'If it can't be measured it's not worth knowing.' Now to celebrate this special Peace meeting I propose to hold the first ever public measuring examination and I choose my brightest student." Turning to the boy he said "Stand up Wilz. You will need your animal length records volume 11 and your tape conversion tables." The circle of the crowd moved in as Wilz scrambled to gather all his material together and set it out on a small table.

The Master took Sis by the hand and stood her in front of his student. "Here is your subject. Now throw your tapes away and working only from your notes tell me the measure of this girl in moles, shrews, weasels and badgers. You have six and one quarter Desmonds. Start now!"

"What does he mean by 'Desmonds,' Delfie?" asked Sis.

"It's a very old system of measuring time passing by using a burning candle. I can't do it myself but the Master does it in his head."

The first three calculations Wilz felt confident he had completed correctly and the other he remembered from the master's own measuring. Nevertheless, he doubled checked every one just to be sure.

"Now say your measures in moles?" "Nine and a half "answered Wilz.

"Common shrews?" continued the Master.

"Twelve and three quarters" replied Wilz and he went on to answer all the questions correctly.

"Very good indeed" said the Master. "Now your final question, and for this I allow you five Desmonds. What is her height, in the ancient measures of fox and stoat?"

On hearing this, the colour drained from Wilz's face. The women standing next to Sis remarked with surprise "No one's used fox and stoat measures for cycles. I wouldn't know where to start!"

"Time starts now" signalled the Master with a haughty wave of his hand. The crowd fell silent and Wilz thumbed through his books and scrambled through his notes, scribbling numbers over everything. He knew these two were difficult. They had never come up in class, not in ten cycles. *They must,* he reasoned to himself, *be 'nearly numbers,' above or below the nearest quarter- but by how many whiskers?*

He sketched and calculated and went over and over his answers, each time slightly altering the whisker count.

"Time's up" the Master called. "I give these answers to our measured guests. They will judge" and he handed folded pieces of paper first to Sis, then to Delfie.

"Give your answer clearly, firstly-the measure in fox".

"Wilz took a deep breath and looking directly at the Master said "Six whiskers over one and a quarter"

"And the written answer in your hand?" he asked Sis.

Sis read out "Six whiskers over one and a quarter foxes." Everyone wanted to clap and cheer but refrained under the glaringly serious look of the Master as his eyes scanned the crowd.

"Secondly-the measure in stoat?" said the Master dramatically"

"It is two whiskers under four and a half." This had been very difficult. Wilz just felt relief now. The crowd could hardly control themselves with excitement and the Master was enjoying this, deliberately waiting before he asked Delfie to read out her answer.

"Two whiskers under four and a half" called out Delfie.

Such a cheer went up that it silenced every conversation in the hall. Even the Singers stopped gargling. Everyone looked over to the Tapers' corner and soon word spread of the brilliant new scholar discovered by the Master. Tapes flew up into the air in celebration before a loud banging on the table silenced the excitement.

"Step forward student Wilz, called the Master Taper formally. Wilz struggled free from his friends' and family's' arms, rubbed his hands across his face and stood before the Master. With exaggerated movements the Master pulled the measuring tape from around Wilz's neck and discarded it on the floor.

"On behalf of the Ancient Tapers I award you 'Taper Trainer First Class' and he hung around Wilz's neck a bright purple measuring tape. "Friends, it is my privilege to present to you the school's newest Trainer First Class- Trainer Wilz" and he held his student's hand in the air and bathed in the thunderous applause.

Sis and Delfie joined in the applause. Even the Supers, for the moment, forgot their anxieties and clapped too. It was a special, shared moment that almost united all of Thanet and everyone in the hall sensed it, and savoured it.

It was also the perfect chance for Attar who, unnoticed, rushed through the noisy celebrations and linked arms with Delfie. In the thick of the crowd the girls hugged.

"This is Attar, Sis."

I'm so pleased to meet you Attar, Delfie's told me so much about you" Sis looked into Attar's face. "You have your mother's eyes Attar."

"How did you know that?"

"I saw her over the other side. She was with Delfie's mother. They looked so happy together, talking and laughing."

"Oh this is such a wonderful day, why can't it always be like this instead of everyone hating each other?" Asked Attar.

"Well isn't this meeting supposed to be about making peace?" asked Sis.

"If everyone was as loving and understanding as you Sis, we wouldn't need peace meetings," said Delfie.

"Do you know the saddest thing of all? I'm sure people want peace but they're frightened of changing their old ways. They don't know how to start," said Attar.

"Yes, and no one wants to be the first to make the change either," added Delfie.

Just then a noisy argument broke out over the other side of the hall. "What's all that about Delfie?" asked Sis.

"Sounds like the 'fence menders'- the group of Singers, Super's and Tapers in charge of maintaining the fence and settling disputes. That's where the arguments usually start."

"Yes" added Attar "and if they don't settle down the Judger will have them all thrown out and then they will have to cancel the Peace meeting yet again."

"What, you mean this has happened before?" asked Sis.

"Happened before? Every cycle since before I was born, according to my mother," answered Attar.

"What's the dispute about anyway," asked Sis."

"My Dad did tell me, he called it 'unsolvable', whatever that means. All you hear now is people saying 'it is a point of honour or a matter of principle'. Doesn't make any sense to me", admitted Delfie.

"Are you staying here with Attar?" Sis asked Delfie.

"Yes. We've got so much to talk about. It seems ages since we met last and we can talk in public here without worrying about who is watching us."

"I won't be long then, I'll meet you back here" said Sis. She had spotted an elderly man sitting alone in the middle of the room, who she guessed was the Judger Delfie had spoken about. He was the only one dressed entirely in black, apart from long grey cuffs to his robe and a broad grey scarf across his shoulders. His clothes were severe but his expression calm.

"Excuse me Sir", asked Sis "are you the Judger?"

"I hope so, young lady, I was invited to be. How can I help you?"

"This is my first time here and I'm trying to understand how a problem can be 'unsolvable.'"

"Understand! That word sounds so sweet to my ears. You're clearly not from here, please come and sit down. I'm delighted to meet someone who does not want to measure me, or sell me a charm to keep the Wingars at bay," he smiled. "And what's your name?"

"Sis, my friend told me that these meetings are held every cycle and yet the problem is never resolved."

"No, no" replied the Judger "it never even gets as far as being unresolved- it never starts! In all the time I have been coming here, we have never reached beyond the opening singing before arguments start and the meeting has to be disbanded. It might be funny if it were not so sad. To be honest, I think there is as much chance of me settling this dispute and removing the fence as there is of seeing a Celfyte"

Sis smiled "Oh! So it's not impossible then?"

The Judger stared at Sis quizzically. He did not speak, only read her eyes. "Well, well, I wouldn't have believed it - you have seen a Celfyte. I know you have. Well, well, well. What else can I say? So there really is wonder left in this crazed world, that's quite cheered my heart up."

"Will I understand this dispute that causes so much argument?"

"Yes of course, it is simple at its heart, but every cycle each side adds on facts that makes the original argument far more complicated. Let me try to explain Sis. Many cycles ago, after endless skirmishes and fights over the fence a Peace meeting was held and it was 'agreed' to tear down the fence and use the wood to build two 'Unity' meeting halls for the whole island. The halls were meant to symbolize the end of fighting, places where all people could meet together in harmony and friendship.

Anyway, the Tapers were responsible for all the measurements of the new hall and in calculating how much wood would be needed. The Singers were responsible for demolishing the fence and moving all the materials. The supers were in charge of choosing and preparing the sites where the halls would be built: one in the East and one in the West. Simple so far, Sis?"

"Yes Sir"

"The problem started with the first site chosen by the Supers in the east. The Tapers said it was too far from the roads and the Singers didn't agree with the first hall being built on the Taper's side. They said it would use up most of the wood and there would not be enough left for their hall. So a compromise was agreed. Both halls would be built at the same time."

"That sounds sensible and fair" said Sis. "Then there could be nothing to argue about."

"Oh, but there was" said the Judger in an exasperated tone." The Tapers accused the Singers of spending more time on collecting wood for the Western hall than on collecting for the Taper's hall in the East. The Supers caused problems for both as they refused to work on the two days either side of a new moon because they said the Wingars were active then and they all had to stay indoors. Then one day a group of Singers went over to inspect the progress of the building in the East and found that the Taper's hall was bigger than theirs in the West. The Singers might not have understood measuring but they could see it was definitely bigger. When they asked for the official measurements of the two halls to compare, the Tapers took it as the greatest insult 'that their measuring couldn't be trusted'. From then on, it was all downhill. Argument followed argument." "So what happened then?" asked Sis.

"The wood was dragged back and the fence re-built and everyone went back to how they had always been - divided by hate. The Taper's however decided to finish their hall, and that's where we are today. This is the only Peace hall ever built in Thanet. Now I doubt if any side remembers the original misunderstanding, they've moved on and both sides keep inventing new facts purely to disprove the other side's reasoning."

"Therefore" ventured Sis, "the longer the dispute goes on - the further away each side moves from the other."

"That's a fine judgerment. Couldn't do better myself" replied the Judger.

"So why bother to go on if you know they will never agree with each other?"

"Ah! But they do," said the Judger. "They all agree on one thing and it continues to unite them in their distrust for each other."

"You mean?"

"Yes, they all agree that they will never agree on the new meeting halls, and the more they argue, the more they agree on the depth of their disagreement." The Judger raised his eyebrows and smiled at Sis as if waiting for another question.

"With respect Sir, I think you have far more chance of seeing a Celfyte.

"I live in hope" he replied kindly.

The Judger had been right. Before the first Singers could open the proceedings, arguments started. The hired Singers representing both sides raised their volume in an attempt to gain attention but it proved hopeless. At one point it seemed to Sis that every single person in the hall was speaking at once and certainly no one was listening to hear the Judger call the meeting to a close. Nobody noticed him leaving either. He pushed through the main door and out in to the fresh air. He let out a deep sigh of relief and shook his head "there's always next cycle" he said aloud to himself. The door behind him opened and Sis emerged from the deafening hall. She had to close the door behind her to speak.

"Everyone was talking and no one listening. How do they imagine they can ever solve problems like that?"

The Judger gave a knowing grin and looked across the meadow to the meandering river. He turned to Sis and confided "After this, Judgering in the animal village, even with interpreters, will be bliss. At least the animals listen even if they don't always understand and they don't have long memories like the folk here so they cannot hold grudges. Thank heavens animals haven't learned how to hate. Yes, I'm quite looking forward to the next few days." "So you are going to animal village soon?" Sis asked.

"Yes, my clerk and I do a regular judgering round there every third moon. We have to take our tents and provisions with us and camp outside overnight. We're far too big to actually enter the village. We stay beyond the fourth ring."

"Why do you need interpreters Sir?"

"Because there are at least two main languages, upper spoke and lower spoke. All the birds, insects and animals that live above ground use upper spoke, any animal or creature living mostly underground or under the water uses lower spoke. Neither group can understand very much Judger spoke so I always need a good interpreter."

"I wish I could go with you Sir, it sounds a fascinating place."

"Don't see why not, we've got a spare tent and if you don't mind helping to carry the provisions. It is a long trek from the river to the village though and there's a big hill to climb. Still interested young lady?"

"Yes, of course" replied Sis.

"That's decided then. Meet my clerk at the landing stage. You'll see our boat, it has blue and green markings along the side. Hard to miss," he chuckled. "You'll have to hurry, we need to arrive there and set up camp before nightfall."

Sis rushed back into the packed hall and pushed her way through the throng. She found Delfie deep in conversation with Attar and Attar's mother. The noise was still deafening so she bent over to almost shout into Delfie's ear.

"Say thanks to your parents and brothers. I won't be coming back with you tonight. I'm travelling with the Judger to Animal village. Have a wonderful time with Attar and I'll see you in a few days." Delfie half listened without stopping talking then called back to Sis "I hope you enjoy yourself too Sis. Watch out for the Wingars!" and they both smiled.

199

Sis found the boat easily enough. A young girl, slightly older than herself, was loading parcels and packets into the small craft. She wore a short black gown with a grey collar and her hair was tied back with a white ribbon. She paused and looked up. "You must be Sis, Uncle told me you were coming. I'm Zana."

"Hello Zana, so you are the Judger's clerk?" Zana caught the slight surprise in Sis's face.

"Yes. Why, did you expect a man? Don't worry, everyone assumes that. I am studying Judgering and Law mending and I think I am the first Thanet girl ever to be trained as clerk to a Judger. Not that it is any easier because he is my Uncle, it's harder in fact."

"He must be very proud of you Zana"

"I am sure he is, but he never says anything directly. He's so careful not to show me any favouritism and always expects more from me than the other trainees. Still there is no wiser Judger to study with. Here, help me with this Sis" Two tents and some bottles were added to the stowage and tied down as the Judger arrived and carefully stepped on board.

"You two met, eh? Good. I will row the first part, you girls the second. Untie the stern Zana. Sis, sit in the front of the boat to balance us. Let's get going."

They moved up river and Sis stared lazily into the muddy water, her hair brushed by the hanging fronds of the weeping willows that lined the bank. The slow rhythmic creaking of the wooden oars behind her and their gentle splashing in the calm surface soothed her and her eyes began to feel heavy. Suddenly she felt a delicate wing touch her hand, then again, and her eyes opened to see Sparcal perched on her wrist. Sparcal put her finger up to her tiny lips and motioned to Sis to get the Judger's attention.

Turning round Sis tapped the Judger gently on the shoulder.

"Could you stop a moment please Sir?"

He pulled the oars in and turned around. "What's wrong Sis?" "Look behind you Sir" invited Sis.

The Judger turned back and his eyes fell on Sparcal who now sat perched on the blade of the oar. Zana turned too and was immediately mesmerized. "A real Celfyte" was all she could say and she just kept on repeating it.

The Judger could not speak. He looked wide-eyed, captivated by this magical creature. His face simply beamed with pleasure. Instinctively he held out his hand and Sparcal climbed on. The Judger held Sparcal up and watched her minute movements. He marvelled at the subtle colour changes that flowed over the Celfyte and were reflected in her whirling wings.

Still the Judger looked on in awe, until the silence was broken as Sparcal spoke. "Your wisdom is well known Sir and your judgements trusted. I am honoured to meet you", she smiled and curtsied to the Judger.

"Zana, Sis! Tell me I am not dreaming" called the Judger without moving his eyes. "It's wonderful, simply wonderful."

"It is no dream" said Zana. "I see her too Uncle. Oh this is pure magic." Despite all his experience of life, despite his age and knowledge, the Judger's heart flooded with child-like happiness. He could not stop smiling.

"I've come with an urgent message for you Sir" said Sparcal. "The animals on the East shore are very frightened and need your help. They have asked for you to go there immediately. They said to tell you that they had seen a serpent."

"But I'm already booked for a Judgering round in animal village. They are expecting me there before nightfall. I can't let them down."

"With respect Sir, may I suggest that Zana and Sis could begin the round so you could go to East Shore? I really believe you are needed there. I have never seen so many animals near to panic."

The Judger looked at Sparcal, then at Sis. Then glancing over his shoulder asked "could you cover for me for half a day Zana?"

"Yes of course Uncle. I'll have all your books to help me and anything difficult I will leave till you return."

"Ah, but what about an interpreter Zana, who will translate for you?" the Judger asked.

"With your permission Sir, I wish to nominate Sis" interrupted Sparcal.

"That would be fine by me if she spoke the languages" replied the Judger.

"She does Sir and all the dialects of the deep burrowing creatures and the sea animals"

"How", asked the Judger astonished. "How is that possible?

"Sis will tell you 'Where all is possible, all is secure'" replied Sparcal reassuringly.

The Judger turned to Sis. Her face radiated confidence as she confirmed "yes Sir, I have been given the knowledge."

The Judger shook his head and smiled. "Any more surprises for me today?"

"Rain is coming" warned Sparcal as she glanced up at the gathering clouds, "if you leave now you will have time to set up camp. Can I go to tell the East Shore animals that you will come to see them in the morning Sir?"

"Yes, I will leave at first light."

"Thank you" said Sparcal, "they will be so relieved." At this she sprang back onto the oar and slid down into the river. She skated across the surface as if weightless and then flew up to hover in front of them.

"Bye Sis, Bye Zana. Till the morrow Judger" and she sped off.

The girls did offer to take their turn at the oars but the Judger was enlivened and rowed non-stop to the upper landing stage. He felt young again, excited and inspired. He even sang as he rowed. Zana had never seen her uncle in such a joyful mood and it continued, even when struggling up Kelvin hill with all the provisions.

Zana and Sis could hardly keep up with him as he raced to get set up before the rains came. They made it just in time and Sis and Zana sat inside the blue tent as the rain hammered down. Through the opening they could see the Judger's tent and through the noise of the downpour faintly hear him singing.

"That's a real miracle Sis", Zana observed. "I can't imagine a better birthday present for anyone."

"You mean it's the Judger's birthday today?"

"Yes. He never tells anyone but I know because my Dad and he are twins."

"Is your Dad a Judger too?"

"He was for a number of cycles, now he trains young clerks in Law mending. He's a very good teacher" said Zana proudly.

As the girls settled down to sleep, Sis pulled the tent flap open and looked across. The Judger was still awake. She could see by his shadow that he was reading by candle light.

"Good night Sir and Happy Birthday" she called across the clearing.

"It's been my best birthday ever thanks to you. Good night Sis.

Goodnight Zana."

The girls awoke shivering. Their single blankets had not really been sufficient even though they had slept fully dressed. Rather than getting up they wrapped the blankets around themselves tighter, trying to warm up as the sky outside began to lighten.

"Why is it so cold Zana?" asked Sis through chattering teeth. "It's only autumn, not winter yet."

"It's the damp from all that rain and don't forget we didn't eat much last night, did we. Do you think it's too early to start breakfast?"

"Absolutely not" said Sis launching herself out the tent and jumping up and down in an effort to get warm. "I'll get a fire started."

That proved far more difficult than she had imagined. There was plenty of tinder and small branches lying about but everything was soaking wet. She had to walk into the woods, pushing through dripping foliage to search for twigs dry enough to burn. She eventually pulled a few dead branches from under a fallen tree and managed to get the fire started while Zana went to prepare the breakfast.

By the time the Judger came out of his tent the clearing was full of dense wood smoke and the water still hadn't boiled in the tea kettle. Sis was kneeling down fanning the flames. She had no idea how dishevelled she looked. Her dress was soaked and mud stained, her hands black with ash and her hair hung down in tangled wet curls. She looked up to the Judger and said "Won't be long Sir." He smiled and shaking his head walked over to where Zana was laying out food on a cloth draped over a large log.

"Good morning Uncle. Did you sleep well?"

"Yes thank you Zana. How long will breakfast b - I have to leave as soon as I can."

"Well it's taking longer than we expected, everything got so wet and" She paused "I'm afraid there's no bread. We left the food bag out by mistake last night and now it's full of water and I just dropped the butter in the mud."

The Judger grinned at Zana who was now looking down dejectedly. Her dress was soaking wet too and her legs scratched and muddy. She had salvaged some apples and damp wheat cake but little else. He looked back at Sis who was still kneeling in the mud, desperately fanning the flames. "Any chance of tea Sis?

"Just come to the boil now Sir. I'll bring it over."

They stood around the makeshift table, warming their hands on the tea cups. *That felt good.* "So you girls are enjoying this outdoors life then?" teased the Judger. Sis and Zana looked at each other. Both were still shaking with cold, both looked thoroughly miserable in the damp dawn's light. *They didn't know if they wanted to laugh or cry!*

"I'd like it better if it didn't rain all the time" said Sis.

"And if it wasn't so cold" added Zana in support.

"What fine Law menders you both look now" he laughed and stooped back into his tent to rustle through his bags. He emerged with a parcel, untied it and laid out a large apple pie on the table cloth. "My wife always makes me a pie on my birthday. This should fill us up." The girls' eyes lit up as the Judger generously divided the pie into three. *It was good, very good.* "What's the point of a birthday pie if you can't share it?"

The sun was above the tree line by the time the Judger set off to walk to the East Shore. The girls had made their way down to the stream to wash and make themselves presentable for their 'legal duties'. At least they had made sure that their spare clothes and towels had been under cover and after washing in the freezing cold stream- they were very glad they had!

'The Haven of Trust'

The sun was warm now as Sis and Zana followed the winding path through the elderberry bushes whose berries hung in heavy bunches of deepest purple. The bushes swayed with flocks of thrushes gorging on their sweetness. Suddenly they took off in a clatter of whirling wings as the girls moved through. They crossed the marshy ground and came to the edge of the third ring.

The goats were already there organising the animals around the ring. It was easy for the birds and squirrels they could sit anywhere in the trees above. The other animals had to be arranged in size order: biggest at the back, smallest in front. Insects were allowed to fly freely as they never stayed in one place for long anyway.

The goats took their duties very seriously indeed and became easily irritated by the squabbling mice and the foxes that never stopped complaining and the young hares and rabbits that seemed to find it impossible to sit still. Then the moles caused problems by insisting they should be given a sitting space nearer the front than their size really demanded. They moaned that their hearing was not so good and as they were famous for their bad eyesight – obviously they needed to be at the very front. Worms were excused these gatherings as they couldn't stay above ground in the daylight. Their views were always put forward for them by the wood lice. But all the beetles and lizards attended, sitting right by the toads, newts and grass snakes.

Sis was absolutely amazed at the sight before her. *This was the kind of scene she might have read of in a story book when she was little- but this was no child's tale. She was seeing this with her own eyes!*

Zana explained proudly. "The animals call these meetings at the third ring their 'Haven of Trust.' Really it's the result of cycles of wise Judgering and the mending of many laws to protect every kind of creature. My Uncle's spent half his working life settling disputes amongst the animals. It's wonderful what he's achieved, isn't it Sis?"

"It really is. I could never in my wildest dreams have imagined all these animals sitting together like this - it's a miracle!"

Now as they walked into the ring all the animals stood up to greet them- led by the goats that made a big show of balancing on their hind legs. They took their seats on a fallen oak log. Zana sat with her pile of books on the left. Sis as translator sat to the right.

Zana waited for the animals to settle then opened the meeting as usual with the 'Haven of Trust Pledge'. "I declare" she announced, "within the four rings all creatures live free from harm, free from fear. Any creature breaking this trust stands banished from this Island for ever." She then announced "the Judgering ring is open, bring the list." It was the badger's turn to read out the cases to be judgered and she started in a loud barking voice, "Spiders' complaint."

Sis walked over to the web in the bush and strained to hear their soft voices. She could see they were shouting but she was unable to hear them. The spiders ran to the edge of the web and started stamping wildly causing the gossamer strands to vibrate. Just then a bat flew down and hung under the branch, squeezing its eyes shut in the bright light.

"I can translate for you if you wish, they are using 'wave spoke.'"

"Yes please do" Sis said gratefully. The bat translated the spider's complaint into upper spoke, Sis translated for Zana.

After careful thought Zana announced her verdict. All animals were to be more considerate to one another. It was not acceptable for larger animals to barge through undergrowth and to thoughtlessly destroy the spider's carefully woven webs. She had particularly harsh words for the pole cats and pheasants who were the main culprits but she acknowledged that the rabbits were sometimes careless too. Her conclusion was a balanced one: 'the animals to take more care, spiders to weave webs a little higher above the ground.'

Zana was just about to ask the badger to announce the next case when there was a commotion in the trees above and a large owl flew in and settled on the log next to Sis.

"The Judger sent me on ahead to warn all the animals that a serpent has been seen in East Shore and its coming this way. The Judger is making his way back here now", reported the owl.

"Did you see it yourself?" asked Sis.

"Only briefly as I flew over the ridge, it was moving very fast and it was big". As if to emphasise the point he opened his large orange eyes wide. "I've never seen anything like it before. The Judger said you should send out a search party to find it quickly."

Sis informed Zana. She spoke quietly and in a relaxed manner so as not to convey any alarm to the animals. "We'll have to tell them" said Zana. "We'll need their help to find it but we have to keep everyone calm."

Sis held out her arm and the owl walked up and on to her shoulder. Then she stepped forward into the ring and speaking in both upper and lower spoke repeated the message from the Judger. Seeing the owl perched on Sis's shoulder was somehow reassuring for the animals. Owls may not have been every animal's natural ally but they were known to be trustworthy and every one respected them.

The grass snakes and vipers shook their heads and mumbled to each other somewhat nervously. Then the oldest viper said "If it's as big as owl says it is, it isn't from here. It's not one of us and I for one won't let my children out to play around here." This note of fear and distrust struck a chord with many other animals and they started talking between themselves in a concerned tone.

Zana was watching carefully and sensed that the animals were becoming increasingly nervous. She stood up and called out confidently "I call this meeting to order. The Judger himself has said that this intruder must be identified before noon and brought before the Haven of Trust to explain himself. Go now and search him out."

The insects were already airborne, the birds followed, led by the sparrow hawks. Along the ground the rabbits bounded off, while above the squirrels raced across the thinnest branches. The foxes held back momentarily then made a showy dash through the tall grasses, scattering the butterflies that were resting in the sunlight. The badgers remained behind in the ring looking serious while the goats continued to patrol the surrounding undergrowth - on high alert now.

"What do you think it could be Zana?" asked Sis.

"If it is not a grass snake or a viper maybe it's a creature that swam over from the mainland, anything's possible." She looked at the owl sitting contentedly on Sis's shoulder and smiled. "If owl said it was a big snake then I believe him. The Judger always jokes that an owl's eyesight is so acute it can even see a mouse blink from across the river." Zana looked at Sis with questioning eyes. "You really talk to animals?" Sis just smiled. "That's amazing, how do you do it?"

"All creatures have much sharper and stronger instinct than us. They sense things we cannot understand and they know immediately if your heart is pure. It takes them time to trust you. That is why in a wood or forest, strangers walking through rarely see many creatures because they watch the strangers approaching and hide. But if you are patient and build up trust, they will come to you. After that learning their language is easy. There may be different languages among the creatures yet they all have one thing in common - they are all languages of the heart."

"Can you teach me Sis, please?"

"I will help you learn and once you have the animal's confidence and trust, believe me they will help you too."

Zana studied the owl with new interest. She realized she had never been so close to a bird that was normally only ever seen fleetingly at dusk. She thought of all the old tales she had heard about owls and how they were supposed to be associated with spirits of the night. A bird many people thought of as unlucky. All that made no sense to her now. She just looked at the beautiful colours of its feathers, its breast of dappled fawns, browns and golds. Its long ear tufts and piercing orange - yellow eyes. The bird shuffled its feet and Zana saw the strong black talons gently holding onto Sis's shoulder.

"He's so beautiful Sis. His feathers look so soft it's almost unreal."

"Yes, owls are very special. Their soft feathers enable them to fly almost silently through the night. "Hold out your hand Zana" asked Sis as she whispered to the owl. Zana lifted her hand and the owl hopped onto her wrist and walked up her arm and sat on her shoulder. Zana was overjoyed. She tipped her head to lay against the owl's wing and closed her eyes to savour the moment of magic.

"That's the power of trust Zana," said Sis. "Wonderful, isn't it?"

The girls strolled around the ring together with the owl perched happily on Zana's shoulder. As they continued on they became aware that the remaining animals were becoming more and more nervous. Even the sniffling hedgehogs, normally preoccupied with seeking out food, huddled together looking worried. It was only when the birds and animals returned to the ring to report they had found nothing that Zana herself began to feel concerned. She turned to Sis "until we find this intruder it is not possible to continue with this Judgering round. Fear does strange things to animals – if panic breaks out the 'Haven of Trust' will be destroyed. Then we will be back in the dark times when all creatures lived in constant fear."

"That would be horrible" agreed Sis. "I only wish Sparcal was here, I'm sure she could help."

"Yes Sis?" Her gentle voice sounded close as Sparcal changed her reflection and appeared on the branch next to her. "I've been here all the time. I always attend the Haven of Trust hearings."

"We have an intruder Sparcal? Can you help us, please?"

"Yes, but if it's what I think it is, there's not only one, there are many. They're known as Cave creepers." Sis could not hide her anxiety at hearing these words and she swallowed hard before she continued.

"What are they, where do they come from?"

"I have no idea, maybe from some distant Kingdom in the past? Now they live in the dark in the deepest caves of Kelvin. Strange, I have never known the snakes to venture out before, certainly not in daylight. Perhaps it's lost? They have poor eyesight and very thin skin. If it doesn't return to the caves soon it will certainly die in the heat of the sun."

Sis paused then said reluctantly "Oh Sparcal, I wish you had told me sooner, we've wasted so much time."

"I'm sorry Sis. But I did tell you as soon as you asked me. Please try to understand, Celfytes cannot interfere in this animal Kingdom otherwise our powers will be taken from us. We have to be invited.

That's how it's always been, even in the Minla Kingdom." Sparcal paused and looked deeply into Sis's eyes. "I see in your heart that you are worried what fear will do to these trusting creatures and I know how long it has taken the Judger to build this haven. Don't worry we will find the creeper for you."

She flew off joined by hundreds of other Celfytes who appeared from every branch. They had all been sitting watching with their reflections off now the very air glowed vivid with their colour-splashed wings.

"Sis, will you tell the animals? Say something to calm them, please" asked Zana. Sis was careful to smile first then explain in a gentle tone that the snake was not an intruder but a lost creature trying to find its way home. The Celfytes were now out searching for it. The mere mention of the Celfytes reassured the crowd and a few isolated smiles broke out. Soon after a whole raft of smiles greeted Sparcal's return and her report that the snake had been found at the foot of the cliff below Kelvin caves.

"I'm afraid he is exhausted and cannot climb the cliff."

"Did you speak to him" asked Zana. "How big is he really?"

"At least as long as you like the Owl said. His name is Megratt and he is a young Cave creeper. This sun is killing him, can't we help?"

"I'll go" volunteered Sis. "Are you coming Zana?"

"Where are you two going?" the Judger called out as he walked into the ring. He looked tired and he sighed with relief as he sat down on the log. All the animals stood up to show their respect at the Judger's arrival and the Celfytes turned their reflections on and off, flashing colours across the ring. The Judger smiled his acknowledgement. "Thank you all," he said.

Zana explained to her Uncle all that had happened. "We're going to try to save him."

"Be careful, both of you. Sparcal, please go with them" requested the Judger.

"All eyes followed the girls till they disappeared into the elderberry grove and the Judger called the round to order again. "Right Badger- next on the list please…"

211

The Cave Creeper King

The girls moved quickly, guided by Sparcal. They ran across the open meadows, then when the vegetation became thicker, slowed to a walk. Then ran off again, ducking under branches and jumping over the coarse grass clumps that grew along the streams. They were on a mission with no time to lose. The cliff was close now and Sis called to Sparkle to fly on ahead to see if the snake was still there. He was.

Sis could not associate all the nightmarish thoughts she had experienced since she first heard the word *serpent* with the creature that lay before her now. He was, as Sparcal had described, as long as Zana and his thick body was covered with thin pearl coloured scales. Maybe it was his pale colouration that lent a kind of innocence to his appearance for despite his size he did not appear to either girl to be frightening at all. Sis bent over to stroke his head. His tiny eyes began to brighten then went dull again. The girls sprinkled warm water over him to moisten his skin yet he remained motionless, half coiled into a tired crescent shape.

Sparcal flew down to Sis's shoulder. "There is only one way up Sis, he'll have to be carried. Remember," she reminded her in a hushed voice, "trust, trust." Sis cradled the creature's head while Zana took the weight of his body and tail. Sis knelt down and the girls lifted the snake over her head and onto Sis's shoulders. She rose carefully and the snake, like a giant shimmering scarf hung down around her. Sparcal darted ahead, hovering around Sis, guiding her every foothold. She needed both hands free to climb and moved gingerly, trying not to make any sudden movements. Zana waited below watching as Sis neared the cave entrance and crawled over the ledge. She squatted down and leant her head forward to let the snake slide off and supported it as best she could as it slid onto the rocks in the shadows of the cave.

"He's home now and safe" said Sparcal, "thanks to you Sis."

Sis rested a while on the ground and was just getting up when she noticed movements in the deep shadows within the cave. She sat back down and watched snakes heads appearing, each with a bright green tongue flickering, tasting the air. Then they came. Pouring out from the entrance, slipping and sliding over each other like water rolling over rapids. The living, writhing carpet spread and covered Sis's feet completely. *There must be hundreds* she thought to herself and out of curiosity started to try to count them.

Sparcal looked on and said "where's all your fear gone Sis?"

Sis replied with a loving glance "What's the strongest force in the universe Sparcal?" They both smiled knowingly, joined in a secret happiness. This was a very precious moment and they felt the mysteries of the Kingdoms flowing together.

Still smiling, Sis returned to her counting, trying to concentrate on the writhing mass. She got to 87 then gave up. She really had no idea how many there were, certainly too many to count. Slowly the tangle began to separate and individual snakes broke off from the formation and slithered back into the shadows. This continued till only two remained, coiled around the rescued creature. They lay closely intertwined till Sis saw their eyes open, then with a flick of their tails they disappeared into the cave together.

Sis had turned and was about to climb down when Sparcal called "they're coming back Sis, wait." Sis remained standing as a long procession emerged from the cave. Each snake slid up to her and coiled gently around her leg twice before retreating back into the cave's darkness.

"It's their way of showing gratitude for rescuing their lost youngster" said Sparcal and then she added thoughtfully, "He must have been a very special snake."

From out of the shadows drifted a soft, scratchy voice and as both Sis and Sparkle heard it they looked at each other in surprise. "He is my son. The heir to the deeps of the Kelvin caves and he owes you his life. For this all- Cave creepers honour you and pledge to protect you."

The voice stopped and Sis and Sparcal peered into the cave entrance. Then he came. Slowly, majestically, a giant Cave creeper slid out from the darkness. He was huge, twice the size of all the others. His scales were of the deepest slate grey. Even with his head now nestled against Sis's ankle his tail was still hidden inside the cave. He remained motionless as Sis closed her eyes and saw in her mind a maze of tunnels, a map of the world of the Cave creepers.

"Remember this well. This is our cave Kingdom. The time will come when you will be in great danger. Then you will turn to us and we will protect you. Never forget this. You Sis are the first being above the earth to set eyes on me. You will be the last." Moving his head towards Sparcal the snake said "Celfyte, I see your heart is pure. I entrust you to watch over her in all the worlds above. I will protect her in all the worlds below." Neither Sis nor Sparcal could respond, they just watched silently as the snake turned and slid into the blackness.

Sis sat back down and Sparkle perched on her shoulder and said to her "that was a wonder for me. I never knew of the snake King and he had the power to read my heart!"

"He knew my name. Why did he warn me of danger in the future?" questioned Sis.

Sparcal shook her head. "I can't explain. It is a mystery to me too, but I believe him. Celfytes have never had the power to see into the future but I could read his heart and what he said was the truth."

Sis sat in silent contemplation while images of the snake King's underground world flashed before her. She learned every entrance, every twist and curve of every tunnel, then the images stopped." Now I am prepared for the future" Sis told Sparcal.

"I believe you are Sis." Come, we must get back. The animals will be wondering what's taken us so long."

Back inside the third ring the Judger was completing his rounds and had managed to settle most disputes. Only one Judgerment had been really difficult and that was deciding how long a woodpecker could claim nesting rights for a hole he had excavated in the old lime tree. The starlings insisted they had every right to nest anywhere by natural law and just because the woodpecker had made the hole, it did not mean he owned it for all time.

The Judger listened to the arguments carefully and noted too the fact that the barking squirrels and tree lizards craftily chose to remain silent even though they were even more frequent residents of woodpecker holes. His eventual decision was to find in favour of the woodpecker who was the original creator of the hole. Woodpeckers would have sole rights to each and every hole they excavated for two breeding cycles. Only then would the hole become common property, available to all creatures. After all this he was relieved and delighted to see Zana and Sis return, especially as they were escorted by two lines of sparkling Celfytes. *Only the water dispute to settle now.*

The Judger called for a break in proceedings. It had been a busy day for everyone. Zana used the time to catch up with recording the Judger's rulings. Sis went to collect fresh water from the stream and to bring back what food remained from the bags they had brought with them. It wasn't much and the girls had to content themselves with an apple and a piece of damp wheat cake. "Not exactly a meal fit for a hero is it Sis? The Judger joked.

The animals were re- assembling now and the Judger called the meeting to order. "This has been a strange but interesting day for all of us," he began. "Before we start the final case for today I think everyone would like to hear the story of what happened to the serpent. I call Sparcal to the ring. The Haven of Trust welcomes you Sparcal."

The Celfyte flew down to rapturous applause and wing flapping. All the creatures fidgeted in anticipation and the eared owl flew down and sat on Zana's arm. The Judger just couldn't believe it!

The animals listened to Sparcal in perfect silence. They were all fascinated by the story, relieved by the outcome and full of admiration for Sis's daring rescue. Sis sat next to the Judger translating for him and Zana. Then she suddenly stopped even though Sparcal was still explaining. She remained quiet while different animals stood up and spoke excitedly. "Why have you stopped Sis? We missed the last part. What were the animals saying?" asked the Judger.

"Oh, nothing important, they were just making suggestions," Sis replied dismissively and she looked down as if examining her shoe.

"Sis, I may not speak much upper spoke, or indeed lower spoke, but I'm familiar enough with the animals to know when they are excited and happy. Please translate for me."

"Oh, they were just saying kind things. It doesn't matter, honestly."

Sparcal had finished now and she flew back and landed on the Judger's hand and said "popular girl our Sis, isn't she?"

"I didn't hear the last part of what was said. Sis wouldn't translate for me." Sparcal smiled knowingly and looked first at Sis and then back to the Judger before explaining.

"The animals want to make Sis a special member of the Haven of Trust and they have asked if you would let her be the Judger for the final case today." The Judger started to reply but Sparcal interrupted. "Sorry, one other thing, they've also asked if you would name this day 'Serpent Rescue Day' in honour of Sis's bravery."

The Judger's face broke into a broad smile, "Any more requests?"

"No Sir, absolutely none".

The Judger sat back laughing quietly to himself. He had seen more strange and wonderful things in the last two days than he had in the last 25 cycles…….. *What could possibly happen next?*

"Please Uncle," whispered Zana. "It would make the animals happy, let Sis judger the last case. I've never seen them so united about anything before."

The Judger listened but his attention was focused on Owl dozing on his niece's shoulder.

What a magnificent creature.

His concentration returned when Sparcal asked. "Will you allow it Sir?"

"If it is the wish of the Haven of Trust and if Sis is willing, then I give my permission."

Sparcal leapt up in a blur of colour and announced the Judger's decision to the animals that immediately crowded around Sis. The Judger looked across to Sis who was smiling gently and nodding.

The Judger called for silence before he formally announced that henceforth this day would be known as 'Serpent Rescue Day' and called for Zana to record it. He further announced that the honour of 'Life member of the Haven of Trust' be conferred on Sis. The animals stood up as Sis walked into the ring and the Judger presented her as the official Judger in the water dispute. "Judger Sis will mend the law" he announced, then withdrew outside the circle.

Sis took her seat on the centre of the log. Zana sat at her side to take notes while Sparcal stood on a branch next to her as her translator. 'Judger Sis' began by taking statements from all the animals concerned in the case while Zana took notes of the bird and insect opinions. Sis then took a break to consider all the facts and read through the opinions carefully. *There was so much to think about, so many different points of view to consider. She wanted to be fair to all creatures.* She closed her eyes and tried to concentrate but nothing came to her mind. Then she heard Sparcal calling to her softly "Trust, Trust" and it all suddenly became crystal clear. She rose to address the animals.

"How many types of water does the Haven need?" asked Judger Sis. It was an open question for everyone.

"Surely, called the badger, "water is water."

"There's only one type of water I know and that's the wet kind," shouted a goat rather rudely.

"The type you drink when you're thirsty" added the shrew in a high pitched whine.

Not to be outdone the fox growled "and the type you jump in and roll about in to wash the fleas out of your coat."

"And the type you swim and bathe in" quacked the black duck who until now had not spoken a word.

"Oh! And the type we lay our egg in," bellowed the frogs.

"And us," squeaked the tiny gnats.

Judger Sis waited patiently until all the comments ceased before asking seriously, "So if there is only one kind of water, you Badger won't mind drinking from the pond after the goats have washed in it?"

"No! It will be dirty, I can't drink from that."

"And you master Hedgehog, would you drink water from the stream the foxes had used to wash off their fleas?"

"Certainly not, there's water for washing and water for drinking" said the hedgehog firmly and all the animals nodded in agreement.

Judger Sis waited again as the animals talked among themselves. Zana glanced around at the animals. *How clever of Sis, guiding them to mend their own laws.*

"So as Judger I ask again, how many types of water does the Haven need?"

"Two" the animals called out in unison.

"Which way does the stream always flow?" asked Judger Sis in her loudest voice.

"Everyone knows that. From the dell, through the Haven and down to the river" answered the goats on behalf of all the animals present.

"Therefore, where should you drink and where should you wash?"

"Drink in the dell, wash where the stream reaches the river" answered Badger.

"All those in favour of Badger's suggestion say yes."

The whole meeting roared its approval, in a range of noises and calls. "Is there anyone against Badger's suggestion?" Judger Sis asked finally. The answer came in a satisfied silence.

Judger Sis and Zana stood up together and Sis began. "I declare and will have written down a mended law, which you yourselves have agreed this day and I now bind every creature to obey. It is the law!" I now declare the Judgering round complete. She bowed slowly to the animals and sat down.

"What a fine ending to a fine day" said the Judger as he joined the girls in the ring. "That was an excellent Judgerment Sis. It was wise far beyond your years. I'm very proud of you. Now let's get back to our camp, we've another early start on the morrow for Animal Games day. Believe me - you really wouldn't want to miss that!"

The Animal Games

With all the activity and excitement of the day Owl had not rested much at all. Now as the evening was falling around them and the group trundled back to the tents, he perched lazily on Zana's shoulders. Rather than being alert for the coming night he could hardly keep his large eyes open. When they reached their camp he flew on to the top of the girl's tent, tucked his head into his chest and immediately fell asleep. Neither did it take long for the girls. They collected their dry clothes from the branches and were soon tucked up inside their cosy blue tent that had been warmed all day by the sun. They did not even hear the Judger calling 'good night' across the clearing. They were already dreaming.

Morning came. Still no one stirred. It was Sparcal who first woke the girls then she flew over to wake the Judger. Even in his half-awake state he smiled. The

Celfyte danced on his hand and flashed brilliant colours around the tent. He eventually emerged with Sparcal clinging to his arm and his face wreathed in happiness.

"Good morning girls" he said. "I hope you slept as well as I did?"

"I can't remember even getting in to bed," said Zana.

"It's wonderful sleeping out in the open when it's not cold and raining" added Sis.

"Fancy a mushroom breakfast?" suggested the Judger. "Sparcal just told me she's found a mushroom carpet deep in the woods. Sis you go with her, it's my turn to light the fire. Here, take this basket and see if you can fill it up," he said with a chuckle. "Tea will be ready by the time you get back and I'll have the hot frying pan waiting."

Sparcal led Sis on a winding route through the woods till they came to a large oak tree beyond which stretched a shaded meadow. Sis followed, firstly crossing through the dew laden grasses that soaked her shoes and then onto the dry leaf litter that crackled underfoot as she walked beneath the towering beech trees.

"There" said Sparcal, "by the mossy bank Sis, see?"

"Oh yes" and she ran over to the mushroom carpet and knelt down to pick them.

"Only the cream-coloured ones with long stems" directed Sparcal. "Don't touch the red spotted ones – they're poisonous." "Shame, said Sis, they look so lovely.

"Certainly lovelier than your hands", answered Sparcal.

Sis looked down. Her hands were black with mushroom stains.

"Don't worry it will wash off," She looked at the overflowing basket. "I don't think that basket will hold any more now Sis, let's get back and on the way we can pick some water mint. That really brings out the mushroom flavours."

"You can't get fresher than that" said the Judger as he handed Sis a wooden plate piled high with steaming mushrooms with the delicate aroma of mint. "Better than yesterday's breakfast eh?" asked the Judger.

They all sat down to eat, Sparcal sitting on the Judger's shoulder, Owl on Zana's. "I feel quite left out, sitting here alone," she said light heartedly.

"You won't be alone for long Sis. I've decided to appoint you as Judger for the Games after you did so well yesterday. Zana and I will assist you. If you thought judgering in the third ring was difficult - just wait till the games!"

"What did you call it Uncle," asked Zana, "wasn't it judgering the impossible?"

"No," he replied laughing "I think I called it - judgering the unjudgerable!"

It fell to the goats again to organise the animals around the small lake where the games would begin. This was infinitely more difficult than arranging seating around the third ring. Games day was totally different. All the animals were excited and unruly and rarely listened to the goats' instructions. They just gathered in haphazard groupings rather than in their teams and each group took advantage whenever the goats' weren't looking to tease and annoy the group next to them. And when Sis arrived with the Judger's list of races and competitions everyone cheered, left their groups and raced up to greet her. "Not alone anymore are you," teased Sparcal.

She had no choice but to wait until they all settled down before she could make herself heard and announce the order of the games. Then she had to speak quite sternly in both upper and lower spoke to all the creatures. She told them that they had to obey the guidance of the goats that had a very difficult task. "The more you listen to the rules, the more games we can play and then everyone will be happy" she told the gathering.

"The first event will be the Celfyte Ferry race. Each team must carry a Celfyte over the water from this bank to the far side of the lake. The heron will be waiting over the other side to decide the first one across without, without," she repeated, "the Celfyte getting wet. First teams line up." She looked at her programme and called: "water voles, little grebes, swans, frogs and- representing the insects in this first round- the dragonflies." Sis walked down to the water's edge and repeated the rules to the teams. "Ready, Go!" As they moved off Sis whispered to Sparcal "doesn't look a very fair race to me."

"Oh, you'll be surprised. The Judger's drawn these team competitions up over many cycles. There's wisdom in his selection, believe me. Just watch."

As Sis expected the birds raced ahead. The swan was fastest, moving effortlessly along with its strong webbed feet powering through the water. The little grebe, or dabchick as it was called in the East, followed in the swan's wake. Its small lobed toes propelled it swiftly as it paddled furiously to catch up. *Compared to the huge white swan the dabchick looked like a bobbing ball of fluff on the lake* Sis thought. Behind them the frog, which had started off at a hectic pace, slowed and sank underwater, leaving its Celfyte passenger to fly back to Sis. "Frog down" shouted Sis and she crossed it off her race list.

The dragon flies were really struggling now. Being so light they had no difficulty in floating on the surface but equally every little gust of wind blew them sideways. They had to keep together and had practised moving across the water with their legs locked together to form a raft. Their Celfyte was balancing as best he could but when a large ripple approached the raft of dragonflies it washed over them and the Celfyte was tipped into the lake. "Dragonflies sunk" shouted Sis and they too were crossed off. Now there were only three competitors left: the birds, who were already half way across, and the water vole some way behind. Yet he was quietly and steadily moving forward with his head held high out of the water and he seemed to be gaining on the dabchick.

"Wait for it!" called Sparcal. "It happens every time."

"What?" asked Sis, as she strained her eyes to follow the water vole's progress in the sparkling water?

"The Judger calls it the 'Conceit'. There, there he goes. He's veering off to the left."

Sure enough the swan had suddenly changed direction and was flapping it wide wings and dipping its head beneath the surface. Then it moved its neck around in circles just above the water. "He's looking at his own reflection" called Sparcal. "Now he's started dancing. He's forgotten the race completely. What's he doing now? Oh no! He's preening his feathers. Why does he always have to show off?"

Sis watched, bewildered. The swan had suddenly given up and decided to clean his feathers *to beautify himself.* As he flapped his wings and raised his body clear out of the water the Celfyte was thrown off into the lake. Still the swan continued performing graceful movements and had now decided to swim back to the start and his friends were moving out to greet him.

The swan's name was crossed off. "Swan disqualified" was all Sis could think of calling out. "Where's the dabchick? I can't see it Sparcal" Sis asked as she stood on tip toe.

"It's dived, as usual. It's in their blood. I've never known a dabchick to swim for any time without diving. They can't concentrate on anything for long," grumbled the old badger who had been sitting behind Sis since the race began.

"The dabchick has dived" shouted a fox and the entire group of animals around Sis started to laugh and then cheer for the water vole - the only contestant left.

"He's still under Sis" said Sparcal "and here come his passenger returning.

As Sis crossed off the dabchick and announced "dabchick disqualified" all the voles and rats started jumping up and down squeaking excitedly. Across the lake the heron was beating its wings and stamping on its long legs to signal the end of the race. "Water vole's the winners!" Sis shouted as loud as she could.

The Judger and Zana, who had been watching the race from the other side of the willow tree, walked round to join Sis. "How's it going Sis?" the Judger asked.

"Sis shook her head. "Well, as you said, not easy."

"The secret is to have the races one after the other in quick succession. None of the creatures are very interested in just watching they want to be involved themselves," advised the Judger.

"I'll try to remember that, thank you" and she walked down to the water's edge to start the race for the second round. While she read out the next four contestants the Judger had chosen she had to clear the starting line of a group of water voles who were splashing around celebrating their first ever win at the games. *They were so happy.*

"Get ready, go!" Shouted Sis and the second team were off. No insects were entered this time, just a fish, a rabbit, a snake and a water bird.

"Who do you think will win Sis?" whispered Sparcal.

"I really haven't got a clue" said Sis honestly. Obviously it should be the carp but after the last race, I don't know. Do you?"

"The rabbit of course, she's the weakest swimmer," Sparcal replied. Sis thought about this but did not answer.

There were more supporters for this race. In the shallows, next to the reed beds a shoal of carp wallowed and took it in turns to roll and jump. The rabbit's supporters skipped and cavorted right around the lake, while the other grass snakes left their sun-basking to slide down to the lake side. The coots were already assembled in a black line half way across the lake and were calling loudly and splashing the surface with their wings. Swallows swooped across the lake, every now and then dipping to touch the surface then soared up again. Above, the kestrel hovered stationary in the breeze. She had the best view of all.

In fact it was kestrel, the small falcon, who witnessed the first Celfyte slip from the back of the race favourite. The fish had carefully swam with his back clearly out of the water with the Celfyte clinging on to his large bronze-black scales. He simply went too fast. As he cut through the water a wave washed the Celfyte off.

"Carp gone," announced Sis as she made the first note on her programme.

Now the coot was in the lead. She had cleverly decided to run across the water- it was faster than swimming. Her Celfyte had to hold on to her feathers for dear life as the coot's wings flapped around her. The line of coot supporters raced alongside her, their white faces glowing against their black sheened feathers. They all called out together 'go faster.' She was getting tired now and her concentration was waning. She stole a glance behind her to see the grass snake gaining on her. That was a mistake as she lost the rhythm in her pattering lobed feet and cart-wheeled into the air. Her race was over. Her Celfyte passenger returned, wet, dazed and grinning. "What a ride" he said to Sparcal "that's another competitor crossed off."

"Coot crashed," shouted Sis. At this announcement even the Judger burst out laughing as he stood behind her.

With the fastest contestants out of the race, attention fell on the survivors. Well ahead, the grass snake swam with graceful sinuous body movements and every now and again would look back to admire the way his sleek body moved.

"What do they say about pride Sis?" asked Sparcal with a knowing look. Sis had no time to answer. The snake had looked back just a little too long and hadn't noticed a log floating towards him- Sparcal had. As he turned back and came face to face with the log he had no choice - he instinctively dived under it. Another race favourite was gone.

"Grass snake submerged."

A great roar of calls from every creature erupted. Suddenly they all wanted the rabbit to win. The rabbit was now everyone's favourite. But he was in real difficulty. He was tired and not a little frightened. Rabbits are not natural swimmers. They swim when they have to but not out of choice. As he struggled on he was having real doubts about his ability to get across and he was feeling very, very tired.

Kestrel arrived first, hovering just above and in front of the rabbit's bobbing head and flapping ears. "Come on, be brave. Everyone wants you to win. Just keep going," she said then flew forward. "Keep your eyes fixed on me – you can do it. I'll stay with you."

The rabbit's brave effort had brought the games alive. Birds and insects flew straight across the lake. Everyone else, Sis, the Judger and Zana included, raced around the lake to the finish. The geese 'honked', the woodpeckers drummed on the hollow trees, the insects 'buzzed' in unison, while the swans and ducks formed a double line as escorts as the rabbit neared the end.

Secretly, and strictly against the game's rules (as passengers in Ferry races were not allowed to talk to the contestants) the Celfyte bent over to whisper in the rabbit's ear. She could sense that he was practically finished, exhausted. "You will be the first rabbit to ever win the swimming games. Don't you dare stop now" and she dug her tiny heels into his back and pulled on his fur. "Go, now!"

That spurred him on. Even so the last short distance was sheer agony for the rabbit. Surrounded by every noise imaginable all he could hear was his own heart pumping. He could feel nothing of his body till…his foot touched the lake bottom. He had made it!

This may have been only the second round but no one cared. It was in fact the water voles who were the first to greet rabbit and declare him winner. His passenger Celfyte broke the rules again by standing on rabbit's head to lead the applause. The Judger just looked at her, raised his eyebrows questioningly, and then broke into a forgiving smile. As the rabbit dragged himself out of the water he collapsed at Zana's feet. She bent down and carefully picked him up to cradle him in her arms. She then walked back to a grassy mound in the sunshine and sat down for all the animals to walk past and congratulate the brave rabbit.

"Will he be alright Sparcal?" asked Sis "will he recover." She waited while Sparcal flew through the crowds and sat on Zana's arm to inspect the rabbit. She was soon back.

"One very tired rabbit. He just needs rest now, and lots of it," Sparcal reported.

"If I were you Sis, I would use this time to arrange the next games." She looked up into the sky. Its mid-day already you know."

"Yes, you're right. I've had an idea, it was something the Judger said earlier and you've just reminded me. Thanks Sparcal." Sis raced off to find the Judger. It wasn't difficult. He was standing by the willow playing host to all the Celfyte passengers who had gathered to sit together on his outstretched hand.

"Look Sis, a handful of magic. I really can't bear to think I have to leave on the morrow."

"Can't we stay one more day Sir, please? I've had this idea. What about having an animal Games day for the children of Thanet: 'A Unity Games' dedicated to peace?"

"So now you are a dreamer, eh Sis?"

"Glancing down at the Celfytes on the Judger's hand Sis said with a cheeky grin "you're never too old to dream, are you Sir?"

The Judger smiled, shook his head and started to laugh. "Well Miss Judger, I'm certainly not in a position to argue with that am I? So what's your idea then?"

"It was while watching all the animals united in cheering- on the rabbit to finish the race and their joy when he succeeded. At that moment there were no differences between creatures. They really were one. And I imagined how wonderful it would have been if it were Super, Singer and Taper children united like that." "Oh, it would be indeed" said the Judger. He looked away and Sis noted a growing sadness in his eyes. "You know Sis, all children are born trusting and loving, it's what they learn from their elders that spoils their innocence." They both stood in silence, thinking, wishing and, yes…………dreaming.

Then a strange sensation flowed through Sis and she distinctly heard herself repeating her 'Promise of the Heart' to the Governor.

....to be true to all worlds.

....to believe and trust – where all is possible, all is secure.

....never to judge another being but only to highlight their goodness that you might help them become yet better.

"Do you know, I reckon if anyone can make such a dream come true, you can," said the Judger as if suddenly inspired. "I'll certainly stay another day to witness such a wonder. What can I do to help?"

"If you would please take over the games and let Zana come with me, we can meet you back at the camp at nightfall." Without allowing the Judger time to reply Sis held onto his arm and stretched up to kiss him on the cheek. "Thank you" she said and dashed off to find Zana.

Zana had been reunited with her owl. As Sis approached she heard Zana talking quietly to the bird and the bird was replying. "The power of trust Sis" said Zana. "Remember, you taught me."

"I'm so happy for you Zana. Now I need your help to make my dream come true. Owl, you can help too. The animals all trust you and it's important we get their agreement.

Sis outlined her plan to hold a special Animal games to which only children would be invited. The animal village was not large enough for an unlimited number and besides, the animals would get nervous when faced with crowds. No, it would have to be restricted. But to how many from each group was the question?

"Well the players won't come; they can't travel far from their homes. And anyway", continued Zana, "they are already united and friends with everyone."

"What about nine from each of the three groups?" suggested Owl.

"You know in the Minla Kingdom the number nine was believed to have mystic powers as it is the perfect number, containing all others" said Sparcal as she appeared on Sis's hand.

"How long have you been here, Sparcal? Asked Sis.

"All the time, I came here with you."

"So what do you think of the idea?"

"I think it's wonderful, Sis. Nothing is as important as freeing young minds from prejudice. But how are you going to organise it by the next sunrise?"

"I'm sending messages with the sparrow hawks and then I was hoping you would fly over and visit my friends." "You mean Delfie and Attar?

Sis was shocked! "How did you know their names, how is that possible Sparcal?"

"Remember" where *all is possible, all is secure.* "And the Super girl, who you have not met yet, is called Rose. She's Attar's other secret friend". Sis looked at Zana who was equally wide eyed with amazement at the Celfytes knowledge. "I'll guide the sparrow hawks who can carry the letters, and then I will speak to the girls and if necessary their parents. So are nine from each group enough?"

It took Sis some time to gather her thoughts after hearing all this. "Yes nine is fine Sparcal" she said hesitantly. "I'll write to my friends and ask them to meet us outside the third ring mid-morning. That will allow enough time for the children to get here. They won't all be able to come by boat; some will be walking cross country.

"More likely running" said Sparcal.

"And all adults to wait outside- agreed? "Yes."

"Don't forget to mention that the Judger has personally invited the children Sis. All the parents know and trust him."

"Good idea, Zana. Owl, can you go and explain this plan to the animals and ask the sparrow hawks to come over. Zana, will you help me write the letters please?

Not long after, Sparcal left with the sparrow hawk messengers. Sis and Zana worked on planning the day ahead while the games continued around them. Every now and then a cheer would go up or they would hear scuffles in the undergrowth as animals raced through. At one time, during a flying race for larger birds, the sky had almost darkened as dense flocks of crows and pigeons wheeled above them.

The light was just beginning to fade as the Judger made his weary way back to the camp and was welcomed with a cup of hot dandelion and mint tea. "Sorry Sir, we've got mushrooms again tonight. But my friends will bring food for us in the morning."

"Here Uncle, can you hold owl for a moment please" said Zana as she stretched out her arm for the bird to walk along and up to the Judger's shoulder. The old man beamed contentedly and brushed his face against the owl's warm feathers.

"You know girls," he said gently with a sigh. "If I live for a hundred cycles I don't believe there could ever be another visit as wondrous as this."

*

Sis had no way of knowing what excitement her plan had stirred up on both sides of the fence. Certainly she would never have imagined the arguments and commotions that it had caused in so many households. The three girls, Delfie, Attar and Rose had very bravely decided to break with all tradition and appear in public together. The trio, each with a Celfyte on their hand had clambered over the fence together and arm in arm marched up to homes across the Isle. They had explained, to shocked and speechless parents, about the animal games and how the Judger had invited the children.

The impact this daring act had on the parents and children across Thanet was electrifying. The children, oblivious to the colour of any girl's dress, hugged the nearest and gazed in total wonder at the magical Celfyte. The mothers witnessing the joy of their children had freely invited the three girls into their homes. It was as if hearts were melting all over the Island of Thanet.

Only the men folk, steeped in cycles of hatred and mistrust, did not know how to react. They merely stood back, almost frightened at this challenge to their way of life. They were confused too. They saw the happiness on their wives' and childrens' faces and were as mesmerized by the Celfytes as the children - maybe even more! Yet they were haunted by what their neighbours would think of them, how it would affect their standing in their community. They instinctively realised as well that this signal act by the girls could never be reversed. Life just could not go back to the way it was before. The security of their traditional way of life was being washed away in front of them - and it unnerved them all.

Morning came and the excited children gathered with their mothers on either side of the fence. As the adults discussed the travel arrangements with Delfie and Rose the children swarmed up and sat on the fence together. There was a loud cracking sound as a section of the barrier buckled under the weight and collapsed. The children rolled over the floor screaming with delight.

Then a strange thing happened. Rather than scolding their children as they would have done before - Singer, Taper and Super mothers suddenly put their picnic baskets down and as one barged against the fence from both sides. Their husbands looked on from inside their houses mortified, as strong hands ripped and pulled the wood apart. The fence shook and as Tapers pulled the Singers and Supers pushed and a whole section came crashing down. The women did not stop there, they continued to stamp angrily, splitting and cracking off the fence's wooden panels.

This time it was the children who had stopped to watch in amazement. They had never seen their mothers so angry. They were too young to understand that for their mothers it was not the fence they were destroying. No, it was what the fence represented to them all. The years of frustration and isolation they had suffered and the stupidity of their separate lives. *Their children did not see differences in each other just because they wore different colour clothes. From this moment on, neither would they.*

The fence was never rebuilt.

The Mothers' picnic

Because she knew the area best, Attar had volunteered to leave before dawn to take supplies to Sis. She had rowed through the darkness alone and was now struggling through the damp undergrowth with two heavy carriers. Owl had spotted her approaching and now Sis and Zana rushed out to help her.

This was truly the strangest and most enchanting breakfast Attar would ever have. She was invited to sit down and rest by the Judger who introduced her to a string of Celfytes who perched on her cup as she drank. Then there was Zana, a trainee Judger talking to the eared owl on her shoulder as she shared out the fresh bread and cheese which Attar had brought. While they were all eating, a succession of animals came and gathered around the tents to talk with Sis. Attar was amazed to hear Sis switch effortlessly from talking to badgers and squirrels back to holding a conversation with the girls. And even Attar herself was naturally feeding crumbs and pieces of apple to the blackbirds that flew in and perched on her knees. Then as she drank her second cup of tea she began stroking the young rabbits that had crept up and were now nestling in her lap.

And the strangest thing of all was that everyone, apart from Attar herself, seemed to accept all this as totally normal!

"Do you know how many children are coming, Attar? Asked Sis.

"Twenty seven in all but we could have brought the whole Island. Everyone wanted to come, except the men of course, their pride wouldn't allow them. In the end we had to flip coins to choose nine children from each group and of course their mothers insisted on bringing them."

"They do know that it is only children allowed in to the games, don't they?" asked the Judger.

"Yes, but Delfie, Rose and I had to promise we would go in with them."

"Of course" said Sis.

"And", Attar continued excitedly, "the women have all arranged to meet outside the third ring and while the children are at the games, they're going to have their own picnic together."

"Oh, that's marvellous" said the Judger and he turned to Sis and put his arm around her. "Do you know if that happens what you would have done, young lady? In one afternoon you would have achieved what all the Judgers of the past have failed to do in generations. Unbelievable - and I don't use that word very often".

"Except when you see a Celfyte Sir, said Sis." The Judger couldn't stop himself from laughing. "True Sis, I have to admit that Celfytes are the exception."

They talked and ate and fed the animals. Word had spread among the birds that a new visitor had arrived and Attar soon found herself feeding a whole flock of inquisitive finches that flew in to see her. When eventually breakfast was finished Sis went over the arrangements for the day. They would all meet outside the third ring with the mothers and children when they arrived, then the three girls, Delfie, Attar and Rose would take the children off to the games, which Sis and Zana would be organising. The Judger would stay with the mothers for a while then come back over to the games later.

"Let's get ready, they'll be here soon" said the Judger. "Attar, it was very thoughtful of you to come so early to bring us food, thank you."

"Yes, thank you" added Sis and Zana together. Attar looked down. "I can't get up, the rabbits have fallen asleep." Zana helped her to carefully lift them up and one by one placed them on the soft grass.

"I think I should thank you all, as well. This is one breakfast I will never forget" said Attar.

They all arrived together. Firstly the sound of excited children came from behind the elderberry grove, and then they all came into view. With Delfie and Rose leading them, the multi-coloured group streamed forward to be greeted by the Judger. Delfie anxiously looked around to find Sis and pulling Rose by the hand ran over to meet her friend. Their excited conversation was cut short as the Judger clapped his hands and asked everyone to sit down.

"Welcome to the animal games. Firstly I must introduce you to Sis. This was her idea, her dream, and seeing you all here today, well - you've made her dream come true." Sis blushed as the whole group clapped and cheered. "Zana, my niece here," he said holding her arm proudly, "has assisted Sis throughout and will be helping to organise the games for the children today." Zana too blushed in the applause.

"But none of this would have been possible," he continued, "without the conviction and tireless energy of three special girls who shared Sis's dream: Delfie from the Singers, Rose from the Supers and Attar from the Tapers. Please stand up girls" As they stood shyly a shower of Celfytes flew around them leading the applause.

When the noise had died down the Judger moved forward and addressing the children said "this is a very special day for you all. The animals have invited you to their games. This is their home and I would ask you to respect that. Please stay with your leader and do not run off and most important of all - never chase any animal - it will frighten them. The quieter and calmer you are the closer the animals will come – just wait and see." He finished with a smile as the three girls stood up to call the children into three groups. As they moved off, each child turned round to look at their mother; all faces glowing with excitement and anticipation.

"I'm delighted you all came. It's quite wonderful to see you all here together." The Judger looked around the circle the mother's had formed. In the middle cloths were being laid out on which they were placing a whole array of food. "At least you won't go hungry" he joked. "Tell me "he asked the group in general, "what was it that made you come today, after all, every other meeting in the past has only led to arguments and more bad feeling between you."

"That's just it" said a Taper mother, holding hands with a Singer and a Super. When the three girls came to my home to invite my daughter to the games and I saw her reaction to them, I believed this could be different. I so wanted it to be different. I'd thought I was the only one who was sick to death of the endless arguments, all the hate. Then when we met at the fence this morning, I found I was not alone. The other mothers felt the same. We all wanted a better life for our children."

"We certainly did", added a Super mother from the other side.

A Singer mother stood up to address the circle. "As we travelled here I talked for the first time to Taper and Super mothers. I really *talked* with them. It made me so sad to realise what we had each missed, what we had denied our children. All the chances to learn from each other, all the things we could have shared together." Her lips trembled as overcome with emotion she sat down. There followed an aching silence.

Then another Singer mother stood and with the sweetest voice began to sing an ancient lullaby. Slowly, one by one the other mothers joined in the beautiful melody. They each knew the song, that had been handed down from generation to generation and as they sang they joined hands together. The Judger too hummed the tune till silence fell again across the circle and the singer returned to her seat.

"That was so beautiful" said a Super mother. "Thank you. If Singers can change - then so can we." The circle looked on in disbelief as the Super gently took out her eye earring and turning round threw it on the embers of the small breakfast fire. Eight other Super mothers followed, removed their superstitious symbols and with genuine relief on their faces consigned their earrings to the fire.

The Judger just watched and listened. He had no further part to play, neither was there anything for him to say. This was a special moment and it belonged to the brave new mothers. For once he was merely a bystander and he simply felt privileged to be there. First one, then two, then all nine Tapers stood up and left the circle together. They walked round the fire and without speaking, dropped their measuring tapes into the flames and returned to the circle.

Delfie's mother stood and nervously walked over to Attar's mother. She bent down to help her to her feet, glanced around and said. "Before you all, I want to publicly acknowledge this brave Taper woman who saved my life and the life of my child many cycles ago. Yes, we have been secret friends ever since, but now I feel only shame that I did not have the courage all that time to openly express my gratitude. I kept my feelings hidden. I am so sorry." She looked into Attar's mother's eyes and said "I owe you everything. Thank you."

Those last two words hung in the still air above the circle. *Thank you* - the simplest of everyday words that all mothers had repeated thousands of times as a commonest courtesy. Yet now they were invested with a new meaning for them all. As Delfie's mother embraced her old Taper friend there was an explosion of tears around the circle. Each mother felt intuitively that she too was embracing something new. It was a new freedom - and it felt wonderful.

For a long time no one spoke. They couldn't. They just felt relieved and grateful. It was only when the Judger moved to get up that a Super mother suggested, "Stay a while with us Sir. Have you ever tasted a Super's apple pie?"

"Apple pie's my favourite. It's tempting, but I really should be going over to the games."

"What about a Singer's plum tart Sir?"

"You can't leave without trying a Taper's blackberry roll Sir. You don't know what you've been missing all this time."

Surrounded by so much warm hospitality the Judger had no escape. Inwardly he was more than happy to take on the role of the circle's food Judgerer! Who wouldn't, with so many delicious offerings? *The children would be fine with the girls, they don't need me for the moment. They've got all the animals,* he reasoned, and satisfied with his own reasoning began his 'food Judgering, with great enthusiasm. The Mothers picnic had begun!

They all happily shared their food and then began to swap recipes. They talked and laughed and quite simply 'felt young again.' "It's a shame your husbands are not here to share this feast" the Judger said to the nearest group of Super and Singer mothers.

"They're probably still indoors worrying about the fence," retorted a Super who immediately started giggling.

"Mine too," said a Singer. "Probably trying to work out where he can go to sing now."

This image fired the imagination of the group and they burst out in uncontrolled laughter. The Judger looked confused. *Had he missed something?* The Taper mother seated next to him looked at his puzzled expression. "You really don't know, do you Sir?" "Know what?" he asked.

"We've pulled the fence down. It's gone."

"No. It's not possible. It can't be!"

"Oh, but it is. We pulled it down with our bare hands." "And stamped on it" added a Singer mother forcefully.

"And broke it into pieces" said a Super. "All the women here today - we did it together." A cheer went up, and then clapping began. "We did it together, we did it together." Everyone joined in laughing and repeating the phrase as if it were their anthem - and indeed it was to become just that!

The Judger, a normally reserved man, whose profession had seldom allowed him to express deep feelings - wept. He sat with his face buried in his trembling hands as a sea of emotions swept over him. From above the trees behind him came the sound of children's laughter.

Sis sat alone beside the lake. Across the water the children played in the bright sunlight. They were in a new world now, their lives had been changed - everything had changed. Somehow Sis felt complete and all the urgency of the past days had left her.

Suddenly whirling colours appeared before her. "Where are you going Sis? I see in your heart a yearning to leave."

"I need to go home Sparcal."

"Then don't be sad. When dreams come true it's natural to feel emptiness inside. Then a new dream is born. It's the rhythm of creation and it is the same in every universe. So go now with all our love that you might return. And Sis - I promise I will be waiting for you."

Sis closed her eyes and whispered…………….. "Tala, Tala."

Coming home

Tala, her guide and friend, was overjoyed at Sis's return.

"It was wonderful Tala. What a journey - if only you were with me."

"If only I could have been" Tala replied wistfully. "But I saw everything Sis. I heard each word and read every dream. Now let's seal it all in your sunlight crystal."

"No wait. Not yet, please."

"Then ask me Sis, your eyes are full of questions."

"At the beginning you told me that some kingdom creatures still exist in Thanet."

"Yes, Celfytes are still here and as secretive as ever. The Waldron's cousins, tiny people called 'Brenders', now live around waste bins in motorway lay-byes. A few hog rats can be found in winter cabbage fields. There are a number of burrowing animals you have not seen yet and the 'Blossom-thieves' still survive in a few isolated orchards along with the Cave-mordons. Ditch cats and Septic toads haunt most drainage ditches. I could go on but we have to save your memories while they are time-pure."

"You mean there are more? Asked Sis."

Tala smiled at her friend's endless curiosity. Then suddenly a voice came from behind them.

"I seem to remember that I once told you that 'above all you must have patience.'" Sis spun around to see the Guardian's beaming face. He stood open armed and without thinking Sis rushed over and embraced him.

"Well, well, well - the Judger returns" said the Guardian. He saw the anxious look on Tala's face as she held out the crystal. "Don't worry, Tala. Sis's memories are so strong they will keep time–pure a little while longer. She won't lose anything. Come, let's sit together before she goes back." The two girls walked with the Guardian and sat around a stone table in the corner of the huge map room.

The Governor cast his eyes across the expansive maps suspended around them. "So many worlds, so very many worlds" he sighed. "And you Sis are the only creature with a key to them all." He looked down at her hand, the butterflies glowed brightly.

"I wish Sis could stay with us a while" said Tala. "We promised to show her our crystals of special things."

"Don't worry Tala, you will see Sis very soon," promised the Guardian. Then he turned to Sis and said "your journeys through the Kingdoms of Thanet are only just beginning. So many realms, so many worlds for you to discover…."

"Now it is time for your return. Tala, hold Sis's hand tight and give her the sunlight crystal."

Simone opened her eyes to the brilliant whiteness of her garden. The snow was falling even more heavily now and was beginning to disguise the shapes of familiar bushes and trees. Everything was fast disappearing beneath a thickening blanket. As beautiful as the scene was she was happy to be indoors and warm. And the cosier she felt looking out, the sleepier she became.

Suddenly she heard a loud stamping outside the front door and the sound of a key turning in the lock. Her Dad was home and she jumped up to go and meet him in the hall.

"You didn't drive did you Dad?" She asked as she took his coat and stood on tip - toe to kiss him on the cheek. "Wow! Your face is freezing!"

"Yeh, I had to walk. Mum took the car to work this morning - the snow wasn't as bad then. Just hope the roads have cleared before she comes home. You're lucky your school closed Sis. Your brother'll be envious – his school stayed open, like our College. A whole day off school, eh! - so what have you been doing?" he asked as they moved into the kitchen.

"I've been a bit lazy Dad. The day's just flown by. Rufous came for his food though. He's getting so tame he nearly took bread from my hand. Would you like a coffee?" she asked.

"Yes please. Mmmm! That was a crafty change of subject. So what you really mean is you haven't done a thing all day?"

"Not that you would really notice Dad, no."

"Well I can't fault your honesty. But you have to make sure you catch up on your homework tonight. It's important," he smiled at her affectionately.

"Dad" she said coyly. He knew his daughter so well. She was about to ask him a favour. So he waited for the inevitable.

"Can my friend stay tonight? I promise I'll do my homework."

"What friend?"

"She's in the lounge. You haven't seen her before but I know you'll like her Dad – she's a real angel. Come and meet her – please." Simone took his hand and led him into the next room. "Dad, this is my new friend - Tala…"

…End…

Author bio

After a varied career in High Fashion sales, John left the West End of London to take a Degree in English at Greenwich University before moving to the University of London for his P/G teaching qualifications. He lectured in Business studies and communications for five years in Bexlcy College before returning to London to work in helping set up a Computer Franchise.

In 1987, combining his teaching and marketing experience he moved to Thanet to take up a newly created post of Principal Lecturer in College Marketing. This was later developed to include the recruitment of International students which involved extensive travel across Asia, the Indian Sub-continent and South America. His dual role was promoting both Thanet College's English language, study skills and academic provision and the locality of the 'Isle of Thanet' as a safe and welcoming environment in which to study.

A few years after taking early retirement from Education he was diagnosed with MS which mostly affected his walking and balance. This restriction on physical activity also had a positive side as it forced him to focus more on creative work and motivated him to concentrate on finishing his trio of novels.

"When asked where I get my ideas and inspiration from I say, firstly my universal outlook as a Baha'i – seeing the world as one country and all mankind citizens of that country - a vision enhanced and blessed by the opportunities I have had to meet people from many differing nationalities, backgrounds, cultures, beliefs and interests. Secondly, my life-long interest in and love for the natural world, the beauty of which inspires my abstract painting, my new passion for flower photography and, of course, my writing."

This novel, "Watched over by Angels" is the first in a series of three books which will reveal the 'true' story of the Kingdoms of Thanet. A previously unknown world, beneath this seaside Isle that had now been discovered by a young Thanet girl. A hidden world where Angels and Witches roamed free and wondrous creatures lived……and maybe they all still do……

Author contact: johnstedmanpublishing@hotmail.com

16299043R00148

Printed in Poland
by Amazon Fulfillment
Poland Sp. z o.o., Wrocław